THE ANGEL OF WARSAW

REBECCA SCOTT

First published in 2025
Concept created by Black Swan Digital. Developed by Annie Kenyon.

INSPIRED BY

On 4 December 1942, in the heart of German-occupied Warsaw, an extraordinary institution came into being. Operating under the Government Delegation for Poland – the clandestine representative of the Polish Government-in-Exile – the Council for Aid to Jews, codenamed 'Żegota', began its mission. It would continue until early 1945 and remains unique in the annals of wartime Europe as the only state-sponsored body in German-occupied territory dedicated exclusively to saving Jews from extermination.

PROLOGUE

Warsaw, September 1st, 1939

The apple tree on the edge of the lane had weathered many summers. Its branches arched low with fruit, the leaves freckled by the slow creep of autumn. Beneath it, on a blanket faded by years of washing, a woman sat with a book in her lap. She had chosen the spot for its shade, and for the way the tree's roots pressed up through the soil and wrapped around the base, like knuckles, offering a kind of backrest.

The morning was warm, with the clarity of late summer. Light spilled over the rooftops in gold sheets, catching in the dust that hung above the cobbles. A cart rattled in the distance. The horse pulling it whinnied twice, then fell silent.

From time to time, she looked up from her reading to watch the children playing in the lane. Careless, noisy, their world no larger than the few streets they had always known.

Two boys, not yet ten, chased a hoop of bent wire, their voices raised in argument over whose turn it was to drive it forward. A girl with a red ribbon in her hair whirled in dizzy circles until she staggered against a fence, laughing at her own clumsiness. A toddler, determined to keep up, toddled in stubborn pursuit of the others, his arms lifted like a windmill for balance.

Their laughter rose like birdsong, and the woman allowed herself to smile. For a moment, she forgot the newspaper headlines, the endless whisper of war. For a moment, she believed peace might linger here, as stubborn as the tree whose fruit had ripened year after year, no matter the storms. But then came the sound.

At first it was no more than a murmur, low and distant, a sound you might mistake for thunder gathering behind the horizon. The children did not hear it. They shouted, clapped their hands, tumbled over one another. But the woman's eyes narrowed. She lifted her head, tilting her ear toward the sky. The sound thickened, swelling into a drone. The earth seemed to rumble with it. Pigeons startled from the rooftops in a scatter of wings. She knew, before she truly saw.

The first plane carved across the sky like a dark blade. Sunlight glinted on the iron cross painted on its flank. A second followed, then a third. Their engines howled, a sound vast and mechanical, louder than anything the children had ever heard. The little girl clapped her hands, thinking it a show. The older boy shaded his eyes to watch.

The woman rose slowly to her feet, the book still clutched in her hand. Her heart clenched with the terrible certainty that the world had just shifted. The air itself had changed.

The planes banked, black specks against the light. Then the first bomb fell. The explosion was not near, but it was close enough to rattle the windows and shake the apples from the tree. The ground jolted. Dust leapt from the cobbles. The girl's applause broke into a scream. The toddler sat down hard and began to cry.

Another detonation followed, closer. The sharp concussion cracked the morning like a whip. Dogs began barking wildly up and down the street. A window shattered.

"Inside!" someone shouted, though the woman did not see who. A man leaned out from a doorway, waving his arms.

The children scattered, instinct overcoming play. The girl seized the toddler's hand, dragging him toward the gate. The boys ran in opposite directions, panicked. Their shouts were no longer joyous and instead they were raw with fear.

The woman pressed her back against the apple tree; her book still clutched against her chest. She wanted to move, to gather the children, to run, but her legs would not obey. She could only watch.

The sky filled with more planes. Their drone was deafening now, a chorus of machines announcing the invasion that newspapers had promised, that politicians had denied, that ordinary people had prayed would never come.

A cart overturned in the street as its horse reared in terror. Mothers shouted from windows. The bombs fell in uneven rhythm, each one tearing a new hole in the city. The air stank of smoke and dust.

The woman's hand slackened. The book slid from her grasp and dropped into the grass. Its pages flared open like wings. She stared down at it, absurdly conscious of the way the print blurred where her eyes filled with tears. A truck sped into view and screeched to a halt and in seconds, a squad of German soldiers appeared at the corner, their boots pounding the cobbles. They moved with a kind of dreadful certainty, rifles at their shoulders, helmets glinting. Their voices rang out in clipped commands. People scattered before them, ducking into alleys, slamming doors.

The woman did not move. Her heart hammered against her ribs, urging her to run, but she stood rooted at the base of the tree, her eyes wide. The soldiers spread down the lane, efficient, methodical, claiming the street as if it had always been theirs.

A boy tripped on the cobbles and sprawled. A soldier glanced his way. For a sickening moment the woman thought the rifle would lift. But another voice called out, an order, and the man turned back. The boy scrambled up and fled. The woman pressed her palm against the rough bark of the apple tree. She could feel it shudder faintly with each explosion, as though the earth itself had caught a fever. Her mouth was dry. She wanted to call to the children, to tell them to hide, to run faster but the words jammed in her throat.

The soldiers halted in the lane, forming a line. Behind them the trucks rattled forward, bringing more men, more weapons. The city would not be spared.

The woman's gaze fell to the book at her feet. Its spine was broken, its pages crumpled where it had landed. She thought absurdly of picking it up, of brushing it clean, of saving it as though words might still matter. But her hands would not move. Instead she stood beneath the apple tree, her shadow swallowed by its branches, and watched as the invasion began.

The children were gone now, vanished into doorways and stairwells, their laughter extinguished. The air reeked of smoke, of cordite, of fear. Above, the sky swarmed with planes. The woman whispered something – it might have been a prayer, or only a name but the sound was lost in the thunder of engines.

Another bomb fell. The ground lurched. The apple tree shook, loosing another apple, which struck the earth beside the broken book. The woman stared at it, her breath locked in her chest. She had known, deep down, that this day would come. But knowing had done nothing to prepare her. She bent slowly, picked up nothing, and rose again, her eyes fixed on the horizon where more trucks rolled into the city.

The war had begun.

1

Warsaw, October 1940

The city had grown smaller. It wasn't the size of the streets themselves, though rubble clogged the gutters where buildings had once stood whole, and soldiers' trucks crowded corners that had belonged to fruit sellers and flower women. It wasn't the rooftops, though many sagged from bombing and neglect, tiles missing like broken teeth. Nor was it the horizon, though smoke hung in an ashen veil, smudging the sky into something that never seemed quite blue anymore.

It was a different kind of shrinking, one that pressed into the lungs and ribs and left less room for air. Irena walked quickly, her boots clattering on the cobbles, her satchel tight against her hip. She pulled her scarf closer against the October chill, though the cold was not what made her shiver. A German patrol rounded the corner ahead, two soldiers in grey-green uniforms, rifles slung casually across their shoulders as if they were strolling across a parade ground rather than occupying a conquered city. Their laughter rang sharp and discordant, cutting across the quiet shuffle of ordinary civilians who had long since learned not to laugh in public. Irena wondered if now, they ever laughed at all.

The street narrowed where rubble from a collapsed tenement still lay in heaps, never cleared. Irena stepped carefully over broken bricks and shards of glass that glittered like ice. The air was thick with plaster dust, a smell she associated with both endings and beginnings. Now, it was endings only.

She kept her head down and her gaze fixed just ahead of her boots as she passed the soldiers. But her eyes flicked up once, briefly. They were young – perhaps no older than she had been when she had sat her final examinations at the university. Their faces were ruddy from the cold, and one had a smear of dried mud across his cheek, as if some ancient god of war had reached out and marked him in a tribal ceremony. They looked, she thought, like boys who should have been running footballs down a field, not herding families through gates.

The patrol moved on, their laughter trailing after them, and Irena let out a breath she'd been holding deep inside. Her steps carried her onward, toward the district where new walls had begun to rise. Already they towered two meters high, brick upon brick, topped with coils of barbed wire that glistened wet in the morning mist. She had walked this street for years – first as a student, later as a social worker, but now it no longer resembled itself. It had been cleaved in two, one half swallowed into shadow. The walls grew higher each week, hemming in more of the city with a patient, terrible finality.

Ahead of her, a line of people shuffled forward through a checkpoint gate. They carried bundles: patched suitcases, pots wrapped in blankets, sacks bulging with bread gone stale.

Mothers held their children's hands too tightly; old men leaned on sticks that tapped uneven rhythms on the stones. Soldiers barked at them to move faster, prodding them with the ends of their rifles as though shepherding cattle.

Irena slowed. Her throat tightened as she watched a boy stumble. He could not have been more than seven or eight. His boots were too big for him and the laces dragged loose in the dirt. His face was pale, hollow, as if hunger had already eaten half his childhood away. He lifted his head, and his gaze met hers. The wire between them shimmered faintly in the mist, a net of light and steel. For a moment it seemed the only thing in the world, that barrier, those eyes. He did not cry, though his lips were pressed so tight together they whitened. He only stared, silent, as though daring her to remember him.

"Move along!" a soldier barked and shoved him forward with the butt of a rifle. The boy staggered, caught his balance, and vanished into the press of bodies.

Irena's hand clenched against the strap of her satchel. Her feet rooted to the cobbles, as though part of her wanted to follow the child into that narrow, darkening passage. But another voice echoed up through her memory, a voice long gone but never forgotten.

She was small again, perhaps eight or nine, walking beside her father on a dirt road outside Warsaw. The air reeked of horse dung and woodsmoke, the steady buzz of cicadas filling the spaces between his words. His hand was large and warm around hers.

They were going to visit one of his patients – a Jewish cobbler who lived in a shack at the edge of the village. Other villagers whispered about the man's sickness, about typhus and contagion, and crossed themselves when they passed his door. But her father never hesitated.

"People are people, Irenka," he told her gently as they walked. His voice was deep, carrying a calm that steadied her even when she felt uncertain. "Illness does not choose by faith or by name."

When they entered the shack, the air was thick with the sour-sweet stench of sickness. The cobbler lay shivering under a blanket, his skin mottled with fever. His wife hovered at his side, her hands wringing the edge of her apron. Irena had wanted to shrink away, to cover her nose, but her father only knelt by the bed, resting a hand on the man's brow with quiet compassion. He spoke softly, not as a doctor above his patient but as one human being to another.

Later, as they walked home in the fading light, she had asked her father why he helped the sick man when he too could become ill. He had smiled kindly, squeezed her hand and said:

"If you see a man drowning, Irenka, you must jump in. Even if you cannot swim."

The words had confused her then. Drowning was for rivers, for lakes, not for fevers and hunger. She had asked what he meant, and the corners of his eyes creased as he replied.

"It means if we are called to help, even when it is dangerous and everything feels impossible, we must still try. Especially then. Remember that."

The memory settled in her chest now like an ember, glowing faintly against the chill of the morning. She blinked back to the street, to the sight of soldiers shoving families through the gate, to the echo of boots and cries. In that moment she knew why the city felt smaller each day – because it was being cut to pieces, parcelled out, marked and claimed. But inside that shrinking space, something pressed outward: the memory of her father's words, the weight of the boy's eyes behind the wire.

Taking a deep breath, she turned and walked on toward her office. Her steps were steady, but in her mind, the ember burned brighter.

That evening the café hid itself in a ribbon of fog and coal smoke, its sign half-shattered, the painted letters flaking like scabs. Inside, the air held the weary perfume of boiled tea, damp coats, and the ghost of coffee that no one had seen for months. A single bulb swung on its wire whenever a tram rattled past, smearing a long oval of jaundiced light over chipped tables and the faces bent over them. Men spoke in the hush of conspirators about ordinary things. A woman at the back stitched a hem by lamplight as if the busily moving needle could put the world back together, too.

Irena pushed through the door and stamped the slick from her soles. The day's grit lived in her throat; the taste of brick dust lingered, as if the city had been ground into powder and she could not help but swallow some of it. The damn walls were even higher now and she had felt them rising all afternoon, as palpable as a change in barometric pressure. Then the streets had grown stranger at dusk, filling with shadows that didn't seem to belong to anything you could name. This was a café she had known for years. A place to go after lectures; after rounds at the clinic; after funerals. It had always smelled of cardamom and burnt sugar, always hummed with the cheerful quarrels of students. Tonight, the hum was there, but it loped, limping, around missing words smothered by fear.

"Here," Jadwiga called softly, lifting two fingers.

Jadwiga sat in a corner where the peeling wallpaper met a cracked mirror. The mirror had been smoke-stained so many times it no longer reflected so much as remembered its purpose and allowed faces to pass through it like thoughts. Beside her, a man rose from his chair. He wasn't tall, not quite, but his presence suggested height. His coat was an old schoolmaster's tweed, rubbed shiny at the elbows and he had a courier's satchel slung crosswise, the strap digging a diagonal into the wool. When he met Irena's eyes, she saw there the bright, restless watchfulness of a man who had learned to read danger as quickly as he read books.

"Irena," Jadwiga said, "this is Samuel." She did not add a surname. Surnames had become too much to carry.

"Samuel," he echoed, and offered his hand. His fingers were cool and steady.

"Irena," she said, because the ritual mattered, because manners held the broken pieces of the old world in the cupped palm of the new. "Thank you for meeting me."

He gave a small nod that might have been a bow if there had been more room. "Jadwiga speaks highly of you."

"Jadwiga always exaggerates," Irena said, sitting.

"Only when it serves me," Jadwiga said. She grinned without cheer and signalled to the woman behind the counter. "Three teas."

Teas arrived in dented cups, steaming, the liquid a thin brown that pretended to be stronger than it was. The steam lifted between them like a veil. Around them, the café eddied with small sounds: the scrape of a chair leg; a throat cleared quickly; the soft clink of a spoon as a man stirred nothing into his drink. Somewhere in the back, a valve hissed and sighed; the walls breathed as if glad to have survived.

"Jadwiga tells me you have access papers," Samuel said, not

quite a question, not quite a statement. His voice was low, a measured baritone; a teacher's voice pitched for a classroom, attentive because the pupils love him, not because they fear him.

"I have papers," Irena said. "For inspections. Sanitation." She wrapped her hands around the cup and felt the heat as if it were someone else's palm pressed over hers. "They come and go as they like, the Germans. We are allowed to go only when it suits and they use disease as their excuse."

"Typhus," he said.

"Not yet an epidemic," she answered. "But it will be. You don't crowd tens of thousands into rooms built for hundreds and expect anything else." She saw again the boy's eyes behind the wire, the way he had locked onto her as if memorising her could be a bridge to salvation of some kind. "They ration them to the point of starvation. And then they put up signs tsk-tsking about hygiene. It's so cruel."

Samuel's gaze didn't waver. His mouth tightened, not in distaste but in a grim agreement. "Jadwiga says you carry more than soap in your satchel."

"She should not say that in cafés," Irena said, and then, because something in his steadiness made her want to be precise, she added, "I carry medicines. And bread when I can get it. Information, sometimes."

Jadwiga sat forward. "Samuel has –" She flicked a glance around the room and changed the word. "Contacts."

"Friends," Samuel supplied, as if softening the diction might blunt the risk. "Priests who don't ask questions they shouldn't. A printer who loves errors more than rules. A seamstress who can make a child's coat look as if it belonged to another child, a long time ago."

Irena sipped her tea. It had the flavour of boiled desperation. "Jadwiga tells me you taught in school."

"Latin, history, and the art of not falling asleep while reading

Cicero," he said, the ghost of humour crossing his mouth. "Until last autumn. There are fewer students to teach now. Fewer schools, and fewer windows left where a child can daydream."

"What made you –" She stopped. The question was too personal for a corner table. What made you stop teaching and start carrying things no one is supposed to carry? What made you look up one morning and put your own life on the line against something you cannot touch? That was what she wanted to ask.

He answered the unfinished question anyway. "They boarded up the doors to the gymnasium. Then they took the boys who lingered to ask why and turned them around and told them the answer didn't matter. I thought of all the declensions, all the dates, all the declamations I'd insisted upon. None of it teaches a boy how to climb a wall. So I learned a new curriculum." He glanced at the satchel strap biting into his coat. "It suits me poorly. But it suits the times."

Silence settled among them like another guest. The bulb wavered. On the wall, the cracked mirror turned their three faces into a collage: the curve of Irena's cheek beside Samuel's eye, Jadwiga's mouth where Irena's should be, a composite expression that belonged to none of them and all.

Jadwiga broke the quiet with the sound of her spoon clinking, deliberate, then spoke as if to the tea itself. "They're saying –" She stopped and swallowed. "They're saying a child died this morning in Krochmalna. They said he lay by the wall with a crust in his hand, and he didn't eat it because he had saved it for his sister, and then he stopped breathing."

Samuel's hands tightened around his cup. He was careful with emotion. He was a man who did not let his movements betray him; she could see that. Even his grief had learned to take smaller breaths. "Rumours amplify suffering," he said quietly. "But rumours don't invent themselves from nothing."

Irena kept her gaze on the tea's surface until it steadied. "I saw a boy today," she said. "At the gate. A soldier pushed him. He didn't cry." She let that be the whole story because the rest was a series of facts that did not make sense unless you had seen them. "There are more children every day wandering away from their mothers when the line moves too fast."

Samuel nodded once. "I carry messages," he said. "Sometimes the message is an address that becomes a chance of life. Sometimes the message is only news of a death. I prefer the first lesson plan."

"Do you carry children?" Irena asked before she knew she would.

"That depends," he said carefully. His gaze flicked toward the door, the windows, the ordinary men bending over their ordinary teas. "On how small they are, and how loud."

Jadwiga's knee touched Irena's beneath the table, a brief, reassuring nudge. "Samuel knows people who know people," she said. "And those people know which door will not close when small knuckles knock after midnight. That is why I wanted you to meet."

"Because I have papers," Irena said, recognising the geometry. "And two hands."

"And a spine," Samuel said. Admiration sharpened his tone, or perhaps it was warning; in these days the two were as hard to separate as twined threads. "Jadwiga told me what you did during the last typhus scare."

"I washed a few children," she said.

"You shouted at a German health inspector in his own office," Jadwiga said, half proud, half appalled. "You told him the lice did not respect his cordons."

"He was going to cancel the soap," Irena said, hearing how preposterous the sentence sounded and not caring. "He said it made no difference. He said lice preferred Jews as if they were gourmands. I told him lice preferred filth and that anyone who had ever had hair would know that."

Samuel's smile was quick and procedural, there and gone, like a password exchanged and tucked away. "That was a risk."

"Everything is," she said, and felt the ember that had lived in her chest all day brighten, fed by his presence.

He leaned in, just a fraction. The lamplight found the small flecks of gold in his eyes, and she wondered, unexpectedly, what his laughter had sounded like before the world taught it to wear a heavy coat. "I should be more direct," he said. "We can use you. We can use anyone who can walk into places the rest of us cannot. We need eyes. We need hands that do not shake when they write a name on a scrap of paper and tuck it somewhere no one will think to look."

"I have hands," she said. "And I write legibly."

"And you understand the cost," he said, and his voice made the room narrower. "Not in glory. Not in songs later, if there are songs."

"I understand enough." She thought of her father's large hand wrapped around hers, the cool evening air scented with woodsmoke and his aftershave. If you see a man drowning... "Tell me the lesson plan."

He exhaled a small, surprised breath, as if he had expected to be arguing still. "First," he said, folding the idea into a teacher's structure, "you do not speak names aloud in rooms where a door could be listening. You do not write them where a uniform can find them. We make two of everything important – two lists, two routes, two plans, and we keep them in two places no one would connect unless they loved the person enough to know where she hides her secrets. Second. We never move two children the same way twice. If a potato sack worked once, it will be searched the next time. If a work permit opens a door in the morning, a man with a different stamp will be standing there by afternoon. Third. If you are stopped, you are what your paper says you are, and you do not volunteer to be anyone else."

"Fourth?" Irena asked quietly, because there was always a fourth rule, and usually it was the one that mattered most.

"Fourth," he said, and took a long breath, "you understand the road is one direction. If you step onto it, the city will not permit you to step off when you tire. Those who love you will not be asked to vote. If you step onto this road, there is no turning back."

Jadwiga's hand, warm and firm, settled over Irena's as if to brace her from a fall neither of them could see the bottom of. The café thinned around them; the lamp glowed, determined to emit some form of warmth. Outside, a tram clanged, dragging its bell through the dusk like a spoon through cold syrup.

Irena felt the familiar shape of fear in her mouth. It tasted metallic, like the edge of a coin or blood bitten from a lip. She rolled it under her tongue and waited for the old reflex – the shrinking away, the excuses, the very reasonable suggestion that she would be more useful if she kept her job, kept her head down, kept herself intact for a later, safer day. The reflex came, and she watched it pass, and behind it, something steadier lifted its chin. She saw the boy's face again, the hollowed cheeks, the lashes pale with dust. She saw her father kneeling by a sickbed no one else would approach, his hand open, as if offering the man his own breath.

"Then I'll walk it to the end," she said.

They sat with the words. They didn't jolt the table or knock over the cups. They did not require a witness beyond the three of them and the mirror that didn't know how to tell on anyone anymore. But Irena felt the line those words drew, as clean and irreversible as a surgeon's cut.

Samuel nodded once, the gravity of his acceptance as formal as a vow. "Good," he said. "We go slowly. We go as if we are crossing a frozen river in the dark. We listen to the ice." He drew the satchel into his lap and took out a small notebook, the cover had been rebound with cloth to disguise it. He opened to a leaf already sliced into the thinnest slips, like communion wafers made of paper. Each bore a single word in a careful, upright hand: a street name; a shop; a code that meant a parish hall and not a grocer. He folded two into Irena's palm. "Memorise these routes."

She turned the slips with her thumb. The ink had bled a little, as if even the letters were hungry. "Who is at the end of these streets?" she asked.

"Today? No one," he said. "Tomorrow, perhaps a woman who has agreed to say she is an aunt to a child whose true aunt no longer has a house. Another time, a nun with hands scratched raw from scrubbing, who will teach a boy to cross himself so he can keep his name for later. The slip tells you where to knock. Not who opens."

"There are rumours," Jadwiga said, her voice more thread than cloth now. "We hear of children –"

"We will not speak of the dead tonight," Samuel said gently. "We will speak of the ones who still have enough breath to cry if you step on their foot. Of the ones who fall asleep standing because it is warmer than lying down. Of the ones who still laugh when you pull a silly face, because they have not yet understood that the city wants to eat their laughter and banish it forever."

Irena swallowed. The tea in her throat had cooled to a dull ache. "How soon will you need me?"

"Soon enough that you should sleep tonight as if you are not already on the ice," he said. "Tomorrow morning, come by the rear door of the parish office on Elektoralna. Bring your inspector's coat. There will be a box of soap for the clinic. The soap will be soap. But underneath, there will be something else that is not soap. If anyone asks, you are delivering soap." He smiled then, briefly, and then the atmosphere in the room shifted just enough to let air move again. "When we decide on a lie, we tell the same one all the way through."

"Who else is in your class?" she asked, and the poor joke, calling it a class, made his mouth curve.

"Today?" he said. "You. Jadwiga. Three more who are not here and must never be here at the same time. If I am taken, they do not know one another's names. If one of them is taken, I do not know the other two's addresses. This is how the ice holds."

"And if you are taken?" Jadwiga asked, and the question wobbled like the light.

Samuel's eyes did not leave Irena's. "Then you keep walking and listen for cracks in the ice, always," he said softly.

The bulb buzzed, cooling, then warmed again. The woman at the back finished her hem and bit the thread with her teeth. She folded the skirt over her lap and stroked the seam as if smoothing a child's hair. The tram bell faded. Somewhere beyond the café's fogged windows, boots clicked in practiced cadence.

Jadwiga took a breath and let it out between her teeth. "We should go," she said. "Curfew is a liar and a bully. It pretends to be a friend until you cross it, and then it breaks your jaw."

They stood, three figures in the mirror's torn silver. Samuel reached for his coat. The satchel settled against him as if it were a piece of him that had wandered and now returned. He hesitated, then slid his notebook back into the bag. "A last rule," he said. "When it is possible to choose the slower, quieter step, choose it. The loudest courage dies first."

Irena nodded. The slips in her palm felt light, almost nothing. "Tomorrow," she said.

"Tomorrow," he answered.

They threaded toward the door, careful not to touch anyone they did not need to touch. Jadwiga pushed the handle and immediately the cold air pressed in. For an instant the fog outside eddied into the café, carrying the smell of the river and coal and night. Samuel stood back, letting the women pass first, and when Irena stepped by him, the brush of their coats was the smallest sound in the room. It made her think of a signal – like two strings twanged quietly in the dark to say we are here, we can still make music.

On the pavement, the world had narrowed again, as it did at evening now. Windows were shuttered; the lamplighter had left his punctuations of yellow along the street, each one too small to hold back the dark. In the distance, along an axis she could feel but not see, the new walls threw their cold geometry against the night. A boy blew on his hands at a corner, then disappeared down a stairwell into the earth.

Irena turned towards her companions as Samuel's smile flashed – a short, human flare in a starved landscape. "Tomorrow," he repeated, and then he was gone, a shadow walking the seam between one pool of lamplight and the next.

Jadwiga slipped her arm through Irena's as they turned the first corner. "We can trust him. He's careful," she said. "I like careful."

"He's a teacher, a professional, so that gives me confidence," Irena said.

"That, too," Jadwiga said.

Irena nodded. A window opened above them and someone shook a rag; dust fell in a fine, glittering rain, catching in their hair. She thought of the boy at the gate, of the rumour Jadwiga had relayed, of the way the café had simmered in near silence. She thought of two slips of paper cupped in her hand like seeds.

"I like being useful," she said at last. "And I like roads that go somewhere."

They walked the rest of the way in a silence. Behind them, the café's bulb burned and burned until someone reached up and turned it off, and the mirror kept whatever it had seen the way old glass does, not reflecting, not telling, but holding on to secrets, dim and stubborn, like the three faces it watched for a short while before they disappeared into the dark.

2

Warsaw, November 1940

In the mornings, City Hall breathed like it contained wild animals penned too tightly: that curled in on themselves in an act of self-preservation, behind doors that swallowed people and coughed them back out with new creases between the brows. The marble floors had been polished for other regimes – governments that had believed their intricate ceilings carved in stone meant something – and now those same ceilings looked down on a new regime, new shadows with the same old hunger for stamps.

Irena stood in a corridor where the walls were a tired yellow, gone the colour of nicotine by years of ministry smoke. A black-enamelled stove ticked in the corner like a clock with a cough. The queue inched forward, each person shuffling a small dossier of their life: reasons for travel, reasons for bread, reasons for living where they had lived all their lives.

When the door of the Permits Office opened, a slice of brighter light cut the corridor, and for a second she could see the room like a stage: desks in regimented rows; Polish clerks hunched at typewriters, a new stoop in the shoulders of men once proud of their penmanship; a German officer near the back, his uniform a study of creases and insignia, his cap on a hook like a bird of prey at rest. Between door swings the sound reached them: the percussive chatter of keys, a rubber stamp thudding, voices clipped short before they became opinions.

Her satchel hung heavy at her hip containing soap requisitions, inventory lists written twice (once for the Germans, once for the truth), a folded letter from the parish doctor using words like sanitation and prophylaxis, as if those words, properly arranged, could pass men through walls. She touched the top flap, as much to reassure the papers as herself and felt the small rectangular pulse of the welfare department's seal.

"Next," the clerk at the door called, and she stepped into the light.

The Permits Office was warmer than the corridor; the stove here worked like a conscript. Somewhere behind the desks a kettle hissed, but no one looked as if they expected tea. Two portraits had once hung on the far wall, white rectangles remained where they had been, leaving ghosts of faces that would not be coming back. Opposite, a notice board sagged with new decrees: a tangle of German nouns nailed over the Polish ones like cages hung on cages.

"I can take you," said a voice at the nearest desk, and when she turned she found a man whose face she knew in the way one knows all faces that work too hard. Wiktor, a municipal clerk who used to recite fragments of Słowacki while waiting for the ink to dry, had trimmed his bushy moustache to something neat, unremarkable and obedient. His eyes, though, held their old quickness, even if they looked sideways more often now.

"Good morning," Irena said. "I have an application."

Wiktor glanced at the German officer, a quick flick of the

eyes that could have been a tic, and then back to her. He held out his hand. "We all do," he said lightly, the smallest of laments tucked in the joke. "Let's see yours."

She loosed the strap of the satchel and drew out her packet. He took it without flourish, as if receiving a letter from a cousin. His fingers were ink-stained; a crescent of black under each nail made the hands look perpetually bruised. He spread the papers like cards and began to read, the muscles along his jaw working.

"Welfare Department inspection schedule," he murmured, so quietly the typewriters could have mistaken it for a breath. "Sanitation." He dipped his pen and wrote the word again in the proper blank, careful, patient letters. "Reason for access: disease surveillance, disinfestation protocols, child hygiene." He slid a glance up at her. "You are very clean, Irena Sendler."

"We try," she said. She kept her face as open as a window with the curtains drawn back. "We are very busy with lice and laundry, pan Wiktor."

He nodded once and turned the next sheet. "You brought a doctor's letter."

"Of course."

He read it, not the words, which he could have written himself in his sleep by now, but the spaces between them: the precise dates that were less precise than they seemed; the sentence that chained one department's authority to another's as if authority were a thing you could braid. When he reached the final line, he exhaled. The breath fogged in the cold patch by the window, then vanished.

"This will go to Herr Oberleutnant Hartmann," he said, almost conversational, and at the name the room seemed to lean a fraction toward the back desk where the German officer sat with a fountain pen that gleamed like a weapon. Hartmann's hair was the colour of winter straw; his skin had the clear, smooth look of a man who had never gone without. He bent over a stack of applications as if the right angle of his spine could support a whole city.

Wiktor squared the pages. "He likes order," he added in the tone of a man who had discovered that water is often wet. "He dislikes adjectives but he likes stamps. Do you like stamps?"

"I adore them," she said.

He smiled with only one corner of his mouth, a movement so small it could have been a twitch. "Good. Let us give him a few." He reached for a stamp, rolled it through an ink pad, and depressed it onto her top page. The red seal bled a little. "And now," he said, rising, "we go to the bird."

He gathered her application and moved toward the back of the room. She followed, careful not to look at the others in line who might wonder why this woman got to skip the waiting. She felt their curiosity like fingers pressing between her shoulder blades. The typewriters nattered on. Someone coughed; someone else pretended not to hear.

Wiktor stopped before Hartmann's desk and stood politely. "Herr Oberleutnant," he said in a serviceable German, "a welfare inspection permit. Sanitation. The doctor has signed."

Hartmann did not look up at once. He finished the line he was writing, sanded the ink, blew on it. When he lifted his head, his eyes were the palest blue, as if even his gaze had been washed and wrung out. "Name," he said.

"Sendler," she answered, keeping her German neutral. "Irena."

"Position."

"Senior assistant, municipal social welfare, child and public health division." She could have said it backward in the dark; she said it now as if repeating catechism.

He read her papers with the same impersonal care she had seen surgeons apply to bones that belonged to other people.

"You request access for inspections," he said, as if narrating a play to a bored audience. “Frequency: twice weekly, variable days.” His mouth twitched with his dislike of adjectives. “Purpose: disinfestation and disease surveillance. The Board of Health approves.” His eyes flicked to Wiktor. “And you bring this to me because?”

“Because the area is restricted,” Wiktor said mildly. “And because the regulation requires your signature on any pass that would allow a Polish inspector to cross that line.”

“That regulation is wise,” Hartmann observed, placing the papers flat as if they might otherwise attempt flight. He tapped the topmost page with the barrel of his pen. “Disease does not recognise walls. People do. When they fail to recognise boundaries, we have... untidiness.”

Irena kept her breathing even. Untidiness. Rats, perhaps; fleas; hunger; the fact that those bodies still carried souls even when a stamp attempted to snuff them out.

Hartmann turned to the letter from the parish doctor. “He recommends regular delousing. Soap distribution,” he said, tasting the native word with faint distaste. “We are not a charity.”

“We are a city,” Irena said before she could fold the sentence back into herself. “Cities need to keep their epidemics small. Who knows where disease can spread and who could become infected.”

Wiktor’s shoe nudged her heel, the gentlest kick under a table. Hartmann’s eyes slid up to her face, not so much surprised as briefly interested, the way a man might be by a moth that insists on landing on his sleeve.

“You are very young to have such opinions,” he said.

“She is very experienced,” Wiktor said quickly, and his knuckles, resting on the edge of the desk, whitened.

Hartmann let the sheets lie a moment longer beneath his hand, as if testing whether the ink would run in fear from his scrutiny. Then, with a sigh too measured to be genuine feeling, he signed where signatures were required. He reached for a stamp the size of a child's fist.

"Twice weekly," he said, bringing the stamp down in a square, wet thud. "You will present yourself at the checkpoint with these documents. You will go where the inspector on duty says you may go. You will not linger." He brought the stamp down again, a rhythm, a beat. "You will not speak to persons not relevant to your task. You will not carry parcels in or out."

"I will have to carry soap," she said. Her throat felt tight and dry, as if the stamp had drawn moisture from the air.

"Soap is permitted," he said. He slanted a look that might have been suspicion and might have been a habit of face. "If I hear that your reports are... embellished... I will reduce your frequency to never."

"I don't embellish," she said. "Especially when I count lice."

Wiktor made a small sound, appreciation or warning, she couldn't tell. Hartmann seemed to have tired of her. He pushed the papers across the desk with a tap of the pen. "Next," he said to the room in general, and a woman with a shawl already stepped forward with a petition for coal.

Wiktor guided Irena a pace away from the desk and only then allowed his jaw to unlock. "You should have said less," he murmured without moving his lips.

"I could have said more," she murmured back.

"You could have come away with nothing," he said.

"Then I would have tried again tomorrow," she said softly.

He handed her the packet, the weight of it out of proportion to the paper. The red stamps bled at the edges like rude carnations. "These are good for thirty days," he said in his clerk's voice. "If the lice remain obediently apolitical, perhaps longer."

"The lice are better at politics than we are," she said.

A typewriter bell pinged; the stove coughed; the door opened and closed like a mouth learning one word.

"Go," Wiktor said. "Before he sets you in his sights. You were lucky he dislikes adjectives more than women."

She tucked the permits into her satchel and fastened the strap. "Thank you," she said, and meant it. "For the assistance," she added, because gratitude needed an object in times like this.

He inclined his head. "It was an honour."

She left the desk and re-entered the corridor, the line swallowing her and parting for her in the same motion. Someone's sleeve brushed her hand; a girl with a plait down her back watched her with the frank curiosity of eleven-year-olds everywhere. A man in a threadbare coat with a clerk's stoop adjusted the scarf at his throat and looked as if he had forgotten what he waited for. The door to the street sat at the end of the hall like a promise and she walked toward it, the satchel bumping her hip, the papers inside rubbing like dry leaves. At the landing a draft slid under the door and lifted the hair at her nape. She paused for the breath's space of a memory, holding the past few minutes in her mind and then headed for the door, ready to face the present.

The corridor at City Hall breathed down her neck, like the monster in a bad dream, pursuing her to the edge of freedom. She stood with her palm on the push plate of the door, the cold of the metal steadying her. She breathed in – and out.

Outside, the day was grey and raw. A wind came up the street, tugging at hats and patience. Trucks growled past, rattling the glass in City Hall's windows. Civilians moved in streams that avoided contact out of habit rather than hostility. Somewhere not far off, a new section of wall had gained another course of brick; the ringing of trowel on stone had begun to sound like the city's own heartbeat. She stepped out and let the door sigh shut behind her. The satchel hung on her hip and she put her hand over it as if a child slept there.

On the steps, a young German private was smoking, his helmet tipped back, his eyes the careless eyes of boys not yet visited by nightmares. He watched her come down, then looked away, uninterested; a Polish inspector in a serviceable coat was no one's romantic enemy. She passed him and felt more than saw, the same sneer Hartmann had not given her in person travel like weather down the chain of command. She cared not and vowed to learn to be small enough to be overlooked and large enough to carry what could be carried. She would carry soap. She would carry her load.

At the bottom of the steps, a woman with a baby tucked inside her coat held out a ration card and a question to no one in particular. Irena could not answer the question. She could not make the card turn into meat. The permits in her satchel knocked softly together like dry bones. She felt the ember in her chest lift its head to see what new air it had been given. The rules were brutal and many; the stamps were real; the officer's pale eyes had seen her and dismissed her.

Good.

She turned her collar up against the wind and set off toward the welfare office, the city unfolding ahead of her like a map she had no choice but to learn by heart. The papers at her hip – heavy with ink and authority, were only paper. But paper, properly used, could hold back floods for a moment, long enough to throw a rope, long enough to teach a breathless body how to breathe again. Long enough, perhaps, to carry a child through a door under the guise of inspection.

She walked faster. The day thinned. Somewhere a bell tolled, then another. The city did not bless her; the city did not curse her. It merely counted her among the footsteps and waited to see what she would do with the stamp she had wrestled from the morning as she made her way towards the Ghetto.

The checkpoint gate rose before her like a wound stitched into the city. It was taller than she remembered from the outside, posts driven deep into the cobbles, barbed wire twisting along the top in cruel spirals. Beyond it, brick walls joined end to end, closing streets that had once flowed with ordinary life. A sign in black German letters, nailed crookedly to the gate, barked a single word: *Verboten.* Forbidden.

The guard on duty checked her papers twice, turning each stamped page as if hunting for a lie that might spring out like a cockroach. He smirked when he read her purpose – sanitation inspection.

"Soap," he said, as if the syllable were a joke. His eyes flicked to her satchel. She let him see the corner of the box packed inside, neat bars wrapped in paper, the odour of lye, pungent and honest. He didn't bother to check deeper.

With a grunt, he handed her papers back and motioned her through. She stepped past the threshold, and the sound changed. Outside the walls, the city had been hushed, grey with the threat of curfew and drilled caution. Inside, the air vibrated with something else: the murmur of voices, the creak of carts, the faint whimper of a child. It was not silence, but it was not life as she had known it either. It was something held under water, breath forced out in bubbles.

The smell struck her first. Rot and damp and too many bodies in too little space. A sourness that seemed to seep from the stones themselves. Lice powder clung to clothing in chalky streaks; urine trickled in the gutters where drains had clogged long ago. The stench of waste and the pain of hunger was everywhere, stale bread, boiled turnips, cabbage gone slimy in its barrel.

The streets were narrower than they had been when she had walked them before the wall. Not narrower in stone, they were the same cobbled lanes, the same leaning tenements –but narrower with bodies. Families pressed against the walls, their bundles at their feet, waiting for something that never came. Children played half-heartedly in doorways with rags tied into knots, their eyes darting constantly toward the gate. Every step she took was hemmed by watchers, people who measured her coat, her shoes, her satchel with a glance.

And then they came. Children swarmed around her, quick as sparrows. Thin hands tugged at her sleeves, small voices rose in pleading Polish and Yiddish: "Please. Bread." The smallest of them clutched her skirt with desperate fingers, faces hollow with hunger, eyes too large for their heads. Their ribs pressed sharp through shirts that had once fit other children.

She froze, the instinct to clutch her satchel to her side like a miser. If the guards saw, if the wrong person noticed... But then she looked down, truly looked, and the caution cracked. She crouched, forcing her expression into calm, and opened the flap with hands steady by will alone. Inside, beneath the stack of soap, she had hidden loaves – small, dense, the crusts browned almost to black so they would keep.

One by one, as discreetly as possible, she pressed pieces into the hands that reached. She moved quickly, eyes darting to the guard at the corner, but the children were quicker. They clutched the bread and vanished, darting into doorways, scurrying down alleys like birds startled from cover. For each one fed, two more appeared, voices whispering, tugging, begging. She had to close the flap at last, her satchel suddenly light, her heart heavy with the weight of all she could not give.

A cart rolled past her, its wooden wheel shrieking against the axle. She turned her head, expecting vegetables or coal. Instead, a child lay curled inside, limbs stiff, eyes half-closed, a ragged blanket pulled only to his chin. A man, his father, perhaps, or his neighbour, pushed the cart, his face hollowed to stone. He did not meet anyone's gaze.

The boy could not have been more than five. His lips were tinged with blue, his hair matted damp against his forehead. One arm lolled over the side of the cart as it bumped along. Irena stopped in the middle of the street, unable to breathe. The sounds of the ghetto dulled around her, as if she had been shoved into a bell jar. She wanted to reach out, to tuck the child's arm back under the blanket, to give him dignity in death if not in life. But her feet would not move, her throat locked.

The cart squealed on. The man's shoes scuffed the stones, steady, resigned. No one cried out. No one followed. It was simply another cart among many. She fought for control, blinking hard, forcing her lungs to fill again. She pressed a fist to her mouth to hold back the cry clawing its way up. Tears stung her eyes, but she swallowed them. Tears were too costly here, too loud.

When her breathing steadied, she lifted her chin and looked around her. At the children peering from doorways, crusts clutched in their fists. At the women bent double over buckets, washing clothes that would never come clean. At the soldiers with rifles at ease, their faces blank with boredom, as if guarding hunger were no different from guarding bricks.

The satchel at her side was nearly empty now, but her hands itched with more than bread. Food would fill bellies for a day, perhaps a few hours. But hope – hope might last longer, if she could carry it in with her, if she could leave it behind like a hidden seed in the cracks of this walled prison.

Her father's words rose again in her mind: *If you see a man drowning, jump in. Even if you cannot swim.*

She could not stop the wall from rising. She could not stop the cart from rolling away. But she could carry loaves, and whispers. She could walk into this place again and again with soap and bread and whatever else she could hide in her satchel, until her legs failed her or her luck did. She straightened her shoulders. The stench clung to her coat, the cries still rang in her ears, but the flame in her chest burned hotter now, catching. She resolved, standing in that narrow street, not just to bring food. She would bring hope.

Night, and the fever was a small furnace in a small room. Her father's cough had a new depth to it, a chasm in the middle of a man who had always seemed made of stone and rich wood. The lamp burned low; shadows gathered at the corners like skinny cats watching for a skinny mouse. She sat on the chair by the bed and held his hand, which was both too hot and too cold.

"You should rest, Tatusiu," she said. "I will sit."

"I have rested enough for ten men," he said, and the smile that went with it was the shape of his old smile, if not the colour. "How many shoes have you worn through this week, Irenka?"

"None," she lied.

He turned his head to the window. Somewhere beyond it, a horse snorted; beyond that, the sky did what skies do even when no one looks. "They asked me to stop," he said, and his breath rasped like paper. "They said, 'Doctor, you must not go to the shacks by the river. You will bring it back to us.' As if the river ended in those shacks. As if you could pin disease to a map and it would stay like a dead butterfly."

"You should have stopped," she said, and the adult in her understood the nonsense of the sentence while the child in her needed to say it. "You should have sent one of the younger doctors."

"I am one of the younger doctors," he said, amusement

flashing and fading. Then he turned his head to her. "I did not stop because I could not stop. Not because I am good." The grip of his fingers tightened. "Do not judge me, my child."

She felt her throat fill with something thick and hot. "I won't," she said. "I will be proud of you always."

"If you see a man drowning," he whispered, his voice a map she could walk by touch, "you must jump in. Even if you cannot swim."

"I remember," she said. She would remember so hard the remembering would itself become a church inside her mind.

"Do not betray the living because you are angry with me," he said. "Promise me."

"I promise," she said, and held his hand until the lamp guttered and the cats in the corners retreated and the little furnace by the bed cooled, leaving her alone to keep vigil through the night.

3

Warsaw Ghetto, January 1941

Snow had fallen two days earlier and lingered in the alleys as grey slush, trampled into the cobbles by desperate feet. Inside the ghetto, even in winter, the smell of unwashed bodies, boiled vegetables, and sickness clung to the walls and seeped into clothing.

Irena left the empty trunk at the bottom of the steps, her cargo of soap already distributed, save for the few bars in her pockets, then climbed a narrow staircase, her breath visible in the chill, her satchel containing what was left of the bread she'd smuggled in, heavier than it had ever felt. The tenement groaned under its burden, snow laden rooftops, doors that no longer closed properly, stairs bowed from too many hurried feet. She ducked beneath a lintel and stepped into a room that might once have held a family comfortably but now strained to contain three, perhaps four.

The stove in the corner was cold, its pipe black with soot. A single window faced the street, frost feathering its edges, glass cracked in two places but patched with paper. A cot leaned against the wall, blankets heaped into a mound where a child's head peeked out, curls dark against the pallor of her cheek.

Miriam rose from her stool when Irena entered. She was no older than Irena herself, though hunger had carved deep lines around her mouth and eyes. Her hands twisted a ragged handkerchief, knuckles raw from cold and washing. She said nothing at first, only gestured toward the child.

"Hanna," Irena said gently, kneeling beside the cot. The girl stirred, eyes opening slowly. She was four, perhaps, though small enough to pass for three. Her cheeks were hollow, her lips chapped, her gaze startlingly large in her narrow face. She blinked at Irena, wary, the way all children here had learned to be.

"She hasn't eaten since yesterday," Miriam said, her voice low, roughened by exhaustion. "I gave her half of my bread, but she pushed it back." Her hand trembled as she reached to touch Hanna's hair. "She is already giving me goodbyes, I know it."

Irena drew a small roll from her satchel and tore it in half. She offered it to Hanna, who took it with slow fingers, nibbling as if afraid it might vanish if she bit too greedily. Irena's chest tightened.

Miriam leaned closer, her eyes searching Irena's face. "Can you take her? Out. Beyond the wall."

The words dropped like stones in the narrow room.

Irena glanced at the window, at the frost tracing patterns on the glass, at the cracked plaster walls. "Miriam –"

"Better she forget me than follow me to where they are sending people on the trains. Treblinka"

Treblinka. The name, spoken aloud, seemed to suck the air from the room. It was only January but already rumours of the camp had spread. Of trains that left full and returned empty, whispers of smoke that clung to the skies of distant villages. No one said the word easily, but Miriam spoke it with the clarity of someone who knew the truth and had already buried her hope.

Irena swallowed, her throat tight. She knew it had been done, and she also knew the risks and the rules. "If I take her, she must never speak her name again. She must learn to answer to another. Do you understand?"

"I understand." Miriam's hands stilled, then clenched. "Better she forget she ever had a mother, than –" Her voice broke. She pressed the handkerchief to her mouth and drew in a ragged breath. "I won't see her grow and the pain of that... But she must grow so I will bear it, for her."

Irena looked at Hanna, who chewed slowly on the crust of bread, her eyes wide and solemn. The enormity of the choice pressed down like a weight on her shoulders. Who was she to take another woman's child? Who was she to decide a girl's future with a forged paper and a knock on a stranger's door? Yet the alternative loomed like the walls themselves. If Hanna stayed, she would shrink further each day until she vanished. The ghetto devoured children. Bread bought hours, not years.

Irena sat on the edge of the cot and reached for Hanna's hand. The girl's fingers were small, brittle with cold. "Would you like to come with me, Hanna? To see the world outside these walls?"

The child nodded, crumbs at the corner of her mouth. She did not smile.

Miriam pressed her hand to her chest, her face contorted as if she could not bear to let the sound of her sobs distress the child. "Promise me," she whispered. "Promise me she will live. Promise me she will be safe."

Irena hesitated. Promises had become dangerous currency. Safety was never certain. But she saw Miriam's eyes, saw the raw plea in them, and she could not refuse.

"I promise," she said softly. "I will do everything I can to keep her safe."

Miriam leaned down, gathering Hanna into her arms, holding her so tightly that the girl let out a small protest. Miriam pressed kisses across her forehead, her hair, her cheeks, as if memorizing her by touch. "My sweet girl," she murmured in Yiddish, words tumbling, fierce, endless. "Remember nothing. Forget me if you must. Just live. Live for me."

Hanna squirmed, uncomfortable in her mother's desperation, but Miriam clung tighter for a moment before finally setting her back down. Her hands shook as she reached for Irena's. "Go before I change my mind."

Irena nodded, her own eyes burning. She adjusted her satchel, mentally preparing herself for what she was about to do. Imagining hiding Hanna's small form inside the trunk she used to transport the bars of soap to the ghetto, already rehearsing the route in her mind: through the gate with her papers, maybe a few scratches to the head and face to repulse the guards who would hurry her through, the faint hope that one small child could pass unseen.

Her fingers brushed Hanna's hair, smoothing it back, and as she did so, a memory tugged her under.

The kitchen table was a fortress. Its wooden legs were thick as trees, its underside a canopy that smelled of bread crust and dust. Irena crouched beneath it, knees to chest, while her father's voice wove stories above.

"Do you know, Irenka," he said, his cough milder back then, "that in the old days, Poland was guarded by a great white eagle?"

She peeked between the table legs, watching his boots shift as he stirred the pot on the stove. "A real eagle?"

"As real as the apples on the tree," he said, smiling down at her. "Its wings stretched wide enough to shade the fields. When enemies came, it cried out, and the people grew brave. They remembered they were not alone."

She giggled, tucking her chin to her knees. "Did the eagle live under a table too?"

"Perhaps," he said, pretending to consider. "Perhaps under a bigger one. With legs like castle towers. Maybe he was hiding, waiting for the right moment to fly again."

She had clutched the table leg then, heart swelling with the idea that even in hiding, the eagle still watched. Even in darkness, there was a guardian.

The memory faded, leaving her back in the cramped apartment, Hanna's hand in hers, Miriam's hollow eyes watching. Irena's resolve solidified. She would not be a rescuer of eagles – she would be the hand that lifted a child through a gate, one after another, until her strength or courage gave out.

She rose, drawing Hanna up beside her. "It is time."

Miriam kissed her daughter once more, then pressed a tiny cross into Irena's palm, fashioned from two sticks tied with thread. "For her," she whispered.

Irena nodded. She met Miriam's gaze – one mother's vow, one daughter's promise.

Then, taking Hanna's small hand, she stepped toward the door leaving the sound of muffled sobs behind. At the bottom of the stairs, Irena couched and opened the lid then placed a finger on her lips before signalling to Hanna that she must get inside. There was large keyhole that she prayed would let in enough air during the next few minutes but also, she hoped Hanna understood the danger.

"We are going to play a game, like hide and seek so you must be quiet, and do not make a sound until I tell you to come out. Do not move until I say those words. Can you do that?" Irena watched as the girls eye's widened and then she nodded.

Climbing inside, Hanna scrunched her tiny body into a ball and closed her eyes as Irena shut the lid. Irena covered her with rags and the rest of her sanitation equipment and prayed the guards would just let her through. Heaving the trunk upwards, she reminded herself that it should be empty so composed her expression so that carrying her load appeared effortless. Taking a deep breath, Irena began to walk.

The street leading to the gate narrowed to a funnel of fear. At its mouth stood two German soldiers with rifles slung easy against their shoulders, a dog straining against its lead, jaws wet with foam. The wire above the gate sagged under snow, but no eye dared mistake it for weakness. Everything here – bricks, boots, breath, belonged to them.

Irena's pulse pounded. Her hands gripped the handles of the carpenter's trunk, the weight of it pulling her arms longer with each step. The wood was scarred and splintered, smelling of dust and old nails. Inside, Hanna lay curled into the smallest version of herself, her knees drawn tight, breath held shallow.

"Do not move," Irena whispered. "You are a mouse in its hole. Mice are very quiet."

Now the box bobbed against Irena's stomach with each step, its weight not only physical but moral, immense, like carrying someone else's beating heart outside your chest. She forced herself to walk as if she belonged here, had nothing to hide, papers in her satchel, soap requisitioned and distributed, an inspector of lice and contagion. She had practiced the gait of authority in her mirror at night, but tonight the cobbles seemed to rise unevenly under her feet, each stone a trap.

"Next," one soldier barked. The man ahead of her shuffled through, presenting his pass. His sack was prodded with the rifle butt, then waved on.

Her turn.

Irena lifted her chin, handed over the stamped papers with fingers that did not tremble. The guard, a square-jawed youth whose cheeks had never known hunger, skimmed the documents. His eyes paused on her name, narrowed, then slid to the toolbox.

"What is this?" His German was sharp, official, each consonant a stone dropped in water.

"My tools," she answered in the same language, though her accent gave her away. She set the box on the inspection table, careful not to let it thud. "Inspector's instruments. Delousing, sanitary checks."

He smirked, amused by the idea of a woman with tools. He tapped the lid with his knuckle. "Open."

Her throat tightened. She reached for the clasp, forcing her hand steady, and lifted it. The lid creaked.

Inside, rags lay in neat folds, brushes and small bottles arranged like the kit of a conscientious inspector. Beneath them, Hanna lay hidden, silent, holding herself as tightly as if she could fold into invisibility. Irena bent low, and made to show the guard the contents, but as she did, with her other hand she began scratching at her head, then her neck, wincing as if in great discomfort.

The guard leaned closer, then on seeing her scratching, pulled back quickly, disgusted, wrinkling his nose. At that moment, the dog lunged forward, teeth bared, barking furiously at the box. The sound tore through the street, feral, insistent.

Irena's heart slammed against her ribs. She snapped the lid

shut with a crack that made the soldiers startle. "Careful!" she barked, her own voice rising sharp with manufactured indignation. She straightened to her full height, planting both hands on the box.

"These are delicate, expensive tools. If your beast breaks one, who will pay for it? I will have to report it to your officer."

The soldier blinked, caught off guard by her audacity. For an instant, she thought he might laugh and order her arrested anyway, but he shifted instead, sobered by the possibility that he might be called before his superiors.

The other soldier chuckled, shaking his head. "Let her through. She's probably riddled with bugs. Not worth the trouble and I don't want to catch whatever she's got."

The guard flushed, handed back her papers without looking her in the eye. "Go," he muttered.

For good measure, Irena scratched her head one more time and then gripped the handles of the trunk, lifting it with both hands. Her knees nearly buckled with relief as she moved past the gate, her steps quickening though she forced them not to break into a run. The dog's barking faded behind her, swallowed by the drone of another patrol marching in formation.

She kept walking, past a row of shuttered shops, past civilians who turned their faces away. Only when she reached the shadow of a narrow alley did she set the box down, her hands shaking as she unlatched the lid.

"Hanna," she whispered.

The girl blinked up into the pale light, her cheeks flushed from holding her breath. She drew in a gulp of cold air and clutched the edge of the box as if emerging from underwater.

"Where is Mama?" she whispered.

The question pierced sharper than the dog's bark, sharper than the guard's suspicion. Irena's throat closed. Words clogged, useless. How could she tell this child that her mother had stayed behind in the grey warren, that she had pressed her lips to her daughter's hair and whispered goodbye in the language of love and loss?

She reached in, lifted Hanna into her arms. The child's body was light, frighteningly so, her bones a bird's beneath the thin wool dress. Irena held her close, pressing her cheek against the girl's curls, breathing her in.

"Where is Mama?" Hanna asked again, softer this time, as if already knowing no answer would come.

Irena's lips trembled against the child's temple. She could not speak the truth, not here, not now. She could only hold her tighter, carry her into the cold light of the free side of the wall, and vow silently, fiercely, that she would not let the promise break. That she would keep her safe.

4

Warsaw, Christmas 1942

Snow sifted down in flour-fine flakes that could not soften the city's hard edges. Somewhere, muffled by distance, a reminder of the looming curfew, a church bell marked the hour as if time were a surviving species that could be counted and fed. The river moved under ice, a slow, dark muscle; the walls stood, the wire scored with frost, and beyond them the ghetto breathed shallowly, as if even air had been rationed.

Irena set a kettle on the iron ring of her small stove and watched the flame nibble at its belly. Her apartment was two rooms, not counting the cupboard of a bathroom, and yet she had learned to live in even less: a corner by the window for reading reports; a strip of table for cutting soap into pieces small enough to pass through a hand without notice; a drawer that locked, an envelope that did not leave smudges when handled. On the sill, she had lined up three apples she'd bartered for with a week's ration of sugar. They were perfuming the air with a faint, stubborn sweetness that fought the stove's coal dust. One would go to a neighbour with a cough; one would go to Jadwiga; the last would be saved for the child who came in a different coat every time.

A knock at the door rattled the glass in the frame. She slid the bolt and opened it as far as the chain allowed.

"Don't you ever just say 'come in' like a normal person?" Jadwiga whispered, her breath smoking in the hall. Her cheeks were red from the cold; her hair tucked beneath a hat that had once been fashionable and now was only warm. She held a paper-wrapped bundle under one arm.

"I am not any kind of normal person," Irena said, unhooking the chain. "And neither are you."

Jadwiga stepped inside and shoved the door with the heel of her hand until the latch caught. "God grant you the sense to be ordinary for one evening," she muttered, unspooling the scarf from her neck. She stomped her boots on the mat and sniffed. "Is that tea or wishful thinking?"

"Both," Irena said, setting two chipped cups on the table. "Sit."

Jadwiga glanced around the little room with the practiced inventory of someone who knew that safety lived in small decisions. Curtains: drawn. Floor: swept of telltale grit. Stove: banked low enough that the glow did not advertise itself to the street. Satisfied, she loosened her coat and laid the paper bundle by the cups. "Bread," she said. "A miracle of yeast and bribery. The baker's wife owed me a favour from the old days when I wrote an article about her lemon tart."

"Lemon tart," Irena repeated, unable to keep the hunger from her voice – not for the tart, but for the memory of a world in which sentences could include such a thing without making you sound drunk on nostalgia.

"We will eat," Jadwiga said. "That is my liturgy for

Christmas. We will eat, and we will not talk about lice while we do it."

"We will eat," Irena agreed. She poured tea – brown, thin, steaming, and set a knife to the loaf. The crust fought her; the bread yielded grudgingly, heavy and proud. She cut two thick slices and placed one on each plate, then halved one of the apples and offered the better half to Jadwiga.

"Saint Irena of the Apple," Jadwiga said, biting into it with audible pleasure. "You spoil me."

"Don't canonise me yet," Irena said. "I'm going to commit a sin of paper."

Jadwiga paused mid-bite. "What kind of sin?"

Irena did not answer immediately. She crossed to the small chest against the far wall and drew open the bottom drawer. From beneath a folded blanket, she lifted a tin that had once held sweets, its lid dented, its painted roses rubbed almost to ghosts. She brought it to the table and set it down between them with a care that made Jadwiga straighten.

"Do you remember Hanna?" Irena asked.

Jadwiga's face softened in reflex. "The sparrow. She put her whole fist in the teacup when I gave it to her."

"She is called Hania now," Irena said. "At least, in the parish ledger. And at the convent she is little Ania to the sisters. She answers when they call; she kneels when they kneel. When she laughs, she sounds like a hinge that has just been oiled." The corner of her mouth tugged upward, then flattened again. "She no longer startles at dogs."

"That is not a sin," Jadwiga said.

"No," Irena agreed. She unclasped the tin and lifted the lid. Inside lay small scraps of paper, each folded into a neat, tight bud. She took one up and set it on the table, then another, and another. "This is the sin."

Jadwiga stared, the apple forgotten in her hand. "What are those?"

"Names," Irena said simply. She unfolded the top scrap, smoothing it with the side of her thumb. "Her true name. The one her mother gave her. The one she must hear again if the world turns and she is allowed to be herself. Hanna Miriam Lewin." She tapped the second scrap. "Her new name. Hania Anna Kowalska. The date I carried her. The place she sleeps." Her finger moved to the third. "And here, the names of her mother and father. A place to start, if there is anything left to start from."

Jadwiga's breath leaked out in a hiss. "Fold them up," she whispered, as if the paper could hear. "Fold them up and burn them."

Irena did not move. The kettle began to mutter on the stove, a low, companionable sound, as if the room contained nothing more dangerous than steam. "More children are coming," she said quietly. "One by one, sometimes two in a bundle like kittens. Each arrives wearing a borrowed name." She touched the little pile, not quite caress, not quite blessing. "If they survive, they must know who they are."

"'If they survive,'" Jadwiga echoed, and then put her hands flat on the table as if to hold herself in place. "If. If." She squeezed her eyes shut for a heartbeat, opened them.

"Irena, listen to me. If they find this, it will be both our deaths."

The sentence hung at a height they both could see: the height of German boots on the stairs, the height of a key turning in the lock. Death, as administrative tidiness signed and stamped and filed. Death as a byproduct of ink.

"Then we must make it hard to find," Irena said, and her voice did not shake. She bent over the tin and took out one more folded scrap. "Read this one."

"I will not touch them," Jadwiga said, recoiling. "I will not put my fingerprints on anything the devil might read."

Irena slid the scrap within her friend's reach. "Read quietly, please."

Jadwiga hesitated, then inched the paper closer with one fingertip, as if nudging a beetle out of harm's way. She unfolded it. Her lips moved, but no sound came: a girl's name, a boy's; a street that used to keep a bakery's hours; the word *orphanage* disguised as *aunt*. She folded the paper again and set it down like a hot coal. "They will hang us," she said hoarsely.

"They will," Irena said, and felt, in the saying, a bitter clarity. "One day, for something. For a loaf we did not log. For a soap bar that fell into the wrong hands. For looking like ourselves when the new rules require us to be someone else. I would rather be hanged for the price of giving a child back her own name."

Jadwiga's laugh was a small, broken thing. "You say that as if I disagree with the result. I disagree with the method." She reached for the knife and cut the crust from her bread with surgical care. "Hide anything you like in your head. Your head is very clever and very hard to search. But paper – paper is a gossip. It tells on you in your own handwriting."

The kettle boiled over into a hiss. Irena rose, lifted it, poured. The steam fogged the glass of the window and made the room briefly a cloud. "Paper can be taught discretion," she said. "In the right tin. Under the right earth. With the right guardian."

"The right guardian?" Jadwiga repeated, wary.

Irena set the cups down and sat. The tin sat between them like a small altar. "Helena's garden," she said. "You know the apple tree, its roots run deep. The soil is easy to dig if you know where the stones are." She touched the top scrap lightly once more before folding it back into its bud. "I will bury the names there in a metal box, sealed. Two copies: one under the tree and one somewhere I will not tell even you. If I am taken, you go to Helena's. Or you go nowhere and live, and the tree holds the ledger until another winter, another year, or forever."

Jadwiga's eyes flared. "You will not tell me?"

"I will not tell you," Irena said. "Because I love you. Because if they catch you, you will talk. So will I. So will saints. So will stone, if you strike it long enough. Better for the ledger that it be loved by fewer people."

"Irena, for the thousandth time, stop," Jadwiga snapped, and then, unexpectedly, she laughed, an unsteady, incredulous sound that turned wet at the edges. She dragged the heel of her hand across one eye. "Fine. Fine. Bury your little treason orchard. But you will make a duplicate and you will put it... in a place even you don't look, or you will give it to someone who can walk away from you and never come back."

She had cut the scraps from ration forms and requisitions, the blank margins of decrees, the backs of cancelled permits. Each one bore two columns in her fine, upright hand: the child's name and the child's other name, the one that fit like a coat borrowed from a cousin. Between them, a line no thicker than a hair and yet it held the weight of two worlds. She wrote Hanna's first, because Hanna had come first; then she wrote the next child, and the next. Sometimes she had to stop to blow on the ink where the room's dampness made it slow to set. Sometimes she paused with the nib hovering, because the name she wanted to write belonged to a child who had not made it through the gate at all.

"Here," she murmured, and announced each without lifting her voice above the kettle's. "Jakub becomes Jacek. Sura becomes Zosia. Chava, Ewa." A last name. A mother's maiden name if she had known it, gleaned from a whisper in a stairwell.

A street. A church. A nun's first letter only, because nuns had names that could be taken hostage. She folded each scrap with four clean turns – corner to corner, edge to edge, until the name became a bud to be planted.

Jadwiga watched, her hands clenched around the cup, warming it, as if that warmth could be banked against a worse cold. "You make it sound like bookkeeping," she said. "As if you could balance loss and gain."

"It is a ledger," Irena said. "But it is not theirs." She did not look up. "They count bodies. We will count names."

"A ledger of Hope," Jadwiga said, the words escaping before she could decide whether to bless or mock them.

Irena's pen paused, then moved again. "So be it."

Outside, a car backfired, or a rifle, answering the unasked question of the street. Somewhere a gramophone, wound too tight, let go of one bar of a carol and then strangled.

Jadwiga set her cup down and stood to pace the short length of the room, three strides there, three back. "If they come –"

"We will put the tin in the stove and boil water for tea," Irena said calmly.

"If they start at your drawer?"

"They will find dishcloths." She looked up, her eyes steady. "Do you think I do not know how men search? I have watched them turn rooms into rags and miss the ring hanging on a nail because it looked like a nail."

"Arrogance," Jadwiga said, but there was admiration in it, rubbed raw by fear. She stopped by the window and hooked one finger through the curtain to peel back an inch. Snow feathered across the street. A shadow moved, became nothing. She let the cloth fall. "I want you to promise me something."

"I have already promised too much tonight," Irena said, and blew gently on the last wet line.

"Promise me that if you are caught, you will say you did not know me," Jadwiga said to the window, her voice as even as if she were ordering sugar from a grocer. "Say I was a woman in a café who once wrote about lemon tarts."

"If I am caught," Irena said, "I will tell them I am a woman who counts lice. And they will not believe me. Because men like Hartmann believe women are either what they see or what they want. They never consider we could be something else entirely."

"That is not the promise I asked for," Jadwiga said, turning.

Irena capped the pen and set it down. "I promise," she said. "I will not know you."

Jadwiga's mouth opened and closed; she nodded once, sharply, as if swallowing a bitter pill. She came back to the table and took a slice of bread and bit so hard the crust cracked. "God help me," she said around the mouthful. "I am the sort of friend who helps dig the hole."

"You are the sort of friend who brings bread," Irena said. "There are worse saints." She lifted the tin and began to return the folded scraps, arranging them in a fan, not alphabetical. She replaced the lid and snapped the clasp shut. The soft click sounded like the closing bar of a hymn.

"Tomorrow," she said. "Before noon." She would go to Helena's, to the garden that had no business being green in winter and yet always managed a stubborn hue where the roots ran rich. She would carry a trowel and a story about bulbs that needed planting. She would fold two oilcloths around the tin and tie them with kitchen string. She would press the earth smooth when she was done and leave a fallen apple to mark the spot for no one but herself.

Jadwiga pulled her scarf back around her neck. "Take care," she said. "Do not let your courage outpace your cleverness."

"They run side by side," Irena said, and tucked the tin into the bottom drawer again, under the blanket, under the ordinary.

They ate the rest of the bread. They split the second apple

and pretended not to notice how their fingers trembled when the knife slipped and kissed skin. They spoke of nothing that mattered – of a neighbour's cat that had learned to open the pantry; of a dress in a shop window downtown that had not yet been requisitioned for an officer's wife; of a rumour that the tram would resume running through Pancerna Street, which meant nothing and everything. They did not speak of the ghetto, though it lay on the other side of the wall like a rotting body on the other side of a door you dared not open.

When Jadwiga rose to go, the bells began again, as Irena helped with her coat, her gloves, her hat. At the threshold, Jadwiga caught her wrist.

"Say it once more," she said. "Before I walk into the street."

Irena understood. She took one breath and let the words settle in her mouth like a wafer.

"If they survive, they must know who they are."

Jadwiga closed her eyes, nodded. "And if we do not?"

"Then the tree will remember," Irena said. "And if I am caught, I never knew your name."

They embraced briefly, fiercely, and then Jadwiga slipped into the stairwell, her steps careful on the boards that creaked. The door clicked shut. The room became smaller again, as rooms do when the person who makes them larger leaves.

Irena stood with her palm pressed to the drawer. Then she moved, because movement was the only instruction her body obeyed when thought spun into fear. She banked the stove, rinsed the cups, set the knife to dry. She straightened the apples on the sill. She sat, finally, and allowed herself one minute, only one, in which to imagine a day when the tin would be opened under a different sky, and a woman who had lived long enough to have grey hair would unfold a scrap and say a name aloud, and a child who was a woman would answer, and the sound would be a kind of resurrection.

The minute ended. She rose and blew out the lamp. In the dark, the city shifted its weight on its broken bones. Beneath a blanket, in the bottom drawer of a modest apartment, the Ledger of Hope began to breathe.

5

Church of St. Klemens, basement crypt – Winter 1942

The church basement was ingrained with the scent of old incense, and held a unique aura, as though the cellars remembered every prayer ever whispered inside them. Candles burned low in saucers, their wax pooled like melted moons; the wicks guttered whenever the winter wind nosed down the stairwell and tugged at the flame. A black crucifix hung crooked on the limewashed wall, and beneath it a long table had been assembled out of mismatched boards set on crates. Around that table sat priests in worn cassocks, a handful of women with sleeves rolled back and eyes sharp as needles, and men whose hands looked as if they belonged to bricklayers but whose voices fell to a conspirator's hush the moment the door closed.

Irena came late enough not to be noticed by anyone who didn't already know her, early enough to catch the rhythm of the room before it could harden into suspicion. She slipped onto a bench near the end and warmed her hands over a candle's breath. Across the table, Samuel lifted his head.

He had lost weight since October: the planes of his face carved sharper, the teacher's tweed coat gone baggy at the shoulders. Even in a cellar he carried himself as if someone might ask him to diagram a sentence on the wall. His eyes found hers and were steady, measuring, and dipped in the smallest of nods. He did not smile. No one smiled much anymore.

Father Antoni, whose hair had greyed in streaks that made him look perpetually surprised, cleared his throat. "We begin," he said, as if he could light an agenda the way he lit a candle. He was the sort of priest who typically kept order by telling stories; tonight, he dispensed with parable. "We are agreed on three matters. First: there are more children than we can count, and not enough doors to hide them behind. Second: papers that passed muster once are suspect the next time. Third: every day we wait, we risk losing a name so we must forge ahead regardless of the risks. Yes?"

Murmurs. The women nodded. One man tightened a knot in a length of twine as if he were cinching up the whole city.

"There is a problem we can solve before we begin again." Father Antoni leaned over the map on the table, a hand-drawn welter of streets, arrows, and initials. "We must create noise. The wrong kind, at the wrong time. Babies hidden under blankets or in sacks do not understand silence as a strategy." His smile was one of tenderness, not humour. "And neither do dogs."

A priest in wire spectacles lifted a finger. "I spoke to Brother Leon at the Franciscan house. He trained dogs before the war, sheepdogs mostly, and once a stubborn hound for a countess who had neither time nor inclination. He believes we can teach barking as camouflage."

"Train them to bark on command," said a woman with a seamstress's thimble denting the pad of her middle finger. "To cover the sound of a child." She leaned forward; the candle set sparks in her black eyes. "Or to warn us if a patrol rounds the corner while a bundle is crossing, so the bundle freezes before the guard hears it breathe. It is a good idea."

Samuel turned his notebook toward the light and began to write in his neat, schoolmaster's hand. "We will need handlers who can move with us. Women are less questioned in courtyards," he said. "A barking dog beside a laundry basket looks like a nuisance, not a message."

"You have passed through many times so what do you think?" another woman murmured and touched Irena's wrist under the table. "You and your soap and a dog."

Irena was already counting how many dogs, how many mouths, how many bribes to kennel-men who now wore armbands and rationed loyalty. "Two dogs per route," she said. "No more, and don't vary the breeds. If we bring the same white terrier past the same gate three times, a bored soldier will remember and presume it's a pet. A strange dog with a familiar handler might arouse suspicion. It has to look natural."

Father Antoni nodded. "Brother Leon can assemble a training circle in the old sacristy yard. We cannot waste food, but broth and bones will make the dog our friend. They are starving, too. He'll teach two signals: a low, continuous bark to 'cover the crying' and one sharp burst which means 'stop, danger.'" He looked around the table. "We agree?"

Hands, gloved and bare, lifted. Decision settled in the room like a blanket.

"Next," said a young man whose barber's hands had learned to file keys instead of nails. "Documents. The last batch passed one day and were rejected and torn the next. We must make them look like real papers with creases in the right place, the right smell. German ink smells different." He produced a stamp from his pocket, cradled in cloth like a relic. "Wiktor at City Hall sent word: Hartmann has changed the registrar's ink pad. It leaves a faint violet halo. We will mimic it with gentian drops.

We will also finger-grease the paper edges. Lick nothing. They could smell that too."

Samuel underlined *gentian* and wrote *grease edges* beside it. When he lifted his eyes, they found Irena again. "Routes," he said. "We move in pairs. The inspector and the assistant. The assistant is a voice. The inspector is a wall. If stopped, the assistant speaks fast and pleasantly, so the guard attends to the mouth, not to the hands."

"I can be a mouth," Jadwiga said from the shadows, surprising Irena because she hadn't seen her slip in. "God gave me one for this purpose and has regretted it ever since."

A ripple, something like laughter loosened the room's shoulders. The crucifix on the wall seemed to lean nearer.

Maps were turned; doors were assigned codes. *Carpenter* meant a left-hand alley with a drain wide enough to swallow a child; *Choir* meant the one-eyed nun who could turn any name into Latin and back again. There were, too, decisions about money: who delivered what envelope to which aunt who was not an aunt. Every choice felt like an egg carried under a coat. If you walked too fast, it would break. If you walked too slow, it would be taken.

"Last," Father Antoni said, "we must speak of limits." His gaze moved from face to face and came to rest, unapologetically, on Irena. "There will be nights when we say no. Not because we are cruel, but because arithmetic is cruel. We cannot promise everyone a door."

Irena felt the ember in her chest heat, banked by habit but still dangerous. "We can promise to try," she said. "And to try again when a door is shut."

"Yes," said the barber-turned-forger. "But we cannot smash our own hands on the door until we cannot sign another paper."

Samuel's pencil hovered, uncharacteristically idle. "We will not argue about willingness," he said, and his voice was honed with sleep loss. “But I would like us to be honest about the math. Every time we move, the net tightens. Every success teaches them where to look next.”

He was looking at her again. Not accusing, just measuring. She looked back. In the candlelight he seemed older than the last time she had seen him in the café.

“You can’t save them all,” he said, and his voice filled the room without needing to rise. “You cannot. And if you insist, you will save fewer.”

The words landed like stones. They were not cruel. They were worse than cruel because they were true.

Irena met them with her own truth. “I understand but if we say that sentence too often, we will save fewer also,” she said quietly. “Because it will make it easier to say no.”

For a moment the room listened only to the tiny tick of cooling metal as someone set a kettle away from the flame. Father Antoni folded his hands. Jadwiga looked between Irena and Samuel and rolled her eyes as if the saints were misbehaving at supper.

Samuel set down his pencil. “I am not asking you to let go,” he said. “I am asking you to consider that some nights we lift the bundle and some nights we leave empty handed. Both are necessary.”

“Leaving without a bundle causes grief to many,” Irena said.

“And in these times grief is something we must learn to bear,” he answered.

They looked at one another a heartbeat too long for modesty.

Father Antoni cleared his throat, the arbiter’s bell. “We will do both,” he said. “We will do them in the right ratio, discovered as we go. And we will not let the devil convince us that argument will do his work for him.”

A few heads dipped: apology, assent. Samuel's mouth softened. Irena let her fingers unclench under the table, then balled them again to trap the tremor. The seamstress slid a scrap of folded cloth across to Irena's hand, something to occupy a nervous thumb. It was the hem of a christening gown, yellowed, delicate as old breath.

"Very well," the barber said briskly, relief turning his voice practical again. "Dogs. Brother Leon can begin teaching tomorrow at Vespers. Handlers, raise a hand." Three women and one slight man lifted theirs. Irena added hers to the small forest. "Good. You will meet in the yard with no more than two dogs each. No names. Dogs answer to whistles, not to words. We will cut three lengths of rubber tubing for each whistle," he added, holding up a bit of bicycle valve. "They can be worn around the wrist."

"Routes," Father Antoni continued. "Irena, you and Samuel take Elektoralna to Place Mirowski; we have two addresses there. One child is the size of a loaf and twice as loud; the other is nine and will not be separated from his sister. You will improvise. Very quietly."

Samuel wrote without looking up. "The nine-year-old goes first," he said.

"Agreed," Irena said.

"Money," said a quiet priest who had handled so much cash he now smelled faintly of other people's hands. "We have enough to bribe two gate guards twice this week, with a third bribe in reserve. No one goes to Pawiak to haggle. You will not charm your way out of Pawiak."

"Dogs will get us further than zloty this week," the seamstress said. "Dogs and timing. The patrol on Nalewki is late when the sergeant smokes. He smokes when the woman in the fourth-floor window lights hers and keeps him occupied with a wave and a hint of something more."

"Then we watch the window," Samuel said, already drawing a tiny cigarette in the margin of his map.

"And we pray for weather that makes men lazy," Father Antoni added. "Cold helps. Snow helps. Rain too."

They moved through detail until candles burned down into their saucers and had to be pinched with wetted fingers as a small brass clock hiccupped its way toward midnight.

When the meeting dissolved, it did so the way fog lifts, no single motion, a quiet thinning. Scarves were wound up; hats pulled low; chalk marks erased from the map with a damp rag. The crucifix watched them go: unsleeping, unsentimental.

Samuel waited for Irena at the base of the stairs, his hat in his hands. Near them, dogs – two lanky mongrels and a stoic shepherd with a biscuit-coloured chest stood with Brother Leon, learning patience as a first prayer. The shepherd glanced at Irena and thumped its tail once, as if committing her smell to memory.

"Walk?" Samuel asked.

They emerged into the night. Snow flurried in a slow, stingless drift; puddles had skinned over; the lamps made small halos as their footsteps stitched a line between pools of light. Neither of them spoke at first. They did not have to because silence had been trained to be useful, not awkward.

"You were right," he said finally, without looking at her. "About learning to let go but it frightens me."

She tasted the air, coal and ice and the faintest trace of candle wax on her coat. "You were right," she answered. "About bearing grief. And it also frightens me."

A tram clanged somewhere behind the wall, carrying no one who needed rescuing. He tucked his chin deeper into his scarf. "I had a boy once," he said. "Twelve. Stubborn as April. He hated Cicero and loved Horace because Horace sounded like a drunk uncle telling the truth. He would have been the one to talk to the guard while the rest of us walked past carrying Jupiter in a laundry basket." He huffed a breath that wanted to be a laugh. "He is gone. I have no ledger for him."

"I have a ledger for others," she said. "I will write his name in mine, though I never met him."

"Do," he said, and the word sat in the air like a coin for a saint. "Call him Marek. He hated his baptismal name and wanted to be called something shorter, as if a syllable could make him reborn."

They turned onto Elektoralna; the sound of their steps changed as the paving changed. On a window ledge, a cut Christmas tree leaned at an angle, a ribbon drooping like a tired smile. Somewhere a piano was being tuned with stubborn optimism.

"You know," he said, after a beat of silence, "I meant what I said in there. You cannot save them all."

"I know," she said.

"And you meant all that you said."

"Yes."

He shoved his hands in his pockets. "It is strange, isn't it? How an argument can unexpectedly make a room warmer and broker understanding."

She looked at him then, really looked: the night hollowed his cheeks, the lamplight put a candle in his eyes. "It is stranger how not arguing would make it colder, push people apart" she said.

He smiled – there, finally, the human thing she had wondered after. It transformed him from a diagram into a story again. "You make me less certain of the safety of my mind," he said lightly. "I value you for it."

"And you make me less certain of the safety of my heart," she returned, surprised at her own honesty. "Perhaps that is a fair exchange."

They walked on. Their shoulders occasionally brushed, not

by design but because streets are narrow and people are larger than their coats. At an alley mouth, a stray cat erupted from a bin and fled, tail up, the city's smallest survivor. He reached out reflexively as if to catch it, and his hand grazed the back of hers.

They both stopped. The world did not. Somewhere a door closed; boots passed at the far end of the street; a window shade snapped down. Between the two of them a square of cold air vibrated. Her glove against his glove had been nothing, wool to wool, friction, a whisper. But her skin felt the echo of it with embarrassing clarity, as if her body had unlearned what human heat was supposed to do.

He cleared his throat, that careful, schoolroom sound. "I am sorry," he said, and did not look particularly sorry.

"There is nothing to be sorry for," she said, meaning it more than she meant almost anything else she had said that day.

"Still," he said.

"Still," she echoed.

They resumed walking. The sidewalks narrowed again where rubble had been shovelled against the curb, making a high ridge that insisted people pass close if they were walking the same way. They passed close. At the next crossing he put his hand out automatically, an old habit from a city that had contained trams that killed careless children; his palm hovered near her elbow without gripping it. She let it hover. The gesture, lighter than touch, did not go unnoticed by her lungs. At her building, he stood on the step while she unlocked the door, which stuck in damp weather and just when she'd hoped to linger, it opened for her on the first try.

"Tomorrow," he said.

"Tomorrow," she agreed.

He hesitated. He wanted to say be careful, and she wanted to say, you too, and both of them knew those words sounded thin, like watery advice.

So instead he said, softly, "If you need to choose between carrying the bundle and ..." He stopped, searching for an ending that did not exist.

"We won't choose anything yet," she said, saving him the labour.

He nodded. "Yes."

"Good night, Samuel."

"Good night, Irena."

They did not shake hands. They did not bow. They did nothing at all. He stepped backward once, twice, as if to see her turn and vanish through the door, as if to keep her in sight until sight itself became an extravagance. Then he turned up his collar and walked into the seam of darkness between lamps, and she went inside, closing the door slowly so the latch would not click and wake the landlady's bad temper.

Up in her room, she did not light the lamp. She stood by the window until his shadow passed the next corner and was edited out of the scene. Then she sat at the table and opened the drawer. The tin lay there, obedient, small. She took out a slip and wrote *Marek* in the first column, nothing in the second, and folded it so the name was hidden.

On the sill, her remaining apple made a brave scent in the cold. In the sacristy yard, across town, a shepherd lifted its head, pricked its ears, and gave one soft bark into the night as if answering a question only it had heard.

6

March 1943

The garden crouched beneath a skin of frost, stubborn shoots pushing up like thoughts that would not be suppressed. At the far end stood the apple tree, its branches bare, its bark furred with lichen the colour of old coins. The roots rose out of the soil in slow, muscular arcs, veined and knotted, the anatomy of a survivor.

Irena came through the back gate with her coat buttoned to the throat and a small, heavy bundle held close under her arm. The morning pretended at gentleness, light diffused through pale cloud, a thin sun polished to dullness, but the air still sliced. She closed the gate softly and looked toward the kitchen window. Helena's face appeared there, ghosted by steam, then vanished. A moment later the door opened and Helena stepped out, wiping her hands on her apron.

"You look like a woman who has brought trouble wrapped in tea towels," Helena said without preamble. Her hair had greyed at the temples since autumn; her jaw had a new set to it, as if it had made a decision in the night and never told her face. She glanced at the street beyond Irena's shoulder, then back to the bundle. "Come. We'll do it quickly, and then we'll drink something hot and pretend we have nerves of steel."

They crossed the narrow yard together, skirts brushing the dead stalks of last year's lavender. Helena's boots left firm stamps on the rime; Irena's left none, as if the morning had decided to erase her as she walked. Under the tree the ground held a different cold, the kind that remembered snow lying here even when the sun insisted otherwise.

Irena knelt. The bundle was a tin, once painted with roses now mostly rubbed to history, wrapped in oilcloth. Inside, folded into precise buds, lay the scraps she had written by lamplight: children's names paired with children's other names; parents; addresses that were no longer addresses; churches and convents; a dated breath held on paper. She set the tin on the earth and traced the apple tree's bark with her fingertips, the gesture almost a greeting.

Helena stood with her arms folded. She had always been the solid one: the girl who kicked off her shoes to wade first into any stream; the teenager who argued with a teacher twice her size and made him blush with his own ignorance; the young woman who married a gentle man and buried him when influenza took him in one cruel week. "I hate this," she said quietly.

"I know." Irena unwrapped the oilcloth. Her hands shook, though not from the cold. "It is the best kind of hate. Productive and reactionary."

Helena huffed a breath that fogged and dissolved. "Do you remember when we were twelve and we dared each other to sleep in the orchard?" she asked, voice turned sideways, as if speaking to the past would keep the present from listening too closely. "You told me the tree roots were veins and the earth was a body, and if we listened hard enough we could hear it breathe."

"I said a great many foolish things at twelve," Irena answered, opening the tin. The scent that rose was of paper and iron and the faintest breath of apples, as if the box had been sleeping under a fruit tree for years already. "Some of them keep being true."

Helena crouched, her skirt falling around her like a gathered pool. "Let me." She took the trowel from Irena's bag and pushed it into the soil between two rising roots. The ground gave grudgingly, clods breaking with a soft, wet sound. "I hate them," she said again, more fiercely. "Every uniform. Every shout. Every joke they make in our streets, as if language were theirs to bully. Last week I saw a boy trying to sell matches by the tram stop. A soldier took the whole bundle and then dropped them one by one into a puddle until the boy cried. It was entertainment." She spat the word like gristle. "I have hated things before, like moths in the pantry, the price of onions, but this is different."

Irena bowed her head over the tin. "Why didn't you leave when you could?" she asked softly, though she knew the answer. They had walked around it for years, the question that visited every kitchen.

"Because this is my house and my apple tree, and I do not ask permission to breathe the air that belongs to all of us and nobody," Helena said. Then, after a beat: "Because of you." She glanced up, a quick flash of warmth. "Because you look at me and I hear your father's voice telling us stories under your kitchen table, and it reminds me I am made of more than fear. Because you needed a place to put the things you can't carry alone. Because I would rather hate them here than hate myself somewhere foreign."

The earth deepened under the trowel. Irena unfolded the top scrap and read it once, just once, committing the shape of the letters to the eye's private archive. *Hanna Miriam Lewin → Anna Kowalska.* She folded it again with four precise turns and placed it in the tin. Another name: *Sura Basia Goldberg → Zofia Gwiazda.* Another: *Marek (no second name) → Marek (kept).* For those without paper parents left to record, she wrote whatever truth she could hold, "blue birthmark behind left ear"; "sings to himself before sleep"; a string tied to future recognition.

"Do you remember," Helena said, working, breath quickening, "the day your father came to fetch me when I fell out of the apple tree and cracked my arm? He scolded the tree, not me. He said, 'You must hold on to girls who climb you. They are rare fruit.' He set my arm and then told me the story of the princess who slept inside a hill because she was tired of princes. He made me think I had chosen falling as a way to listen to the earth."

"He made us all braver than we were," Irena said. "And kinder than we knew how to be." She placed another scrap in the tin. "He would have hated this war and died anyway."

Helena's trowel struck a stone; she levered it out and set it aside with an apology to the root she had nicked. "He would have loved what you are doing," she said. "And hated that you have to do it. Both things can be true." She looked toward the house reflectively. "Do you want a spade? This will take all morning with my little finery."

"The smaller the hole, the less the ground remembers," Irena said. "If they come—"

"They will not," Helena interrupted, and the certainty in her voice was an act of mercy. "And if they do, I will be so difficult to move they will leave out of frustration."

"You will not be difficult. You will be clever and polite and say you are boiling potatoes." Irena took up a handful of soil and rubbed it between her fingers. Grainy, damp, a scent of iron.

"And if I am not here, you will not know where the second tin is buried."

Helena snorted. "You and your second tin. You think you invented caution. I was smuggling cigarettes past my mother before you had learned how to lie without blinking."

"I still cannot lie without blinking," Irena said. "I am blessed with an honest face."

"You are blessed with a stubborn one," Helena corrected. "You could plant a field with that jaw."

They worked without speaking for a time. The hole widened, deepened to the width of Irena's hand and depth from wrist to elbow. The roots curved around it like rib bones. She could imagine, if she wished, the tin resting there like a heart beneath ribs, the tree's sap rising and falling over it, carrying the ghost of names upward into the leaves.

At last she lowered the tin in, the oilcloth crinkling softly. She pressed her palm flat to the lid. The cold leached into her skin. "If they survive," she murmured, a prayer she had worn thin with use, "they must know who they are."

Helena laid a hand on her shoulder. It stayed there, heavy and steady, the weight of years. "They will," she said. "Because you have decided they will."

They pulled earth back over the tin, smoothing it with the sides of their hands, tucking it down as if putting a child to bed. Helena sprinkled the surface with last year's leaves so the newness of the disturbance would look like ordinary untidiness. Then she pressed a fallen apple into the soil, a brown, collapsed thing that still held the memory of sweetness. "In case you forget the exact spot," she said.

"I won't," Irena said, and then, because she was human and not a saint, she bent her head and breathed once, and allowed herself a single, grief-muffled sob that sounded like a laugh torn at the edges.

Helena turned and pretended to scold a sparrow at the fence. "I hate them," she said again, a mantra that meant she loved fiercely what they threatened. "For my father they took to labour and returned to us in a box. For my husband they took with fever and no doctor because he was the wrong kind of sick in the wrong kind of winter. For my child I never had, because there was no safety for babies in a year that demanded bravery of their mothers before birth." She faced Irena again, eyes bright and uncompromising. "And for you, because they make you carry a shovel when your hands should be full of books."

"My hands are full of names," Irena said. "It amounts to the same thing."

The bell at St. Klemens tolled the hour. They stood and brushed soil from their skirts, then linked arms and walked back toward the kitchen door, two women who had been girls together, who had balanced on fences and run in the rain and dared each other to jump from the lowest branch of the apple tree. Inside, steam wreathed the window again; a kettle began to sing. They paused on the threshold, both turning back without planning to, both looking at the place where the ground had been smoothed and disguised. They went inside, shut the door softly, and left the tree to stand guard.

By late afternoon the sky had thinned to the colour of watered down milk. A melt had set in, turning the alley ruts to shining wounds, the snow at the curb to slush that wore the prints of boots. When the bell rang at Helena's front door, she wiped her hands and peered through the peephole before unlatching the chain.

Samuel stood on the step with his hat in his hands. He looked perished, coat collar turned up, cheeks wind-burned, eyes bright with some private flame. "Good evening," he said to Helena with teacherly courtesy. "May I steal your friend for a short walk before the curfew tightens its belt?"

Helena smiled in spite of herself. "Bring her back with all the pieces in the same place," she said. "And if you must talk of dangerous things, do it with your mouths closed."

"We will speak of weather and the price of potatoes," he assured her, straight-faced, and then to Irena: "Will you come?"

She took her scarf from its peg and wrapped it around her neck. The thought of the river had come to her earlier, unbidden, as she read the last two names before the tin closed: a long, dark line that had always promised some other shore. "Yes," she said.

They walked past the square where a woman in a headscarf sold matches. A policeman turned his back in a way that was almost kind. They spoke at first of things that had learned to live in winter: crows that swaggered like magistrates; the cat who stole bread as if it were meat; a chimney that had puffed without rest for three days and announced a new widow.

When they reached the riverbank, the world opened a little. The Vistula lay broad and bruised, slabs of ice drifting like pages torn from a book. The willows at the edge that had their feet in water; their hair, uncombed, rattled when the wind pressed through.

"I used to think," Samuel said, hands in his pockets, "that you could learn a city the way you learned a text. Keep at it long enough, memorise the corners, and the meaning would eventually arrive. Then the war came and added footnotes, endless, contradicting footnotes, and now I am always aware that the book might be burned before I reach the end."

"The city is a mischievous teacher," Irena said. "But it still teaches." She looked down at the water and saw the sky break in it, mended, then break again. "When I was small, my father told me the Vistula was a spine, and Poland's stories hung from it like ribs. He made it impossible for me not to stand up straight when I walk along it, in case it needed help to hold itself together."

"I never met him," Samuel said, "and yet I hear his voice in your defiance." He smiled at the look she gave him. "That was a compliment."

"I chose to take it as one," she said primly.

They walked together in companiable silence interspersed with brief insights into each other. The river carried on as if it could not be convinced to do anything else. He told her of the boys he had taught – how Marek's mind moved sideways when everyone else marched, how Piotr hid poetry in his Latin homework, how Dawid whistled in the corridor to test the echo because he wanted to understand how space changed sound. "They would be men now, if the world had kept its promises," he said.

"It will become honest again," she said. "Perhaps not in time for us to see. But it will remember those it owes a place in history." She did not say that she had written *Marek* on a slip and folded it and placed it where a root could guard it. Some acts did not need a witness to be real.

He touched her hand lightly in the crook of her elbow, a guide's touch more than a lover's, and then did not remove it. The pressure worked like a second pulse. "What were you like," he asked, "as a girl?"

"Hungry for everything," she said, surprising herself with the speed of the answer. "Books, yes. Stories, yes. But also running in the rain and being the first to put my foot on the next stepping stone in the stream. I wanted to hold every hand. I wanted to solve every quarrel. I wanted to make the world stop crying, even if it meant shouting louder than it did." She laughed once, short. "I have not improved."

"I like you noisy," he said.

"And you?" she asked. "What were you like?"

"A serious boy who counted fence posts on the way to school and believed that if the number came out even the day would be good. I learned to read by listening to my mother sing. I learned to argue by watching my father avoid it poorly. I learned to want by standing outside a bookshop window and reading prices as if they were the first lines of a romance." He glanced at her, rueful.

"I like hearing about your before life," she said.

They stopped where the bank dipped into a small, unobserved cove of reeds. The city's sound thinned here; the war kept its voice a block away. Above them, evening was a bruise brightening to purple. He turned toward her as if pulled by a string from his shoulder to her face.

"You cannot promise me anything," he said gently. "I know. The road we walk is one direction and does not point to the bridges ahead."

She exhaled. "I cannot. But I can tell you what is true right now." She looked at his mouth, then away, then back. Honesty had always been her hardest melancholy. "I... would like to keep walking with you. As far as the road allows."

He lifted his hand, as cautious as if he were reaching for a bird that might startle and touched the edge of her scarf where it framed her jaw. His fingers were cold; the warmth of her skin shocked them into tenderness. "Good," he said, the word both prayer and decision.

She did not close her eyes. She wanted to see the exact world she kissed in. The smudge of river on the air, the stubborn reeds, the first shy star smudging the horizon. When he bent, she met him with the steadiness she saved for moments when she needed to be sure. The kiss was not stolen. It was chosen. It was two people agreeing to a brief interlude. After, they did not step apart quickly like children worried about being scolded. They stood with their foreheads close enough that their breath made a squall between them. He smiled, visible even in near-dark. "I am teaching my hands to hold tight and let go at the same time," he said. "It is an advanced course."

"You will pass. I'm sure of it," she said.

A curfew bell rolled over the roofs, shaking a flock of crows into the air. He dropped his hand, reluctantly, and they turned back toward Helena's street, walking faster now. On the corner he paused and took her fingers again, briefly, the touch a signature.

"Tomorrow?" he asked.

"Tomorrow," she echoed.

They did not say *if*.

Outside Helena's gate he left her with a bow that would have been old-fashioned even in a gentler year. She watched his figure shrink along the pavement until the dark possessed it. Then she let herself in.

In the garden the apple tree stood, untroubled by human arrangements, its roots netted through earth like blue veins. Under it, the tin with its names rested where human hands had decided it should rest. Wind moved through the branches with the patience of nature. If the roots could speak, they might have said what all guardians say: I will hold and protect what you give me, for as long as I stand.

7

April 1943

The morning fog clung to everything, making the lamps look like ghosts that had no home. Irena pulled her shawl tighter around her shoulders, the cold sinking through wool to bone. Ahead, another checkpoint loomed, its iron frame slick with dew, a German flag limp against the still air.

Beside her, Piotr steered the handcart. He looked older than his twenty-five years, his jaw gaunt, his eyes shadowed from too many nights without rest. The cart rattled under its load: two bulging potato sacks stacked on top of one another. The smell of earth clung to them, convincing enough if you didn't look too closely.

But Irena knew. Beneath the burlap, folded into silence dressed in rags and riddled with fear, lay two toddlers, smuggled out of a tenement before dawn, their mother whispering prayers as if each breath might be the last. The guards were already restless, shifting their weight, stamping feet against the cold. A German shepherd strained at its chain, its muzzle wet, its eyes bright with suspicion. One of the soldiers yawned and rubbed his nose. Another paced, rifle slung loose, scanning the line of civilians with a boredom that could kill faster than anger.

"Keep steady," Irena murmured to Piotr in Polish.

He gave the barest nod, but his hands tightened on the cart's handle. They reached the front of the line.

"Papers," barked the officer.

Irena presented hers, stamped with the red seal she'd coaxed from City Hall. She kept her expression calm, her voice clipped but deferential. "I'm returning from an inspection, welfare department. Soap and sanitation."

The officer skimmed the permit, his lip curling as if even paper offended him. His gaze dropped to the sacks. "What's this?"

"Potatoes, I'm delivering them to the church, as a favour to the priest." Irena said simply.

"Potatoes," he repeated, as if testing the sound for lies. He stepped closer, nudging one sack with the toe of his boot. The burlap twitched, just a shiver, but enough.

Then it came. A muffled whimper, small and rising. Irena's heart lurched. Beneath the coarse weave of the sack, one child had woken. The sound became a cry, thin and unmistakable.

Piotr's face drained of blood. His hand twitched toward the cart as if to flee, but Irena's palm pressed against his sleeve, firm, commanding stillness. Her mind raced. If the sacks were opened, both children were dead. So were they. She stepped forward sharply, her hand closing around the leash of the mutt at her side, a rangy mongrel she had trained for weeks in the convent yard. With a snap of her wrist, she gave the signal.

The dog erupted. It lunged against its rope, barking in a frenzy, each sound tearing the air like a whip crack. Furious, insistent, drowning out everything else. The shepherd jerked its head toward the racket, ears swivelling, distracted.

"Quiet!" Irena shouted, her voice pitched with convincing irritation. She cuffed the mutt's flank, though lightly, as it continued to bark with savage persistence. "Stupid beast, always whining for food, he thinks you want to steal his potatoes. He thinks he's a guard dog, like yours!"

The soldiers glanced at one another. The officer sneered, shaking his head. The shepherd barked once, confused, then whined. The mutt answered with another volley, covering the toddler's sobs beneath burlap and cloth.

One of the guards laughed, the sound short and ugly. "Crazy Poles. Even their dogs guard potatoes."

The others joined in the laughter as the officer shoved the papers back into Irena's hands. "Go, before your beast gives me a headache."

Irena tugged the leash, still muttering curses at the mutt, and motioned Piotr forward. They pushed the cart onwards, the rattling wheels a drumbeat under her ribs. Only when the checkpoint shrank behind them did she let the breath leave her chest as they turned into a narrow alley. Piotr sagged against the cart, sweat beading his temple despite the cold. Irena knelt, fingers working the knots in the sacks.

The first child blinked up at her, cheeks damp, eyes huge in the half-light. The second whimpered, clutching at the other.

"Shhh," Irena whispered, smoothing their hair, her throat burning. "You are safe now."

The mutt sat at her heel, panting, tail wagging faintly, as if proud of the lie it had barked into the morning.

The flat was lit by two candles stuck in bottles. Wax dripped down their sides in frozen rivers. A map lay spread across the table, corners weighted with mugs. Irena sat with her coat still on, hands wrapped around a tin cup of lukewarm tea. The day's danger clung to her like another garment she could not take off.

Across from her, Samuel stood by the window, arms folded. His jaw was tight, the scar by his ear white in the candlelight. Jadwiga perched on a stool near the stove, fiddling with a matchbox, though she said nothing.

"You take too many risks," Samuel said finally, his voice low but cutting. "The Gestapo are not fools. A barking dog is clever once. Twice, perhaps. After that, it's a pattern, and they will pounce."

Irena's hand tightened on the cup. "If we hadn't used the dog today, those children would be corpses by now and so would I."

"You were lucky," he shot back. "If they'd searched the cart? If the guard hadn't laughed but looked closer? You gamble not only your life but all of ours. Every name in your tin. Every family who trusts you. Do you understand the scale of the fire you play with?"

His words stung because they were true. She wanted to throw them back, but anger twisted into something perilously close to fear.

"I understand That I'm playing with fire," she said, forcing her voice steady. "But I also understand the cost of doing nothing. And I am also tired of having this conversation."

Samuel's eyes blazed. He took a step closer, his voice fierce but trembling at its edges. "And if you burn with them? What then? Who carries the next child? Who keeps the ledger? Who tells the truth if your voice is silenced?"

The room hushed. Even Jadwiga stopped fidgeting, her gaze flicking between them like a spectator at a duel.

Irena looked down at her hands. Her father's voice rose in memory, strong even in sickness: *Do the right thing, Irenka. Live a good life. Even when the cost is high, you will know it is right because your heart will not betray you.*

She remembered sitting at his bedside, his cough rattling through the cold night, his palm resting over hers with all the warmth of a promise as his body gave up the fight even when his soul desperately wanted to carry on. She had been naïve then, certain that goodness was a clear road. Now the road was broken, mined, deadly, but the echo of his words had never left.

She raised her head. "I cannot choose safety over the right thing, Samuel. My father taught me better."

For a moment Samuel's face softened, the fire cooling into grief. "He sounds like a man I would have liked."

"You would have argued with him," Irena said, a faint smile tugging despite her exhaustion. "He welcomed arguments. He said they made truth show itself."

Samuel's shoulders lowered a fraction. He came to the table and sat opposite her, his hand splayed over the map as though steadying it. The candlelight caught his eyes, tired but fierce.

"I argue with you," he said, quieter now. "Not because I want to stop you. But because I am terrified of losing you."

Her breath caught. The words landed not like stones this time, but like balm poured on a wound she hadn't admitted she carried. She felt seen in a way that was both comfort and exposure, as if his gaze reached past her coat, her bones, to the ember within that had kept her walking.

"Then argue," she said softly. "So long as you walk beside me after."

Their eyes held across the table, silence settling like a truce. Jadwiga cleared her throat loudly, muttering something about saints and fools, and went to the stove. Samuel's hand brushed hers briefly, deliberately, across the wood grain. It was the lightest touch, but it tethered her, reminded her she was not carrying the ledger, or the children, or her father's words entirely alone. Outside, boots clattered on the street. Inside, two candles burned steadily, their flames bending but unbroken.

8

April 1943

The courthouse was an in-between place, built to hold disputes about bread prices and property lines, but now pressed into a darker service: a stone corridor between two worlds. One set of doors opened onto Warsaw proper, streets still battered but not yet strangled. The other, guarded, shadowed, led directly into the ghetto. Its foundations had not shifted, yet it carried a new burden in the form of a passage where lives could be smuggled through on the hinge of a door and a heartbeat. In another story, in another time it would have been magical. A gateway to another realm, paradise maybe. Now, the doorway signified stepping into a place of misery or stepping out and taking a chance on freedom.

Irena adjusted her hat, smoothing the edge of her scarf against her cheek. The boy at her side clutched her hand, his fingers cold despite the wool mittens she had borrowed from Jadwiga's cousin. He was seven, maybe eight, his hair cropped short to pass for a gentile child, his wide eyes dulled by too much hunger and too little sleep. On the papers she carried, he was her niece's son—*Janek Nowakowski*, travelling under her protection for medical reasons. On the street, he was just another boy trying not to cry.

"Stay close," she whispered.

He nodded, though his small jaw trembled.

Inside, the courthouse hummed with the bureaucracy of occupation. Clerks hunched over desks, their pens scratching as if they could write order into chaos. Piles of papers shifted from one blotter to the next like sand in an hourglass. Typewriters clattered in a back room, each letter a small hammer of authority. The walls reeked of ink, dust, and the cold sweat of people praying their documents would pass.

Irena led the boy forward, presenting her permit with the ease of someone who had done so a dozen times before. The guard at the inner door glanced at it, bored, and waved them through. But the real test waited at the clerk's desk by the far wall.

"Papers," the clerk said without looking up. His glasses perched low on his nose, his hair slicked flat with pomade gone rancid. He had a reputation for being particular, and particularity could kill.

Irena handed over the forged identity sheet. She had written it herself that morning, her hand steady though her heart had bucked against her ribs. A single misspelled word, a date out of sequence, could unravel everything.

The clerk adjusted his glasses, frowning. "This stamp is faint."

"The parish seal is worn," Irena replied evenly. "They have petitioned for a new one, but you know how long such requests take."

He grunted, unimpressed. His pen scratched across the page. "And the mother?"

"Unwell," Irena said. "I am escorting him for treatment. Surely you see the sense in that."

The boy pressed closer against her hip. His silence was perfect, but silence could also draw suspicion.

The clerk narrowed his eyes. "Unwell, or dead?"

The word cut the air like a knife.

Irena leaned forward, lowering her voice just enough to imply discretion without secrecy. "In times such as these, what difference does it make? If you wish to write *dead* in your ledger, do so. But I will not have the boy punished for it."

The clerk blinked, unsettled by her bluntness. He dipped his pen again, signing with a flourish more annoyed than convinced. "Very well." He stamped the page, the violet ink bleeding faintly around the edges.

Her breath slipped out slowly. She gathered the papers, tucking them back into her satchel with a nod. "Come, Janek."

They moved toward the side door, the one that opened onto the safer street. Safety was relative, but compared to the ghetto, it was another planet. She had nearly reached the handle when a figure blocked their way.

A German officer, tall, polished, his uniform creased to perfection. His boots shone like mirrors; his eyes, pale as glass, fixed on her with sharp curiosity.

"What is this?" he demanded in German, gesturing at the boy.

Her pulse jolted, but she met his gaze. "My nephew," she said, switching languages smoothly. "We have permission." She held out the stamped paper.

He skimmed it, his mouth twisting. "Children wander in and out like rabbits now? And all under the banner of sanitation?"

She forced a thin smile. "Would you rather they wander sick and spread lice to your men? We catch the disease here, Herr Oberleutnant, before it reaches your barracks."

His brow furrowed, weighing irritation against practicality. The boy's hand clutched hers tighter, a tremor betraying the lie.

The officer's gaze lingered too long. He tapped the papers against his palm. "You seem very sure of yourself."

"I have to be," she said quietly. "Incompetence is not tolerated by you, or by my superiors and I need this job."

For a breath, the world balanced. She could feel it tilt either way: exposure or escape. Then, with a dismissive flick of his wrist, he shoved the papers back.

"Go," he said.

Her legs carried her forward, her spine rigid with effort not to hurry. The side door opened onto cold air, the sound of trams rattling somewhere beyond. She guided the boy down the steps, his breath puffing white beside hers. When the door closed behind them, she let herself breathe.

"Where are we now?" he asked in a whisper.

She bent to meet his eyes. "On the right side of the door," she said. And silently, in her head, she said, *for now.*

The café was little more than a darkened room with blackout curtains drawn tight, the glow of a single lamp staining the smoke-stained wallpaper. Its tables were scarred wood, its chairs mismatched but it was warm, and warmth meant sanctuary.

Samuel sat in the far corner, his shoulders tense, his cap on the table beside a chipped mug. He looked up when she entered, his relief so sudden it softened his whole face. He rose before she had reached him, pulling out the chair as if she were a guest in a more gracious world.

"You made it," he said, the words edged with breath he had been holding too long.

She sank into the chair, letting her satchel drop to the floor.

"Barely. The clerk was suspicious. And an officer stopped me at the door."

His jaw tightened. "Irena..."

"But I got him through," she cut in. "The boy is safe."

He exhaled, running a hand through his hair. "You gamble with knives pressed against your throat."

She allowed herself a weary smile. "It is the only way to win, isn't it?"

For a moment he only looked at her, eyes searching, full of words he did not yet say. Then he reached for the pot of tea, pouring into her cup. The liquid was weak, more tinted water than drink, but it was hot, and heat mattered more than flavour.

They sat in silence at first, sipping, letting the world shrink to the small circle of table between them. The room thrummed faintly with muffled conversations, but here, in their corner, there was only the sound of breathing and the scrape of china.

Then Samuel chuckled, low and incredulous. "Do you realise? If anyone looked at us right now, they'd think we were two ordinary people meeting after work. A teacher and a social worker, drinking tea in a café."

She laughed softly, the sound foreign in her own ears. "Ordinary. Imagine."

The laugh caught, turned to something solemn, but she let it linger. It felt like a rebellion as much as the forged papers.

He leaned closer, elbows on the table. "When I didn't see you on time, I thought –" He broke off, shaking his head. "I thought I'd lost you."

Her throat tightened. "You haven't."

Silence stretched between them again, but it was different this time: charged, fragile, alive. His hand shifted, brushing the back of hers where it lay on the table. She did not pull away.

"Irena," he said quietly.

She met his gaze. His eyes held both fear and longing, the

same twin fires she felt in her own chest. She thought of her father's voice, urging her always toward the right thing, and wondered if love could be right even when it was dangerous.

"We can't promise tomorrow," she whispered.

"No," he agreed. "But we can claim tonight."

He leaned across the table, and she met him halfway. Their lips touched, tentative at first, then steadier, the kiss a fragile truce against everything pressing in from the outside. His hand cupped hers, warm, anchoring. For a moment the war receded, leaving only the taste of tea and the heat of his breath.

When they pulled back, they did not speak. Words would have broken it. They simply sat, hands entwined on the scarred wood, two people daring to carve a sliver of tenderness from the ruins.

Love was a risk. So was hope. But tonight, she chose both.

9

May 1943

Oberst Karl Ritter preferred silence to noise. Noise was sloppy and boots clattering out of step, papers shuffled in nervous hands, typewriters striking without rhythm irritated him. Silence was discipline, and discipline was what carved order from the chaos of Warsaw.

The headquarters on Szucha Avenue was quiet this evening, just as he liked it. Gas lamps glowed along the corridor, their light thin, clinical, washing colour from the walls. Behind his office door a map of Warsaw hung above his desk, its surface punctured by coloured pins. Red for patrols. Black for arrests. Blue for "concerns." The pins multiplied each week, a constellation of unrest.

He leaned over a stack of reports, his gloved finger tapping at the columns. Children, it seemed, were vanishing. The ghetto's ledgers recorded them one day and not the next. Families swore they had gone missing overnight, runaways they said. Patrols insisted no bodies had been found. Yet the numbers added up to absence.

"Impossible," Ritter muttered. His German sharpened the word until it sounded like a blade.

Across the desk, two Gestapo officers shifted. They had learned not to interrupt him when he read, but he felt their unease prickling the air. Ritter looked up, pale eyes narrowing. "You have all the walls, all the dogs, all the eyes. And still –" He snapped the report shut. "The children seep through."

One officer cleared his throat. "Perhaps disease, Herr Oberst. The bodies buried without record. You know how Jews –"

Ritter raised a hand, silencing him. "Do not insult me with excuses. Disease kills, yes. But where are the bodies? I do not believe they burn them or that children have somehow managed to run away. Someone is producing forged papers stamped with parish seals. Someone is placing children in Polish homes under new names. This is the only answer." He leaned back, steepling his fingers. "Someone moves them. Someone clever. A network."

He stood, pacing to the map. His shadow stretched across the pins. "You need to pay attention, watch, listen for stories as I do, which is why I heard a new one. A woman, a mouse darting through walls, carrying children in toolboxes and potato sacks. The ghetto believes in ghosts, but I believe in mice. And every mouse leaves droppings."

The younger officer shifted. "What would you have us do?"

Ritter's mouth curved, not in a smile but in a grimace of hunger. "We will set traps. Informants inside the ghetto. More in the Polish offices, welfare, sanitation, courts. Clerks love to talk when given cigarettes or fear. We will listen. We will wait." He jabbed the map with his finger. "And when the mouse scurries, we will catch it. Then we will let the city watch what becomes of anyone who dares to cheat the Reich."

He turned back, eyes glinting cold. "I want names. I want whispers. And when you bring me this mouse, alive –" His voice dropped to a whisper that was more dangerous than a shout. "I will enjoy watching it squirm."

The officers nodded, spines stiff. Ritter sat again, opening a fresh file, but the air in the room shifted. The hunt had begun.

When they arrived at the church crypt, candles struggled for life in glass jars, throwing restless shapes across the walls. The table was cluttered with papers, routes, forged birth certificates, ration cards smudged from too many hands.

Irena sat among them, her scarf pulled tight, her satchel at her feet. Samuel leaned against the far wall, arms crossed, listening with his schoolmaster's patience. Around them, the members of Żegota spoke in urgent whispers, their words snapping like twigs underfoot.

"They are watching more closely," said Piotr, voice taut. "Two guards stopped me yesterday, demanded to know what I carried on my cart. They searched for far too long."

"They know something," murmured the seamstress, her hands twisting the hem of a christening gown she was altering for a disguise. "Perhaps not everything. But enough to look harder."

"We cannot ignore it," added Father Antoni. His face drawn by sleeplessness. "The Gestapo is not blind forever. Someone whispers in their ear. Perhaps we are almost betrayed. Perhaps they will come for us anytime now."

Silence shivered through the room. Eyes darted, quick glances, not of guilt but of fear.

Jadwiga slapped her palm against the table. "Paranoia kills

faster than bullets. We cannot start suspecting everyone amongst us. That is what they want."

"Yet we must be cautious," Piotr argued. "If one of us is careless, or worse, is captured –"

The words trailed off. Everyone knew what worse meant.

Samuel pushed away from the wall. "Caution, yes. But not paralysis. If we stop moving, the children already hidden will starve in their cupboards waiting for the next loaf."

Irena lifted her chin. "Then we keep moving." Her voice was steady, though her pulse skipped. "The walls are more guarded, the patrols tighter, and still we must carry on. If we falter, the children will die. Stopping is the same as killing them ourselves and they are our future."

The words rang harsh in the silence. Samuel's eyes flicked to her, dark with something more than argument. He didn't answer at once. The meeting limped on, assignments divided, maps folded away. But when the others drifted out into the night, he caught her arm and pulled her into the protection of the stairwell.

"You can't keep this up," he said, his whisper harsh, urgent. "Irena, every trip is a gamble, and Ritter is not a fool. He is circling. Can't you feel it?"

She pulled her arm free, bristling. "Of course I feel it. Every time I walk through a gate, every time a guard looks too long at my satchel. Fear lives in my throat. But what should I do? Stop? Watch children die and know I could have carried them out?"

He stepped closer, his voice fierce but shaking. "You've done more than anyone. More than enough. If you fall, everything collapses. The ledger, the routes, the faith. They need you alive, Irena. I need you alive. Even if all you carry is bread, even if you only hold my hand."

Her breath caught. His words cracked something in her chest. She wanted to lean into the warmth of his worry, to let it shield her. But her father's voice rose again, steady as ever: *Do the right thing, Irenka.*

She steadied her gaze. "If I stop, Samuel, I might as well have pressed my hand over Hanna's mouth that day in the box. Or pushed Janek back through the courthouse door. Stopping is killing them myself. I cannot. I will not."

For a heartbeat he only looked at her, his eyes searching, as if memorising her resolve even while fearing it. His hand lifted, then dropped, curling into a fist at his side.

"You terrify me," he whispered.

She almost smiled, though it trembled. "You keep saying that."

"Because it keeps being true."

The candle nearest them sputtered, throwing Ritter's imagined shadow across the wall. Irena felt it settle there, cold and patient. The hunter had set his traps, and though they whispered in crypts and kissed in corners, she knew the game was closing. But still, she would continue.

10

June 1943

The ghetto at night was a mouth closed tight around its own cry. The streets narrowed into passages of ebony fear, their cobbles slick with recent rain, the stench of rotting refuse souring the air. Windows glimmered faintly with candle stubs; beyond them, silence was broken only by the faint cough of a fever or the scuffle of rats.

Irena kept her steps light, one hand steadying the small bundle at her side. The girl was no older than six, her hair a matted halo, her cheeks hollow. She clutched a doll so worn it was little more than cloth and stuffing, its button eyes mismatched, one arm dangling by a thread.

"Hold tight, Basia," Irena whispered, her breath ghosting in the cold air. "We're almost there."

The parents hovered behind, fear making their movements jerky. They had agreed to the plan after long persuasion, their desperation outweighing terror. The mother's lips were cracked from fasting; the father's hand trembled on the girl's shoulder. Both looked at Irena as if she were not a woman but a saint.

She led them along the wall toward the gap she knew, where rubble piled against brick, creating a path that could pass for collapse if one didn't look closely. Her papers were in her satchel, her story rehearsed. If stopped, she would claim the child was sick, needed to be removed to avoid the spread of disease and medicine that may cure her. She had said the lines so often she could hear them in her sleep. And then her worst fear became reality.

The boots came first, striking stone with the sharp rhythm of inevitability. Then the voices – German, laughing low, careless. A flashlight beam slashed through the fog.

"Run," Irena hissed, but the word was swallowed by panic. The parents froze, then bolted in the wrong direction. Shouts rang out. The beam swung.

"Anhalten!" Stop!

The father shoved his wife forward, screaming her name. The patrol surged. Rifles barked, deafening in the narrow street. Irena spun, clutching Basia. The doll slipped, caught, dangled. She saw it all in fragments: the mother dragged by her hair, her cries torn to rags in the night; the father beaten down, his arm breaking under a boot. The girl's mouth opened in a scream, but Irena clamped a hand over it, muffling the sound into her coat. Then she ran.

She ran through the cracks of the street, heart hammering, the child heavy against her chest. Behind, the patrol shouted, the German words sharp as bayonets. A shot cracked stone beside her. Another sparked off metal. She turned, ducked into an alley, lungs burning. The doll caught on rubble.

Basia screamed, reaching, twisting in Irena's arms. "My doll!"

The fabric tore. Half of the doll remained in Basia's grip, the other half dangling on the stones, soon to be trampled by boots closing in. Irena did not stop. She could not. She pressed forward, the girl sobbing against her, the torn doll clutched like a talisman.

At last she stumbled through a broken fence, into the skeletal remains of a yard. She crouched, pressing the child against her chest, listening as the patrol thundered past, boots fading into distance. Only then did she allow her breath to shake free. Only then did she know, admit, that the parents were gone. The child was saved. The doll was broken. And she would carry the sight of it all forever.

Samuel's apartment was a single room above a cobbler's shop, its walls thin, its ceiling low, its safety more imagined than real. A spare cot looked forlorn in the corner, the half-dried laundry strung on twine. Irena stumbled in, clutching Basia, her coat spattered with mud and blood. The child's sobs had dulled to hiccups, her small hands still locked around the ragged half of her doll.

Samuel rose from the table so abruptly his chair toppled. His face blanched at the sight of her. "Jesus, Irena –" He reached for the girl first, then drew back, as if afraid she might shatter. "What happened?"

She sank onto the cot, pressing Basia into the blankets. "Patrol. Shots. They took the parents." Her voice broke on the last word.

Samuel's jaw tightened. He knelt, his hands trembling as he touched the child's brow. "She's alive." Relief warred with fury in his eyes. He stood, whirling on Irena. "And you... look at you. Blood on your coat. You could have been killed!"

"I wasn't," she said flatly.

"You weren't because God blinked," he snapped. His voice

cracked under the weight of his fear. "Do you think you're indestructible? Do you think the Gestapo will look at you and see mercy? I can't –" His voice broke. He pressed both hands to his face, dragging them down until his eyes shone with tears. "I can't lose you."

She stared at him, her own breath shuddering. The anger in his voice was love twisted raw, and it unravelled her more than the night's terror. She rose, stepping close, her hand brushing his sleeve.

"You won't," she whispered, though she didn't believe it. "Not tonight."

Their gazes locked, two fires feeding each other. He seized her arms, then dropped his grip, ashamed of the roughness. She lifted her hands to his face, her thumbs brushing the tears at his temples.

Their mouths met with desperate force, the kiss a collision of grief and relief, of fury and longing. It was not gentle. It was survival, an act of claiming something human when the night had stolen everything else. His hands tangled in her hair, hers clutched at his shoulders, pulling him close as if closeness itself could ward off death.

The room blurred, their fear turning to heat, their fight dissolving into passion. Clothes tumbled, the cot creaked. For a while, they forgot the walls, the patrols, the ledger of names. For a while, they were only man and woman, clinging to each other against the dark.

When at last they lay tangled in the blankets, her cheek against his chest, his breath ragged in her hair, silence settled over them like a fragile truce. The child slept, clutching the half-doll. The candle burned low.

Irena closed her eyes. A memory rose, unbidden: her father sitting by the hearth, his cough softened by the fire's crackle. She had been ten, curled at his side. *Love,* he had told her, voice thick but steady, *is the only fight worth losing. Remember that Irenka. The only fight worth losing.*

She opened her eyes. Samuel's hand stroked her hair. She lifted her head, searching his face.

"There's something I must tell you," he said quietly. His voice trembled, not with fear of her but with the cost of truth. "I am Jewish."

Her breath caught. The room tilted.

He held her gaze, unflinching. "I hide behind papers, behind a name typed on paper that says Szmuel. The Germans would see me burned for being Samuel. You deserve to know. You need to know before you risk another step with me."

She reached for his hand, threading her fingers through his. "It changes nothing," she said. "Except that I love you more."

His eyes closed, his forehead pressing against hers. Outside, boots clattered down the street, the war marching on. But inside the small room, under the blanket of truth and loss and love, two hearts beat stubbornly against the dark.

11

June 1943

The garden had surrendered to night, but not to silence. The wind rustled through the untrimmed grass, carrying with it the faint scent of lilacs from a bush that refused to die. Somewhere in the distance, an owl was answered by another, until the sound was swallowed by the rattle of the occupied city. Yet here, within Helena's gate, all that seemed to exist was the apple tree, the lantern, and the object in Irena's arms.

The tree loomed over them, its crooked branches black against a pale wash of moon. In summer, it would swell with fruit, its roots drinking deeply of the soil. But tonight its branches were bare claws, reaching upward as if in supplication. Beneath them, Irena knelt, her knees pressed into damp earth, the lantern throwing a trembling halo of gold around her.

In her lap sat the tin. Once it had held sweets but now she stroked the lid with her thumb, as though to soothe it, though what needed soothing were the names folded within. Each slip of paper was a fragile tether to a child remade for survival: the identity they were forced to wear, and the identity they might one day return to.

She felt Helena's gaze from a few paces back. Her friend stood with her arms wrapped tightly around herself, her shawl pulled high on her shoulders. She hated this part. She hated the burying of names, hated the thought of secrets placed in soil like corpses. But she had agreed, because she loved Irena, and because friendship sometimes meant holding a lantern steady while another dug into the dark.

"You must hurry," Helena whispered. Her voice carried in the still air like the crack of a twig. "Neighbours watch from their windows. Too many questions could be asked."

Irena didn't answer at once. She had dug into the earth with her small spade, carving out a hollow where the roots bent like arms around a cradle. The soil was damp, rich, smelling of iron and decay. It clung beneath her nails, filled the creases of her hands. She'd

unwrapped the oilcloth, the crinkle of it loud as gunfire in the night. The tin was cold against her palms as she placed more names inside then lowered the tin back into the hollow. The click of metal against stone was muffled, intimate, like the drop of a ring into water. But she didn't cover it yet. Instead, she pressed her palm flat against the lid and closed her eyes.

Her lips moved, whispering.

"Jakub. Sura. Hanna. Dawid Basia..."

One by one she spoke to them all – the real names she'd memorised, the ones stripped from the children at the ghetto gate, the ones erased on forged papers and ration cards. She whispered them as if breathing them back into existence, as if the sound alone could draw them from the abyss. Her voice cracked on some, steadied on others. Each name hung for a heartbeat before the night devoured it.

Helena flinched at the sound. She turned her face away, her

arms locked tighter. "You'll bring down God's notice," she muttered. "Or worse, theirs."

"They must be spoken," Irena said, her voice rough but resolute. "If no one says their names, they vanish. And I will not let them vanish."

She whispered more, words spilling like prayer beads through her fingers. A girl who used to sing lullabies to her brother. A boy who counted stars at night. A baby whose first word had been "bread." Details too small for records, too sacred for silence.

Finally, she covered the tin, pushing the soil back over it with both hands. She smoothed it down, packed it firm, her breath coming hard, as though the act had stolen her strength. Her fingers trembled as she scattered dry leaves across the fresh earth, disguising the scar of disturbance. The mound vanished into the garden's untidiness, another imperfection in a world full of them.

The lantern flared, catching the bark of the apple tree. Its surface glistened in the light, grooved with scars. The roots below seemed to pulse with hidden life, curling around the buried tin like veins protecting a heart.

Helena stepped closer. She crouched, her hand settling on Irena's shoulder. Her grip was firm, almost bruising. "You must take care," she said quietly. "They are watching you."

Irena froze, her eyes on the mound of earth. "What do you mean?"

"I hear it," Helena said, her voice shaking though her words were sharp. "Whispers on the street. The neighbour's talk. German patrols linger by your door. They ask after your comings and goings. You walk with your head too high, Irena. They notice."

Irena sat back on her heels. The damp seeped through her skirt, the cold clutching her bones. Her hands were filthy, nails black with soil, but she kept them pressed flat to her thighs. She stared at the tree as if it might answer for her.

"If they notice me," she said finally, "then I am still here. Still useful."

Helena's hand tightened. "But for how long?"

The lantern guttered, its light stuttering over their faces, leaving them half in shadow, half in flame. In that trembling glow, the garden felt less like sanctuary and more like a place of judgment. Irena lowered her gaze back to the earth, to the secret she had just planted. The tin lay hidden, its names muffled, its truth locked away. She whispered one last vow into the night, too soft for even Helena to hear:

"I will keep speaking you, even if it kills me."

The apple tree stood silent, its roots clutching the secret like veins wrapped tight around a beating heart.

Gestapo Headquarters, Warsaw. July 1943

The corridors of Szucha Avenue carried their own kind of chill, a cold not born of weather but of cruel intent. The walls sweated with damp despite summer heat, their plaster stained from years of damp boots and whispers smothered against them. The silence here was not peaceful. It was the silence of waiting, of prey holding its breath.

Oberst Karl Ritter sat in his office, jacket placed neatly over the back of his chair, shirt sleeves rolled to the elbow. On his desk lay a collection of reports: pages smudged, ink still fresh on some, faded on others. Across the top of each ran the same word: *Kinder.* Children.

He turned the pages slowly, like a priest with scripture. One report spoke of an infant smuggled out in a carpenter's box. Another described forged baptismal papers found in a dead courier's pocket. Yet another, a rumour whispered by a starving boy in exchange for bread: a woman with clever eyes, always carrying soap, always walking too steadily for someone in wartime.

Ritter's mouth curved. Not a smile, for he smiled rarely, but the anticipation of one. "The mouse again," he murmured.

At the edge of the room, a junior officer cleared his throat. Ritter ignored him, leaning back in his chair. The pins on his wall map gleamed, a constellation of suspicion. He tapped one with a knuckle. "They slip children out beneath us. Dozens. Perhaps more. Do you know what that means, Lieutenant?"

The younger man stiffened. "That we are not thorough enough, Herr Oberst."

Ritter shook his head slowly, enjoying the discomfort that followed. "It means we are being mocked. Someone moves in and out of my city, my ghetto, carrying lives like contraband, and leaves me nothing but rumours. That is not sloppiness, Lieutenant. That is insult and I will not be insulted."

He rose and paced to the map, his shadow blotting Warsaw. His finger traced from the ghetto to the outlying streets, to the suburbs where Polish families lived quietly. "She spirits them away and conceals them," he said softly, almost to himself. "She thinks she is clever but soon, I will unravel the entire web."

The Lieutenant swallowed. "We have planted informants, sir. In the offices. In the parishes. Even among the sewer workers. They will come back with names."

"They had better," Ritter said. He turned, his pale eyes glinting. "Because if they don't, I will begin to choose names myself. And I will not choose carefully."

The officer flinched. Ritter let the silence stretch; the cruelty beneath it clear. Then he returned to his chair and lit a cigarette, the flame throwing his face into harsh relief. Smoke curled upward, veiling the reports as though ashamed of them.

He exhaled slowly. "The mouse will make a mistake," he said. "All prey does. Perhaps she speaks too long at a door. Perhaps she takes one wrong turn. Perhaps a neighbour wonders who is visiting late at night."

He stubbed out the match, eyes fixed on the smoke. "When she does, I will be waiting. And when I catch her, I will not kill her at once. No. I will let her speak first, until every name she knows is dragged from her lips."

The Lieutenant nodded, face pale.

Ritter leaned forward, resting his elbows on the desk. His voice dropped to a near whisper, but every syllable carried. "Warsaw believes itself clever. It believes it can bury secrets, hide children, whisper between church walls. But I do not fear them. I accept the challenge."

He closed the report with a sharp slap. "Go. Tell your informants to listen harder. Tell them to watch the woman with too much purpose in her step. Tell them the Reich does not tolerate collaborators."

The officer saluted quickly and hurried out, boots tapping on the cold floor. The door shut, leaving Ritter alone with the smoke, the papers, and his own patience sharpened to a blade. At his desk, he drew a small circle on the margin of his map, just outside the ghetto wall, where the gardens spread along the riverbank. His pen pressed hard, ink soaking through.

"The mouse thinks she can hide forever," he murmured. "Not from this cat."

The smoke from Ritter's cigarette curled toward the ceiling, a thin thread dissolving into the dark. He leaned back in his chair, watching it unravel. There was satisfaction in smoke – its obedience. One spark, one breath, and it rose exactly where he told it. Unlike children. Unlike Poles. Unlike Jews.

He had learned early in life to value obedience above all things. Bavaria, 1905. He had been twelve when his father's hand first cracked across his cheek for leaving a boot unpolished. "A man is measured by discipline," Herr Ritter had barked, his voice thick with beer and pride. "If you cannot master your own shoes, you cannot master your own life."

Karl had stood ramrod straight, refusing to let the sting bloom into tears. That was the lesson: pain made you weak if you showed it. Pain made you strong if you bore it. His father had nodded, satisfied, and handed him the rag. He polished until the leather gleamed so brightly he could see his own reflection staring back at him: a boy already trying to be a man.

Later, at the academy, discipline became more than a household virtue. It was a creed. The other cadets bent rules when they thought no one watched. Karl never bent. He rose before dawn, laced his boots until they cut into his ankles, memorized regulations as if they were scripture. He believed then what he still believed now – that order was the only antidote to chaos. That Germany needed men like him, who could see weakness and crush it before it spread.

Warsaw, to him, was chaos incarnate. A city that stank of rebellion even under occupation. He despised its twisting alleys, its huddled masses, its stink of smoke and cabbage. And yet it fascinated him. Like a chessboard overturned mid-game, pieces scattered but still dangerous.

The children were the worst of it. In Berlin, when he had been posted there briefly, Jewish children had cried in the streets when their fathers were dragged away. In Warsaw, they did not cry. They watched. Hollow-eyed, silent, their gazes followed him like ghouls. It unsettled him more than he cared to admit.

He tapped ash into the tray, frowning. He did not believe in innocence. Every child grew into a body that could either obey or resist. Better to snuff them out young than allow defiance to harden into adulthood. And yet someone was determined to keep them alive. To smuggle them out like contraband, to erase their Jewishness with new names, new homes.

That infuriated him more than the smuggling itself. It was an insult to his creed. Someone thought they could out-discipline him.

He thought of his father again, the man who had beaten order into him, who had died before the war began, never seeing how his son rose. Ritter's lips tightened. He would prove himself to the memory of that iron man. He would show him that discipline was more than polished boots and that it was mastery over life and death.

The mouse would slip. They always did. And when she did, for he was convinced the collaborator was a she, he would crush her under his heel. Not swiftly. No, swift death was mercy. Slowly, with questions, his special methods, breaking her silence. He stubbed out his cigarette and opened the next report. A whisper from a parish clerk. A rumour from a neighbour. A suggestion of a woman seen lurking on the cobbles at night.

He circled the word. Slowly. Deliberately.

"Yes," he murmured. "Let us see where the mouse runs."

12

July 1943

The crypt of St. Klemens was colder than it had any right to be in July. Irena sat at the long table; hands folded tightly in her lap. Her satchel rested by her boots, heavy with papers that never seemed to lighten no matter how many names she carried. Around her, familiar faces looked different tonight, tighter, paler, their eyes flitting too quickly from one to the next.

Father Antoni cleared his throat, the sound echoing strangely in the vaulted space. "There is news from one of the routes," he said, his voice grim. "Bad news."

The barber-forger leaned forward, the candlelight sharp on his hollow cheeks. "What route?"

"The Nalewki passage," Antoni replied. His hands, clasped on the table, were white-knuckled. "A family tried to cross last night. They were stopped. The parents taken. The children..." His pause stretched long enough for everyone to fill the silence with what they feared. "...gone. We don't know where."

A ripple ran through the group, like wind shaking brittle

leaves. The seamstress crossed herself rapidly, lips moving in silent prayer. Piotr slammed his fist into the table, the sound dull against wood.

"How?" Jadwiga demanded. Her voice cracked, her bravado stripped bare. "They knew that alley was safe. We checked it ourselves."

"It was safe," Antoni said. "Until it wasn't."

"Unless," Piotr muttered darkly, "someone told them."

The words hung, poisonous, between the stone walls. Irena's stomach turned. She looked around the table. Eyes darted, suspicion blooming like mold in damp corners. Even the priest's face carried a hint of doubt. Trust – the one thing that kept them alive, was splintering.

"No one here would betray us," Jadwiga snapped. She leaned forward, glaring at Piotr. "We bleed for this work. You think anyone would risk all we've done?"

"That's the point," Piotr growled. "Who else would know? The Germans don't guess so precisely. Someone is betraying us."

Samuel had been silent, standing half in shadow near the wall. Now he pushed away, stepping into the dim circle of light. His eyes swept the group, steady but troubled. "We cannot tear ourselves apart," he said. "If we let suspicion rule us, we do their work for them."

But even as he spoke, his gaze found Irena's across the table. For a heartbeat too long, their eyes held, her heart stuttering with the weight of what neither dared say. Trust was slipping, and once gone, it would be near impossible to reclaim. She dropped her gaze, but the silence was louder than words.

That night, Irena stayed awake in her narrow apartment, staring at the ceiling beams blurred by darkness. The city murmured faintly through the shutters, distant footsteps, a child crying, the metallic groan of a tram forced to labour past curfew. Her body was weary, but her mind clawed at the night, restless.

She lit a candle, shielding the flame with her hand as the ledger sat open on her table, the scraps spread before her in neat columns. She dipped her pen, the nib scratching across paper.

Jakub → Janek. Sura → Zofia. Anna → Ania.

Each line was both anchor and lifeline, the transformation of truth into survival. Each name she wrote was a rebellion against erasure. Her hand faltered, memory tugging her backward. She was eight again, standing behind her father's legs as he argued with the villagers in the square. They had cornered him after he returned from treating a sick family on the outskirts – Jews who lived in a shack by the river.

"You'll bring their disease to us," one man spat, his face twisted with fear and loathing. "Why waste medicine on them? They are not like us."

Her father stood tall, his doctor's bag still in hand. His coat was smeared with mud, his eyes rimmed with fatigue, but his voice was steady. "A life is a life," he said calmly, though steel ran through his words. "No one is lesser. Not Jew, not Pole, not child, not beggar. If you see a man drowning, you do not ask his name or where he is from before you pull him from the river."

The men muttered, dissatisfied, but none challenged him further. Irena remembered clutching his hand, the warmth of it, the quiet certainty that made her small chest swell with pride. Now, in her dank apartment, she laid down the pen and touched her father's words as if they were carved into the table. *A life is a life.*

"I will not let them erase you," she whispered, her voice hoarse. "Not while I can still write."

She folded each slip with precise corners, stacking them neatly into a new tin. Her hands shook, but her resolve did not.

Outside, the street lay hushed. She thought herself alone. But she was not. Across the street, a man stood in the deeper darkness beneath the eaves of a shuttered shop. His coat collar was turned up, his hat brim shadowing his face. He watched the flicker of her candle, the silhouette that bent and straightened inside. He did not move. He did not need to. His task was simple: observe, listen, report.

And when he turned away at last, slipping soundlessly into the night, he carried with him not just the image of a woman writing by candlelight but the sight of her defiance. He carried it straight toward Ritter.

13

August 1943

Dawn crept reluctantly into Warsaw, pale and thin, as if even the sun feared to look too closely at the city. The air smelled of coal smoke and sewage, clinging to every wall. Irena walked briskly toward the ghetto gate, her forged pass was tucked carefully into the inner pocket of her coat. She had learned to wear confidence like a second skin, but inside her chest her heart drummed too quickly.

At the gate, the guard glanced at her permit, eyes dull from fatigue. He barely nodded her through. She entered, and the world changed. The streets inside were narrower than memory allowed, hemmed by walls that blocked light and air. Dawn barely touched the cobbles. The ghetto still slept, or tried to, children curled in corners, mothers already stirring thin soup in pots with little more than water and bones. The smell of rot, of hunger, of despair never left.

Irena tightened her grip on her satchel. She had come to see Miriam, the mother of Hanna – the little girl she had carried out once in a box, hidden and trembling. Hanna was older now by months that felt like years, her face thinner but her eyes still wide, still alive. But as she turned onto Krochmalna Street, the morning shattered. Boots thundered, the sound rolling like drums. Shouts split the air – German orders barked sharp, unrelenting. Doors banged open. Screams rose, high and panicked.

A raid. Her blood froze. Soldiers poured into the street, rifles slung, bayonets glinting. They dragged people from houses, shoving men against walls, yanking women by their arms. A child cried out, then was silenced with the crack of a rifle butt. The air filled with terror, raw and choking.

Irena's first instinct was to run. Her second was to hide. But her third, the one her father's voice always fed, was to protect. She darted into the alley where she knew Hanna's mother lived.

Miriam was there, barely bones now, already clutching a ragged blanket, her eyes wide with terror. Irena grabbed her, pulling her close. "Quiet. Stay quiet."

The soldiers' boots drew closer, pounding against the cobbles like a monstrous heartbeat. Irena pushed open a cellar door half-buried under debris and dragged the woman inside. The space was small, dank, stinking of mildew. She closed the door above them, plunging them into darkness.

The sound above was deafening, boots stomping, wood splintering, screams tearing the air. Miriam trembled violently, her breath hot against Irena's neck.

"They'll find us," she whimpered.

"No," Irena whispered fiercely. "Not if we are still."

She pressed Miriam tighter against her chest, rocking her slightly, feeling the brittle bones beneath the clothes that reeked of poverty, as if the motion could soothe them both while Miriam's tears dampened her collar.

Above, soldiers shouted. A crash rattled dust from the

beams. Someone sobbed. Someone begged. A gunshot cracked, loud and final. Miriam flinched, a muffled cry breaking from her throat.

Irena covered her lips gently with her hand. “Shhh. Listen to me.”

Her father’s voice rose in memory, strong even through the fog of years. *If you see a man drowning, you must jump in. Even if you cannot swim. And when you cannot keep your own head above water, tell a story, words are air, and air keeps the lungs alive.*

So she whispered, low and steady, weaving the tale he had told her when she was small, hiding under their kitchen table.

“Long ago,” she breathed into Miriam’s hair, “our land was guarded by a great white eagle. Its wings stretched so wide they could cover the whole of Poland. And when enemies came, the eagle would cry out, and the people knew they were not alone. They stood, even when they were afraid. They stood, because the eagle stood with them.”

Miriam’s breathing hitched, then steadied. “Was the eagle real?” she whispered, her voice trembling, childlike and afraid as she clung onto the words of the story.

“As real as you,” Irena said. “As real as me.”

Above them, the boots moved on, pounding toward another street. The shouting grew fainter. The cellar held its breath.

Irena rocked Miriam, repeating the legend, her voice no more than a thread in the dark. Outside, the city was tearing itself apart, but here in the small, dank hollow, she tried to stitch one woman’s courage together with words.

Time slowed. Dust fell. The world above eventually quieted, but she did not move. Fear still pinned her to the dirt floor; her arms locked around Miriam. Only when the light through the cracks shifted, turning from grey to the pale gold of morning, did she dare push open the cellar door. The street was empty except for broken doors, scattered belongings, and blood streaking the cobbles.

She took Miriam's hand. "Come," she whispered. "We must go."

The alley behind the ghetto gate stank of urine and ash. Piles of rubbish pressed against the wall, rats darting through the shadows, maggots and flies adding to the grim tableau. Irena clutched Miriam's hand tightly, her satchel slung heavy across her body. Every step felt like stepping onto shards of glass.

"Keep your eyes down," she told the woman. "You are no one. You are invisible."

But invisibility could vanish with one look.

Two soldiers blocked the alley, their rifles slung, their eyes sharp. "Halt," one barked in German. "Papers."

Irena froze, heart pounding. Her forged permit lay in her satchel, but Miriam had nothing.

The soldier's eyes narrowed. "Who is this?"

Before Irena could form a reply, a voice cut across the air.

"A friend," Samuel said smoothly.

He strode toward them, tall and calm, his forged work order in hand. His coat bore the dust of a foreman, his face the stern impatience of a man interrupted in his duties. He handed the paper to the nearest soldier without hesitation.

The guard scanned it, frowning. "You are a carpenter?"

"Yes," Samuel said crisply. "This is my apprentice's niece. I was supposed to meet her here but I am late. I was ordered to escort her to work detail so she may remain under supervision. Do you question a signed order?"

His tone carried just enough irritation to sound authentic, but not enough to provoke.

The soldier glanced again at the paper, then at Miriam, who looked on the verge of collapse, silent, her eyes wide but her lips pressed tight as instructed. The guard smirked. "She does not look like she can hold a hammer."

"Nor could you, if you were starving," Samuel replied coolly. "But she will learn quickly. And she will eat."

The other soldier snorted. "Always more mouths." But he waved them on, bored. "Go. Before I change my mind."

Irena's knees almost buckled with relief. She grasped Miriam's hand tighter and followed Samuel quickly past the soldiers, keeping her head down until the alley curved and the danger was behind them.

When they reached the narrow street beyond, Samuel pulled them into the shelter of a doorway. He pressed his back to the wall, his chest heaving though his face remained composed. Irena leaned against the doorframe, Miriam squashed between them, her own breath ragged. For a moment, they said nothing. The silence was filled only by the pounding of their hearts.

Then Samuel reached for Irena. He caught her shoulders, pulling her against him with a fierceness that startled even her. She let herself collapse into him, her forehead against his chest, his arms locking around her as if he could keep the entire world at bay by sheer force of will.

"I thought I had lost you," he whispered into her hair. His voice broke on the words. He stopped, unable to finish.

Irena closed her eyes; her cheek pressed against his coat. The warmth of him seeped into her, calming the tremors that shook her bones. She felt Miriam beside them, her skeletal body wedged against her hip, the only proof that they had won anything this morning.

"We are here," she murmured. "All three of us. That is enough."

He drew back just enough to look at her, his eyes fierce, dark with fear and love entwined. He cupped her face in his hand, his thumb brushing dirt from her cheek. "Every rescue binds me to you tighter. Do you know that? Every time, the risk grows. Every time, the cost rises."

Her throat ached. "Then we will pay it," she said. "As long as there are people to save."

For a moment longer they held one another in the doorway, clinging as if their hearts could keep each other alive. The war pressed in from all sides, the danger thickening like storm clouds. But in that narrow space, they stood together, two lives stubborn enough to defy the darkness, a desperate woman pressed between them, alive. And though the cost loomed higher with each rescue, neither would step back from paying it. Not now. Not ever.

14

August 1943

The city felt older than it had the night before, and Irena carried the events of the ghetto with her still, the echoes of boots overhead in the cellar, the woman's sobs muffled into her chest, the terror of almost being found. She carried it like a second heartbeat.

When she reached Samuel's apartment, her steps faltered at the door. It was a narrow building above a cobbler's shop, the stairwell dim and steep. Each step creaked beneath her as though the wood itself wished to whisper her presence. At the top, she knocked twice in their agreed rhythm. The lock clicked. Samuel opened the door, his expression shadowed by fatigue, but when he saw her, something eased in his face. He stepped back, letting her enter, and closed the door quickly behind her.

Irena slipped off her coat, laying it across the chair. Samuel gestured to the table, where a pot of tea sat cooling. "Sit," he said. His voice was soft, but something in it held a tremor.

She did. Her hands shook slightly as she wrapped them

around the chipped mug he placed in front of her. The warmth steadied her, though the taste was faint as dust.

He didn't sit immediately. He went to the small wooden chest at the foot of the cot, opened it, and returned with a photograph pressed carefully between cardboard sheets. He laid it on the table in front of her. It was a group portrait, faded at the edges. Boys stood in rows – some grinning with crooked teeth, others solemn, their hair neatly combed, their jackets patched but clean. Samuel stood behind them, younger, less hollow in the cheeks, his expression proud, protective.

"My students," he said quietly.

Irena touched the photograph carefully; afraid the paper might dissolve beneath her fingers. "So young, so much to live for."

"They were, and they did," Samuel said. His voice thickened. "Twelve, thirteen, fourteen. Bright as matches. They asked questions faster than I could answer." He pointed to a boy with unruly curls, "he was convinced Horace wrote only for him. Dawid whistled when he translated Cicero, because he said the words sounded better with a tune. Stanislav –" He tapped another face, solemn-eyed, "wanted to be a lawyer, though he was always the first to break rules."

He drew in a breath that trembled at the edges. "When the war came, they vanished. Some fled east. Some were shot in the street. Some were taken with their families. I never saw them again."

Silence thickened around the table. The photograph seemed almost to vibrate with the absence of the boys, each face a wound still open.

Irena lifted her gaze to him. His eyes shone, though no tears fell. "You carry this with you."

"Always," he said. "To remind me why I fight. Not for vengeance. Not for pride. For them. For their voices, silenced too soon. If I save one child, one, perhaps I pay a fraction of the debt I owe them."

She swallowed hard, her throat tight. "You do more than that, Samuel. Every day."

He gave a small, weary smile. "Not enough. Never enough."

For a long moment they simply looked at each other, the photograph between them like a shared prayer. Then Samuel reached into his coat pocket and drew out something small. He set it gently on the table. It was a locket, oval, its silver worn dull, the clasp slightly bent.

"I want you to have this," he said.

Irena hesitated. "What is it?"

"Open it."

She did, carefully. Inside, behind glass no bigger than a coin, was a photograph –Samuel's face, younger, softer. The image had faded slightly, but the eyes were unmistakable.

Her breath caught. "Why give this to me?"

"Because I cannot give you safety," he said simply. "I cannot promise you tomorrow, or even tonight. But I can give you something of myself to carry, in case..." He trailed off, the words unfinished, too heavy.

Irena closed the locket, her fingers trembling. She pressed it against her palm, feeling its small weight. "You think I want to carry a reminder of loss?"

He shook his head. "Not of loss. Of love."

The word hung between them, fragile, defiant.

Her eyes blurred. She reached across the table, taking his hand. His fingers curled around hers, warm, strong. "Then I will carry it," she whispered. "Always."

He leaned across, brushing his lips against her forehead, lingering there. She closed her eyes, the locket pressed against her palm, the photograph of his students still on the table as the room filled with ghosts and love in equal measure.

~

The corridors of Szucha Avenue were never silent enough for Oberst Karl Ritter. Men whispered too much, boots struck stone with uneven rhythm, papers rustled without order. But his office – his office was an oasis of calm. The desk was clean, the maps secured with pins, the cigarette smoke drawn neatly toward the window. Tonight, however, his patience thinned. The informant stood stiffly before him, hat in hand, sweat beading on his brow despite the cool. He was a small man, his coat too large, his eyes darting like a rodent's. Ritter disliked him on sight, but vermin could still serve a purpose.

"Well?" Ritter asked. His voice was soft, but it carried the weight of command.

The informant licked his lips. "I have seen her. Many times. A woman. Blonde hair. She wears a plain coat, carries papers. Often with children. She says she is a welfare worker."

Ritter's fingers steepled. "Blonde. A welfare worker. Always with children." His mind ticked like a metronome. "Name?"

The man shook his head quickly. "Irena Sendler, Herr Oberst. She works with the city offices. She enters the ghetto. She leaves with bundles."

Ritter rose, pacing to the cabinet at the wall. He opened a drawer, pulled out a thick folder. He leafed through, pages whispering. His pale eyes scanned until they stopped on one file. He drew it out, set it on the desk, and opened it. The photograph was grainy, clipped from an identification form. A woman's face, young but steady, her gaze direct. Her hair was fair, her mouth unsmiling. Beneath it, the name: Irena Sendler.

Ritter's lips curved into a sneer. He reached for his pen, dipped it in red ink, and circled the name slowly, deliberately, until the line thickened into a noose.

"The mouse," he murmured. "At last."

The informant shifted, nervous. "What will you do with her?"

Ritter's gaze never left the file. "I will let her scurry a little longer. Let her lead me to her holes, to the others who shelter her. And then..." He closed the file with a snap. "I will end her story."

He dismissed the man with a flick of his hand. The door shut. The office was quiet again.

Ritter leaned back, his eyes on the circled name. He tapped the file with his finger. "Irena Sendler," he said softly. "The city whispers your name as if it were hope. Soon, they will whisper it as if it were fear."

Far across Warsaw, in Samuel's apartment, the candlelight clung on faintly. Irena sat at the table, the locket resting in her palm, Samuel's hand covering hers. She smiled, softly, briefly, her laughter breaking through the darkness like a fragile flame.

The warmth that followed the locket's click didn't feel like permanent. It felt like a pause between waves. Samuel's thumb traced the ridge of the metal where years had softened the engraving, then he let her hand go as if afraid of pressing too much meaning into a single object.

"Stay," he said. "I can't bear the thought of you on stairs and streets while my hands are empty."

She nodded. "I'll stay."

They moved in the choreography of people who have learned the mercy of small tasks. He fed the stove two splinters of wood. She adjusted the kettle until the flame licked it evenly. He rescued the laundry from the twine line, pressing a warm shirt flat with his palms; she folded it, smiling at how stubbornly his collars tried to be straight without an iron.

Domesticity came to them like a dialect they both knew and had almost forgotten.

"Will you wear it?" he asked finally, eyes flicking to the locket.

"Not around my neck," she said. "Too risky." She found a narrow length of blue ribbon in the mending tin, threaded it through the little loop, and stitched the ribbon inside the lining of her coat above the heart with quick, neat bites of the needle. "Hidden but close."

He watched her sew. The candle burnished the curve of her cheek, the intent furrow between her brows. "You mend with the same focus you use to argue," he said, softer than teasing.

"I argue with the same focus I use to mend," she answered without looking up. "Both keep something from unraveling."

When she finished, she pressed her palm to the spot and exhaled. The locket's weight was faint but certain, like a word spoken in another room that you nonetheless hear.

"Now you," she said, reaching for the photograph again. "Tell me about them. More than their Latin."

He obeyed, gladly, she realised, as if saying their names kept their faces from fading further. Marek had once stolen a plum from a vendor and returned it, cheeks red, because he'd felt the pit in his pocket and realised the fruit hadn't yet ripened for anyone to enjoy; Dawid had carried in his rucksack a pencil whittled to a dangerous stub because he refused to throw away an object that still wrote; solemn Stanislav could not clap in rhythm but could recite, flawlessly, a law about river commerce from 1846 that he'd found in a battered encyclopaedia.

"You loved them, didn't you," she said, when he paused.

"I love them," he corrected softly, and the present tense set itself like a stone in the room.

They ate what passed for lunch, two slices of bread, thin pickles from a jar rescued from a barter, tea made bold by the fiction of calling it tea. He spread the photograph on the table again while they chewed, the way people set out cutlery when guests come.

"I've been thinking of routes," he said, tapping the table's scarred wood where he'd once chalked a map. "The one through the courtyard with the broken pump is watched now. We need to shift to Elektoralna two days early. And the dog –"

" – barks twice for cover, once for stop," she finished, a weary smile ghosting her mouth. "Brother Leon will be proud of us."

"He already is. In his way."

They bent over details: how to grease paper edges so they felt handled, which seamstress could stitch a parish stamp into the hem of a child's dress so the fabric itself bore the permission, what word they would use if a meeting place turned unsafe – stale bread for abandon; warm soup meant proceed.

"If I don't come," she said, when the practicalities thinned, "and no one knows why–"

"Don't," he said, too quickly.

"If I don't," she persisted, gentler, "you go to Helena's garden and water the tree. Nothing else. Don't dig. Just water. She'll understand. She'll invent a reason if anyone asks."

He looked at her for a long time, as if the shape of her face might be something he could memorise deeply enough to carry if the city tried to take her away. "I thought love would make me foolish," he said finally. "It makes me desperate and scared."

She laughed, surprised by the sound in her own throat. "It makes me unbearable," she said. "Every street now belongs to two maps, the one for bundles and the one for getting back to you."

He stood and, with a suddenness that startled her, pushed the table back against the wall to clear a patch of floor. "Dance with me," he said.

"Now?"

“Before the world forgets how to.”

He lifted her hand; she rose. There was no music, only the frayed rumble of the city: somewhere a hammer, somewhere a cough, somewhere a door closing with care. He counted under his breath, one, two, three, and they turned slowly, bodies learning each other’s balance. She felt the locket shift inside the coat, the photograph watching from the table like a chaperone who had decided to look the other way.

“Where did you learn to dance?” she asked, when his palm found the small of her back with the ease of knowledge.

“At a wedding,” he said, smiling into the air above her head. “A summer before the war. The bride had daisies in her hair and the groom had two left feet. I remember thinking the day was a mirage and the world was precarious, and I was right.”

“And now?”

“I would give anything to go back to that day and enjoy the mirage.”

They swayed, pivoted, swayed. They bumped the cot and laughed, too loudly, both shushing the other, and then laughed again, softly. He kissed her then, not with traces of last night’s terror, not with the fever of “we might die,” but with the slow gravity of a decision being made. She leaned into it, and into him, because constancy was also a kind of rebellion.

A knock sounded below, faint as a thought. They both froze. The shop door. A customer? A patrol? A neighbour with a question they dared not answer?

They stood still until the boards stopped talking to one another. The knock didn’t return. They exhaled at the same time and began to laugh, quiet, apologetic, at their own bodies’ readiness to leap to windows and fire escapes that did not exist.

“Sit,” he said again, but neither did. The room had grown smaller for having almost lost it.

"Tell me a true thing," she said, to push the air back into place.

He ran a hand along the back of his neck, thinking. "When I was sixteen, I practiced signing my name as if I were already a headmaster. I liked the taste of authority even when the ink was cheap. Another true thing: when I teach now, quietly, in rooms that are not classrooms, I hear how my voice wants to be stern and how my students need it to be soft. I am learning to be both."

She smiled. "A true thing from me: when I am most afraid, my fingers itch to make lists: doors, faces, routes, rice, names. Like an obsession."

"That's not obsession," he said. "That's dedication."

She took the photograph again and held it beneath the window so the stingy light could find the boys' faces. "I wrote Marek," she said. "In the ledger. In the first column only. Sometimes a single name is the truth, no matter how many papers try to dress it otherwise."

He swallowed. "Thank you."

They worked side by side for an hour while he sharpening pencils to nubs, she trimming the ragged edge from a form so it would look torn from the middle of a stack. Every small decision felt like a prophecy. When the kettle sighed, he poured and she sugared his cup with one of the last grains from a paper twist saved in a drawer. They watched the last crystal dissolve like a snowflake on a warm palm.

"Promise me something," he said suddenly, as if the notion had struck and might flee if not trapped in words. "If you're taken –"

"Samuel –"

"Promise me," he insisted, voice still quiet but bearing command. "Promise you will not be brave for the sake of being brave. Be clever. Be small. Be what they expect, until you are not."

"I promise to be unbearable and organised," she said, and the echo of their earlier joke softened what neither of them wanted to name.

"I bought something," he said, almost embarrassed, reaching under the chest in the corner. He produced a bar of soap wrapped in brown paper – real soap, fat and pale and smelling faintly of lye and lavender, or something pretending to be lavender.

"Did you sell a kidney?" she asked, genuinely astonished.

"A button," he said. "And two lessons in Latin to a policeman's son who will never need Latin."

"His father believes otherwise," she said, unwrapping the soap as if it might jump. "We'll use it now, so we know it wasn't a dream."

They washed their hands in the enamel basin, water gone cloudy and precious. She scrubbed the black from beneath her nails until the crescents were clean again; he lathered his palms as if rinsing away more than city. When they dried their hands on the same towel, their fingers tangled a moment, brief, domestic contact that hit her harder than kisses. Future, it whispered, traitorous and sweet.

"Stay tonight," he said, as the light thinned to curfew. "We'll sleep with our boots by the bed."

"You snore," she said, smiling.

"I deny it."

"You do. It sounds like," she considered, "– a small saw arguing with a knot in wood."

"I don't believe you," he said, his eyes laughing into hers.

She did stay. They ate the rest of the bread; the last slice turned into a sacrament by how carefully they shared it. He read to her in a low voice from a print of Mickiewicz so faint he had to guess at the lines, and she corrected him where memory knew what ink had forgotten. When the dark pushed into the room, they left the candle unlit longer than was practical.

In the cot, they lay facing one another, nearly touching but not quite, and told each other truths made more profound by whispering. He confessed he sometimes planned lessons for imaginary classes, lining desks in his head and calling on children whose names he'd invented. She admitted she had begun to measure distances in heartbeats – gate to alley, alley to door, door to hand, hand to hand.

"Another true thing," he said into the seam between their breaths. "If I am taken first, I want you to be angrier than you are sad. Anger builds resilience."

"Another true thing," she replied. "If I am taken first, I want you to be sad. A little. At least long enough to keep from doing anything stupid in my honour."

He laughed softly. "Unbearable and organised."

"Stubborn and kind."

Sleep came as it does to people who do not trust it: in increments, with checks at the edges. He woke once and lay listening to the city; she woke once and lay listening to him. At some hour with no name, a patrol's boots clattered the street below. They held still until the sound passed. They lay wrapped together, unaware that across the city, her name had already been marked in red. Unaware that Ritter's hunt had turned her into prey.

15

October 1943

Irena came up Pawiak Street with her toolbox in hand and the wind at her back, cold enough to freeze bones. Her forged pass lay in the inside pocket, warm against her ribs. The locket stitched into her coat lining pressed a mild circle into her breastbone, steady, familiar, small as a word you say to yourself before opening a door.

The gate looked the same as it always did, the iron mouth, the two posted guards, the snarling dog at the end of its lead. A sign rattled against chain links with each gust: *Nur mit Erlaubnis.* Only with permission. The bricks to either side were slick with the oil of many hands. Someone had chalked a Star of David on the wall and someone else had smeared it away. The queue was short today, fewer shoulders, more hats pulled low, a quiet too deliberate to be ordinary. Irena made herself walk as she always did – shoulders square, toolbox low at her thigh so it could swing and say *weighty, useful, boring.*

She had chosen her skirt for its pockets. Her hair was pinned in the plain roll of women who have no patience for vanity. In the toolbox: the tools of her lie and her truth both – delousing brush, two small vials of carbolic, a folded strip of flannel, a child's sock with a name stitched in the cuff. She was bringing in medicines for the day after a fever and meeting a woman who would press into her hand a name for the ledger. The plan was a pencil line. She had walked along pencil lines for four years.

At twenty paces she knew something was wrong. The guard on the right was new. Not the one with the scar through his eyebrow who always scratched the shepherd behind the ear when he thought no one looked. This one wore his helmet exactly as the poster showed and kept his mouth hard. The other guard she recognised but not the posture; his boredom had been replaced by a stiffness that made his uniform look newly ironed. The dog did not look at pigeons. It watched the street. The street watched back.

"Papers," the new guard said when she reached them, the word snapped clean.

She passed the permit across before he finished the syllable. He didn't glance at it the way men did when they were tired or bored. He read. He read the violet halo of the stamp. He traced with one finger the line that granted her access "twice weekly, variable days," and let his fingertip rest on the word *variable* as if he could bruise it into confession.

"What is your purpose today?" he asked in German, eyes not on her face but on the corner of her mouth, like he'd been taught that mouths betray.

"Sanitation inspection," she said in the same language. "Lice control. Soap distribution."

"Open the box."

He said it differently today, flat, as if the words had sat on his tongue all morning waiting for her. She set the toolbox on the trestle that passed for a checkpoint table and slid the brass latch.

The lid lifted, the hinges giving their usual tired squeak. Brushes. Bottles. The folded flannel. The sock. Beneath them, the false bottom she had sanded to fit so perfectly only a man's thumb and suspicion could find a lip.

He did not reach for the tools the way men always had, to prod and joke, to feel important near the business of work. He looked at her instead.

"Remove everything," he said.

Her breath stayed even. She took out the brush, the bottles, the flannel, laid them one by one in obedient line. She placed the tiny sock last, as if it were nothing, a rag, and felt the dog's breath appear at her calf, wet and alive. The guard leaned, tipped the box so the light slid along the grain. His thumb found the seam.

He smiled small.

"Lift it," he said.

She lifted the false bottom. An empty space looked back, the size that could conceal anything from a baby's curled body, a loaf of bread, a hundred acts of rebellion. It looked like the outline of a crime.

The new guard's smile went away. He did not look surprised. He looked confirmed.

"Frau –" he began, then corrected himself with a little pleasure, "Fräulein Sendler. How efficient you are."

Her body knew the name before her mind let it in. Skin went cold, then hot, then nothing. The second guard shifted his weight. The dog's nails scratched the dust. Behind the gate someone cried out and was silenced.. Irena put her hand flat on the table to keep it from reaching, on its own, to the inside pocket where paper lived like a bird.

"Who told you that name?" she asked.

"Me," said a voice from the shadow of the gatehouse.

He stepped into the light like a photograph developing:

collar, boots, the pale stripe of hair; the posture of a man who thinks about his appearance. The smile that wasn't. The eyes that read for misprints in people. Ritter. She had imagined him with different faces, all cruel; she had given him no face at all, to rob him of the dignity of reality. The reality was worse for being neat. He could have been a banker. He could have told a child to stand up straighter without raising his voice.

"Fräulein Sendler," he said with the faintest of nods. "We have been expecting you."

Her throat fluttered once against air that had turned to wool. She looked at him as she would look at a splinter she meant to take out of a child's hand: directly, not melodramatically, because truth had to be looked at before it could be handled.

"Then you have wasted your afternoon," she said in German that did not wobble. "My inspection time is logged. If you impede me, you will have lice in your barracks by Monday."

He took a step closer, the leather of his glove creasing softly. "Monday is not my concern. The next ten minutes are."

He lifted his hand and the guards moved as if the gesture had been practiced: not rough enough to make a scene before the gate, rough enough to say *done*. Fingers closed around her upper arms, the efficient pinch that promises bruises made by authority. The dog's breath came up between them, meat-sour.

Irena did not pull back at once. She allowed herself one heartbeat in which to cash all her plans. The dog whistle sat soft against her wrist under her sleeve. The street was thinner than usual. No laundry line to duck under and tangle a soldier's legs. No cart to tip and create noise. The men at the tram stop to the left wore caps pulled down past expression. A woman across the way had turned her face to the wall and was studying its paint intently, as if memorising the colour might be useful later. There was nowhere to run.

"Papers," Ritter said lightly, as if offering her a courtesy. "Humour me."

She slid her hand into her coat, slow as winter, and drew the permit. The violet halo around the stamp was faint; the edges were oiled the way Wiktor had taught them so paper felt like paper that had lived in other hands. She put it on the table beside the flannel and the small sock. The guard took it to Ritter the way an altar boy takes a paten.

Ritter did not look at the seal first. He looked at her handwriting.

"You write neatly," he said. "Schoolmistress neat." He tapped the line that said *child and public health division.* "Such compassionate nouns." He handed the paper back without examining the stamp at all and nodded, once, to the guards.

They turned her. The grip bit. Her body knocked the toolbox; one of the bottles rolled, glinting, fell, cracked, and the sharp clean smell of carbolic rose smoke-like into the sour air, a ridiculous whiff of cleanliness. A soldier's boot ground the permit into the dust without malice.

She remembered to make her mouth speak.

"You will have a report," she said, absurd, stubborn, the only shield left. "On Monday."

He smiled, for himself this time, not for any audience.

"We will speak before Monday," he said. "You and I."

They began to move her toward the truck parked half behind the gatehouse. Canvas sagged over its frame like tired skin. The engine ticked as if counting. The smell from it, diesel, tar, hot rope, made the world shrink.

She dragged her heel once, enough to shift their rhythm. A little, and only once, because men notice when you make their job feel longer. In the drag she let the inside pocket open and the sheaf there slide. Not the ledger, never carried. Not the names, never at the gate. Just permits she could afford to lose and copies of ration cards that no one would be able to eat, dropped like leaves. Paper fanned against ground and lay there blinking. The wind lifted one and carried it under the trestle, where it caught on a splinter and hung like a small flag of surrender.

The guards did not stop. One did kick the toolbox shut with a bang that felt gratuitous. The dog barked once and was silenced with a jerk. The sound of that small, mechanical obedience made something break and then re-knit inside her.

They walked her past the chalk mark that had been a star. A child on the far side of the wire watched her with the stillness of the very hungry. He held something in his hand, a twig or a piece of bread or the imagination of either. He met her eyes. She did not nod; nodding would make it into a thing. She let her mouth soften for him alone.

"Careful," a guard said, not to her but to his companion, because she had gone too quiet and quiet people sometimes turned into trouble at the wrong moment.

Ritter fell in beside them without hurrying, gloved hands behind his back, boots exact. "It astonishes me," he said conversationally, "how much you accomplished with very little. There is almost art in it."

"Am I to feel flattered?" she asked.

He tilted his head. "Perhaps." His eyes travelled to the seam of her coat where the ribbon lay stitched. She didn't think it possible to feel a needle pass through cloth and into skin that had already healed around it, but she did.

"Search her at headquarters," he said to the guard, and his voice never rose. "Not here." It was almost courtesy. It was mostly control.

The truck's tailgate yawned, then the canvas parted like breath. Two men sat on the back plank, one with spectacles askew, one with a nose that had bled long enough to dry.

Between them, a woman stared at her own hands as if reading her palm and hoping for good news. No one spoke. The truck held a heat that did not come from sun. It came from fear trapped in a small space.

The guard nearest Irena put his hand on the back of her neck to press her duck under the canvas. The pressure was efficient; it found the knot of bone where you push to make a body obey. Her locket pressed against her ribs so firmly she thought for a second it might leave its oval in her skin forever, a brand in reverse.

As she lifted her foot to the step, she turned her head and looked back once because you always do. The table sat there with its line of tools, prim as school, the small sock at the end of the row. The permit lay mashed into the dust where motes swam up through late light, up and up, as if they could float away to a happy place.

She ducked and climbed. Inside, the wood was splintered and she took her spot on the plank because there are right places to take your spot even in trucks for prisoners. The canvas breathed in and out. The guards' steps thudded; ropes creaked; the tailgate. The first cough of the engine kicked the air; the second woke the truck; the third turned the street, and then the gate.

Ritter's silhouette paused in the opening before the canvas flapped shut. Every story required a last look from someone. He did not speak. He didn't need to. He touched two fingers to the brim of his cap in a salute that was not respect and let the flap fall.

Irena's hands found each other's wrists the way hers did around children in crowds. The woman beside her turned her face a fraction, enough to let her profile be known. The woman's eyelashes were thick with dust. She was maybe thirty.

The truck lurched. She smelled petrol. The road under the

wheels turned smoother as they left bricks for paving. She had walked so many maps into herself that even blind she could put her finger on a city and tell you where you were: here, near enough to Szucha where the trees along the avenue had learned not to rustle too loud.

The woman with the dusty lashes whispered something without turning her head. "Name?"

"Sendler," Irena breathed back, because there was no point now in being otherwise. "Irena."

The woman made no sound that meant recognition. She did not need to. The man with the spectacles shifted to ease a shoulder. The man with the set nose let his eyes close. The truck took the corner too fast and all of them swayed together and then corrected, the way people will move as one body when given no choice. Irena felt the locket's oval a second time against bone and thought, ridiculously, of apples. Of roots gripping tins. Of a garden that would need watering even if the sky did not consent. She imagined Helena at her window, waiting.

When the brakes finally took, the stop pushed her forward into her own hands. The canvas flapped up. A square of sky looked down without interest. A courtyard.

"Out," a voice said.

Irena stood on legs that remembered, stupidly, to be firm. The building's windows watched with eyelids of glass. The door ahead waited like a mouth that knows your name. She did not look for Ritter. He would be there. He would have a file open already and a pen uncapped. She fixed her eyes instead on a crack in the stone where a weed had planted itself without permission and pressed up a leaf the size of a fingernail into air. She bent quickly and put the green in her mouth, an impossible taste, and swallowed it like medicine.

~

He was running before he knew he'd left the curb. The clatter of the truck had snagged his ear a block away, a sound like a door slamming on the sky, and something in his spine knew before his mind did. He cut down Krochmalna, shoulder-first through a knot of men at a tram stop, the dog whistle striking his wrist bone with each stride.

Then the gate came into view, iron black against the sideways sun. The trestle table. The dog. The two guards. And the truck, its canvas already yawning, ropes hauled taut by hands that had learned too quickly how to tie people into the backs of vehicles. The canvas flapped once – just once before the tailgate slammed.

Samuel saw her in the gap that remained, not her face, not fully, only a slice: the line of her jaw, the sweep of hair pinned severe, the angle of her shoulders as she climbed. Enough to confirm what his body had already decided: Irena. He lunged.

"Samuel!" A hand caught his sleeve, nails like hooks. Jadwiga. She'd come out of nowhere, or out of a doorway. "No, please, don't –"

He shook her off with a violence that surprised them both and kept moving. The guard to his left half-turned, bored, but the other snapped his rifle higher on his shoulder. The shepherd's ears pricked.

"Back," the guard barked in German, flat with habit.

Samuel didn't even hear the word; he only saw the canvas mouth swallowing her, the rope's knot sitting like a clenched tooth. The engine coughed, then settled into its loud, ugly breathing.

Jadwiga slammed into him from behind. She wasn't strong enough to move him, but she was clever enough to shift his balance, a hard kick into his knee. He stumbled back one step, then another, his fingers smearing dirt up the metal as the truck lurched forward.

"Samuel!" she hissed, her mouth at his ear. "They'll take you too, stop, think –"

He roared. It was not a word; it was an animal torn out of him. The sound leapt down the street and came back thinner, ricocheting off windows, a desperate thing looking for a place to live. The men at the tram stop looked away. A boy on a bicycle froze, one foot on the ground, then pedalled hard in the opposite direction. A curtain twitched.

The truck jolted past him, the side panel close enough to skin his knuckles as he ran two steps beside it like a madman trying to board. He saw through one slit in the canvas a hand hold a plank and then let go. Her hand? Someone's hand. He ran until his lungs caught fire and his ankle rolled on a loose cobble and the truck took the corner too fast and was gone, leaving the smell of diesel and rope and the far-away grind of gears.

He stumbled to a stop. The gate swam, then steadied. He bent double, hands on his knees, spit bitter in his mouth, vision pulsing at the edges. The world became very loud and very far at the same time: a woman arguing with a baker, the mutter of a priest's bicycle chain, the creak of signboard hinges in a wind he had not noticed.

"Samuel." Jadwiga again, softer now, her hand on the back of his neck. She knew where to touch to hold a person together. He flinched anyway.

"She was here," he said, ridiculous, pointing at the place where her body had been two pulses ago. "She was..."

He straightened. The world tilted, then righted. He looked at the trestle table. The line of tools he recognised, brush, bottle, flannel, and at the end of the row, a child's sock no larger than his palm. Her permit lay in the dust, a boot tread pressed flat. A page, one of many, had skidded under the leg of the table and stuck there, paper tongue between wood teeth.

He crouched. His fingers shook as he worked the sheet free,

careful, as if he could pull a person out instead of pulp. A ration card copy. Grease at the edges. Her tidy hand. He slid it inside his coat without looking at it because looking would break something and because hiding things had become his way of breathing.

Jadwiga tugged his sleeve. "Come. Into the alley. You look like a fuse."

He let them pull him into the shade between buildings where the smell of urine and coal dust made a narrow, safer air. The dogs bark was duller here, the soldier's laughter, too. He pressed his back to brick because men stand better when something holds them up, and let his head knock the wall once, on purpose, to reset whatever inside him had come loose.

"Irena!"

Jadwiga pulled his hands down gently. "Enough," she said.

She touched his sleeve again. "One more instruction," she said softly. "Go home. Remove what you cannot bear them to find if the door opens. Then come to my house at dark and pretend to want soup."

He looked at her, and because he was a teacher and not a fool, he nodded. "And you?"

"I will wait. For you, for them. And think of new lies."

They turned to go, each peeling off into a different street. Samuel took three steps and then bent, sudden as shame. He straightened and set off, walking too fast, then forcing himself to slow because speed looked like guilt. At the corner, he stopped and looked back only once. The gate was a stage with the actors struck; the trestle stood like a prop. The guards had returned to their posts. The dog had decided to watch pigeons again.

He tasted iron. It took him a heartbeat to understand it was his own mouth. When the scream came this time, it wasn't a roar. It was her name again, but ground down, the way a mill takes the weight of grain and makes it into something else. It went up, struck stone, and fell back over him, not mercy, not answer, just sound, which was the only weapon the moment allowed. People flinched. A child covered his ears. A policeman half a block away paused, head tilted and then lit a cigarette.

Samuel lowered his hands, pulled his coat tight, and began to walk. Every step felt like dragging a net through a river. He set his jaw the way he did before a class that needed him to be unafraid. He counted, door, door, window, corner, not because numbers mattered but because order did. Behind him, the truck's rumble had dissolved into the throat of the city.

He did not look up at the sky; it would only tell him the hour. He did not look into shop windows; they would only offer him his own face, and he did not want to meet the man who had just watched someone he loved being taken and done nothing.

At the mouth of the alley that would carry him home, Jadwiga's voice floated from behind, winded but steady. "Tonight," she called. "Soup."

He lifted one hand in acknowledgment without turning, an agreement, a vow, a thread thrown back to hold them together. Then he disappeared into the thin shade the buildings offered and let the city close over the place where he had stood and shouted, as cities do, erasing and remembering in the same breath.

16

October 1943

The cell was nothing more than limewashed walls, a single bulb hanging from a wire cage, a bucket, a wooden chair, a smear of straw and a ring in the wall set at ankle height, black with old iron and old skin.

Irena's wrists were cuffed in front, the chain short enough to make any gesture a calculation. Her left cheek had dried to a crusted tackiness where a guard's ring had kissed bone. She sat. She counted the heartbeats between footsteps beyond the door, teaching herself their rhythm so surprise would not have the pleasure of finding her unprepared.

Boots stopped. The latch lifted with an official click. Two men came first – orderlies with truncheons, faces arranged in blank obedience. Behind them and in no hurry, Ritter. He had shaved. The neat white line at his collar was knife-clean; his leather gloves creaked when he clasped his hands behind his back. The room steadied around him the way frightened things steady around a predator that is patient.

"Fräulein Sendler," he said. His voice was not unkind. "I hope you slept."

She did not lift her eyes all the way. She gave him the forehead and the line of her mouth and saved the rest. "I did," she lied.

He smiled. It did not reach his eyes because nothing ever did. He moved the chair so that it sat between her and the door, then sat as if beginning a lesson. The orderlies stood to either side. One rocked slightly from heel to toe; the other had the swollen knuckles of a man who had made having huge fists into a livelihood.

"Names," Ritter said, as if asking for chalk. "We will start with the simple ones. Your colleagues. The couriers. The priest who thinks himself untouchable. Say them and you will go to a hospital. I will write the order myself."

She swallowed. The motion tugged skin under dried blood. "A hospital," she repeated, as if tasting a new word.

"Clean sheets," he said. "Real tea. A bedpan instead of that." He flicked a gloved finger at the bucket as if offended by untidiness. "You have done enough damage. Now be sensible and earn clemency."

She thought of a locket sewn inside her coat and hoped the seamstress's hand had been stingy with thread; of a tin under roots; of Samuel's laugh when he tried not to laugh. She let none of it to her face. Instead she gave him bureaucracy.

"I work in sanitation," she said evenly. "I count lice."

He studied her. "The children, then," he said softly. "Where do you keep their names because surely you do not let their, *heritage*, blow into the wind?"

Her heart thumped once against the bracelet of bone. *Be strong,* she told it. She answered aloud in the same patient tone with which she had turned away questions from suspicious clerks. "In my head."

"Your head can be opened," he said, and for the first time he let his voice show the shape of his thinking. He stood without hurry. "Begin," he told the orderlies.

They pulled her to her feet. The cuffs creaked. A strap looped the ring in the wall; the chain shortened. The room tilted, then found its axis again when her shoulder hit the stone. She decided to look at the bulb and not at their hands. The filament inside the little iron cage glowed like a line of molten writing she could not read.

The first blow landed in the soft meat of her thigh. The second, lower, a precise punctuation. She closed her teeth before her body could split into sound. In the pause that followed, perhaps they thought it courteous – she heard some other woman on some other corridor choke a scream, for Irena or herself, she did not know.

"Names," Ritter reminded, as if they had paused a lesson to let a child catch up.

She turned her head enough to see him. "I am having trouble remembering," she said. "Perhaps it is the stress."

He nodded to the taller orderly. "The legs," he said mildly. "She is fond of walking."

They sat her on the chair and brought a short bench – a carpenter's offcut, a tool like any other, and slid it beneath her shin. The wood smelled of sap even in this room. She thought of men who had once made cradles with such benches, of the curve of a runner on a child's sled. The image arrived uninvited and went blessedly away when the first strike came down.

The truncheon was rubber over iron. It gave only to make the return sharper. The crack that answered was not like the sound of wood. It was wetter. Her breath fled and took her vision with it. She didn't faint. She was busy staying alive in a different place, where the world narrowed to a square of light and a voice.

Her father's.

It did not come in as memory. It rose as present tense, as if he were in the cell with his sleeves rolled, the way he was when fever ran the neighbourhood. *Look at me, Irenka.* She did. She focused on the scuffed toe of Ritter's boot, because an anchor is where you find it.

Never betray the innocent, her father said, in a voice that had calmed men on roofs in storms. *Even if you stand alone.*

The second leg was just as neat. They had learned how not to waste strength. The room yelped white around the edges and then settled into a more complicated grey. She tasted metal so thick it seemed the bulb must be leaking. The bench skittered sideways under her heel; someone nudged it back.

Ritter waited. It was almost considerate, the way a doctor waits at the end of a contraction. "Children, names," he said.

She did. She thought them in order. She said none of them aloud. When she had breath enough to speak, she spoke words he would recognise. "Go to hell," she whispered, because defiance must be fed even when your body is starving.

He had the grace not to sigh. "Fingernails," he said, bored now, the way headmasters get bored when a boy insists on his lie.

They moved to a table. The pliers were small, precise, a jeweller's tool that ought to have mended a clasp. The orderly with the thick knuckles held her hand as if he were a brother. He was careful not to bruise the wrong places. The first tug moved nothing; the second found purchase; the third tore.

The pain felt like a cut rope in the centre of her body: everything that had been held up fell. She made a sound then – ugly – and hated it and forgave it in the same heartbeat because refusing to make sound would have been pride, and pride wasted air.

Ritter watched, as men with tidy hair have watched other men stack bricks. He misread nothing in her face. He misread everything.

"Your priest," he said, after the second nail. "The seamstress. The one with the spool. The lawyer who writes beautiful letters. They have vanished and I want to know where the vermin hides."

She blinked the world into two and then back into one. "I do not know," she said. "I do not care."

"Names," he repeated.

She set her jaw and breathed in through her nose like a woman refusing to sneeze during a sermon. She thought of the apple tree and its roots, of Helena's hands in earth. She thought of Samuel's boys in the photograph, their hair parted, shirts starched, shoes polished. She thought of the small sock at the edge of a table, clean as a whistle. Each image stepped in front of the next pull and took it for her.

By the fifth nail the room had learned to tilt and stay tilted. She counted backwards from twenty-two in multiples of three. By the seventh she had no numbers left. They stopped long enough to make her hear silence again. It was a kind new cruelty. Ritter approached then, gloves still neat. He took her thumb in his hand not to hurt it but to study the whorl of its pad, as if he might learn the truth from the pattern.

"If you speak now," he said, "I will stop this. You may keep that one." He let the nail bed go and gestured toward the door. "You may have a doctor. He will admire my restraint."

She was shivering, and she hated that he could see it and that he could not know how much of it was rage. She lifted her head and met his eyes the way you look at a man you will never shake hands with.

"Poland teaches its children to be proud, loyal and true," she said. "I am a child of Poland."

Something flickered. Was it annoyance? Or amusement? He nodded to thick-knuckles. "All of them."

They obliged. The world narrowed to the rim of the bucket and then to a pinpoint in the bucket where a fly had trapped itself in old water and could not decide whether to die or drink. She laughed once. The sound frightened the orderly enough that the pliers slipped. It hurt differently. She filed that away in case she lived and needed to tell a story about how men with tools and uniforms could still be the left hand of incompetence.

When it was done her hands looked too clean. The pink ovals were obscene. She folded her fingers toward her palm and blessed the ache for being honest. Each throb was a drum that said *you are still here*.

He crouched so they were nearly level, a confusion of intimacy. "The children," he said softly, close enough that she smelled the mint of his last cigarette. "Where are they?"

He was circling the tree and did not know it. She wanted, wildly, to tell him to go stand in Helena's yard at dusk and dig at the roots. She wanted to ask if he had ever eaten an apple that had fallen early and bruised, if he had known to cut around the bruise and love the rest. She swallowed the lunacy and made a better one.

"In the cemetery," she whispered. "Under a stone older than your grandfather." She paused, let him lean closer. "They play with angels and dance under the stars."

He didn't hit her. He stood and laughed, just once, a clipped thing, and shook his head. "That is unfortunate," he said to the room, not to her, "I have no time for angels or dancing."

He stepped aside. The orderlies returned to their first grammar. Knees. Ribs. The careful punches that leave pretty bodies and ruined insides. She made herself list children's names in order of arrival, then backward, then by the letters of the alphabet because letters had never failed her. When she ran out of lists she climbed down the well inside her soul that her father had dug many years before.

Never betray the innocent, he said again, as if he had set a hand on her hair to quiet her. *Even if you fear you stand alone. I will always be by your side, Elenka.*

"I'm not alone," she said hoarsely, before she could stop the words. The orderly looked at Ritter, thinking she had answered him. She meant the tree. She meant Samuel. She meant Helena washing her hands in a yard where neighbours watched with wary eyes. She meant a city full of children who had learned to be small and hence were larger than any man who wanted to own them.

"Again tomorrow," Ritter said at last, snapping his glove's button smartly as if finishing a practical demonstration. "Leave her wrists. She may want to pray."

They undid the strap. They did not do her the courtesy of lowering her. She slid down the wall like a shawl falling from a chair. Her legs did not argue on the way because arguments were for people with cartilage. Pain found a new room to live in and moved in boxes with neat labels. She put her cheek against stone and let it drink heat from her until it had enough.

He paused in the doorway. "Think," he said gently. "A single name and the doctor will visit. Perhaps even broth. You will be shown mercy."

She lifted her head because she would not answer the floor. "Mercy," she said, and her voice was more rag than sound. "I know its face. It doesn't look like yours."

He inclined his head, as if accepting the correction in a seminar. Then he went, and the orderlies went, and the latch signed the room again. She pressed her bound wrists to her mouth and found the salt of iron and the faint sweetness of the soap Samuel had bartered like a fool for. She let the taste sit on her tongue like a coin.

She was alone, and she was not. The city pressed through the stone in a thousand tiny ways: the bold scuttle of a rat, the drip their bucket had learned to sing, the memory of a tram's bell three streets away, the way light claimed the cage around the bulb and made a pattern on the wall that looked, if she didn't blink, like branches. She shut her eyes and spoke names into the place where no one could hear her. When her mouth stopped working she let her mind do the speaking. It stacked names like bricks and mortared them with her father's aid until there was a wall inside her no hand could move.

Boots came and went in the corridor. Far down, a woman began to sing in a voice too hoarse to be anything but the version of a lullaby that keeps mothers alive when their children are somewhere else. Irena breathed in. Out. Counted to five. Started again. She pictured the apple tree. She pictured its roots around tin. She pictured Helena on her heels, digging with a spoon while a neighbour pretended not to see. She pictured Samuel with his boys' faces spread on a table like a congregation that lived in his heart.

Never betray the innocent, her father said, speaking the line as if it had been the first sentence and the last in their house. *Even if you stand alone.*

"I stand," she whispered, and when her legs laughed at the verb, she allowed herself a crooked smile the darkness could not steal. "Then I will lie for them. And breathe for them. And shut my teeth for them. And if all that is taken, I will still refuse for them."

The bulb kept the faith. The room breathed. Somewhere beyond the door, a clerk sharpened a pencil to record what was happening. Somewhere beyond the walls, a woman watered an apple tree twice. Somewhere, the man she loved put a photograph in his shoe and practiced a calm face in a mirror in case the door opened the wrong way.

And in the cell, on the floor, Irena Sendler closed her eyes and began to recite the alphabet quietly, as if teaching a class of angels, so the next wave of pain would find no place to sit.

17

November 1943

They'd made a secret courtroom out of a storeroom: bare plaster chilled to the colour of old bones, a table elevated on two crates to mimic a bench, three chairs set side by side. The flag on the wall, a rectangle of red insisting on its own authority. The smell was lime and the metallic lick of radiator heat turned low to save fuel. A clerk's pen scratched steadily, as if what it recorded were respectable.

They brought Irena in on a stretcher because the splints made walking into a farce. She asked to stand. The guards looked to Ritter; he made a small gesture – granted. They hauled her upright. Her legs did not agree with her intent so she leaned into the cane a guard half-shoved at her and set her broken stance as squarely as the hardware allowed. The cuffs were gone but purple bracelets marked where they'd lived.

A lieutenant colonel sat in the centre chair and to his left, a major who blinked repeatedly; to the right, a lawyer in uniform with the nervous habit of moistening his lips before he spoke.

Behind them, two windows, nailed shut, let in a threat of light. A Wehrmacht doctor stood along the wall, bored already. The interpreter, a young Pole with sad eyes waited with his notebook open and his mouth closed.

Ritter arrived without haste, the sound of his heels precise. He laid a folder on the table with a measured flatness, as if presenting a lesson plan. When he looked at Irena, there was no triumph on his face. He didn't need triumph. Order was his ecstasy.

"Name," the lieutenant colonel said in German.

"Irena Sendler," she answered, steady. The interpreter did not translate. He didn't have to.

"Occupation."

"Social worker." The splints bit as she spoke so she swallowed the hiss that wanted out. "Sanitation division."

Smiles tilted, thin and contemptuous. Ritter's pen hovered, then fell still. The clerk's nib kept scratching.

Ritter began in a voice meant for parlours and staff meetings. "Fräulein Sendler has used her municipal position to pass in and out of the former Jewish quarter, claiming duties of hygiene. In fact –" He opened the folder. A photograph grazed the paper: her permit; a clipped square of her face, grainy but recognisably unafraid. "– she transported Jewish children beyond the wall, forged their papers, placed them with Polish families and religious houses, and maintained a clandestine index under assumed names. This is not rumour. This is how they operate."

The major examined his nails, perhaps out of solidarity with his profession's neatness. "Proof?"

Ritter pivoted a sheet to face them: a form stamped with a parish seal that bled violet at the edges, too perfect to be innocent. Another: a ration card duplicate in tidy hand. He lifted a photograph of a confiscated toolbox; the false bottom lifted by a thumb in the frame.

"The accused was apprehended at the ghetto gate," Ritter continued, turning his profile toward the bench so they could admire how effortlessly he stayed within lines. "Her 'sanitation box' concealed a compartment of suitable dimensions for a small child. We have testimonies from informants within the quarter. She has confessed to nothing. Her silence is her guilty plea."

The lawyer's mouth pinched. "We've had enough silence from Poles this month."

The lieutenant colonel leaned forward. "Why do you not save yourself?" He meant it clinically; mercy was not a part of grammar he admired.

Irena moved the cane a fraction to keep her balance. "Because a life is a life," she said in German that would have pleased a headmaster. "No one is lesser."

The interpreter flinched. He didn't write. The colonel's eyes sharpened, fatigued interest finding a sliver of entertainment. "Sentiment," he said.

"Fact," she answered.

Ritter's gloved finger tapped the folder once, as if asking it to keep time. "Fräulein Sendler is a Jew-lover," he said evenly, choosing the words as if selecting the correct specimen for an experiment, "and a traitor to the General Government. She steals property of the Reich, human property." He let the phrase hang, enjoying its neat offense. "She has undermined public order, contaminated records, and made a mockery of our patrols."

The major finally looked up. "And the sentence?"

"We ask the only sentence that registers," Ritter replied. He did not look at her now. He looked at the men who would sign. "Death. By hanging."

It was presented like an item on a menu.

The doctor yawned and hid it with the back of his hand. The

clerk wrote, the nib whispering down the page. Outside, a cart rolled across the courtyard stones, the clop of hooves oddly gentle.

The colonel cleared his throat in a way that was, absurdly, self-important. "Do you wish to speak before sentence?" he asked, impatient formality.

Irena's mouth was broken at one corner; smiling tugged it cruelly. She did it anyway, small and clean, because if he meant confession, she would choose disobedience, and if he meant apology, she would choose contempt. She lifted her head and found Ritter's eyes and set the smile there like a pin in a map. It was not bravado. It was a habit: telling the truth with her face. For one fractional second, some long-ago boy stood up inside him and didn't know where to put his hands.

The colonel brought his palm down on the table, bored with nuance. "Irena Sendler," he intoned, as if the name were a case file, not a person, "for aiding Jews, forging documents, undermining the German administration, and conspiring with criminal organisations, this tribunal sentences you to death by hanging. The sentence is to be carried out at the director's discretion."

The interpreter translated, voice steady but frayed at the edges. He did not look at her.

The clerk finished his scratch and blew on the ink. The colonel signed. The major signed. The lawyer signed with a flourish that revealed a man who practiced his name when he was alone. Ritter did not sign; he had already done his part.

"Bring her," the colonel said without looking again at the woman he had just ended.

As the guards turned her, pain bit up her legs; she let a breath out in a careful ribbon. Ritter stepped an inch closer than required, so the scent of mint and leather reached her under the lime and wool.

"Mercy can be yours," he murmured, for her alone. "All I want is a name. A place."

She met his eyes and, with the smallest movement, shook her head. There was pity in it, and it was not for her. They hauled her toward the door. She kept her gaze on the far wall and the narrow band of filthy light under the window where some weed had succeeded in living during the winter. She put it in her mouth the way she had learned to do in the cell: taste it like a sacrament and carry it where no order could reach.

As she crossed the threshold, she turned her head once more because human beings are made to do that. Ritter's jaw had set. The faint smile still sat on her cracked mouth, soft and inexplicable, and it followed him for as long as it could.

The corridor received her and somewhere a woman sang, only the bones of a melody, a lullaby stripped to bareness. The guards' hands tightened.

Never betray the innocent, her father had said once, holding her hand so her small palm lay snug under his. *Even if you stand alone.*

She walked, if that was the word for what a body does on splinted legs, and let them take her back to wait.

The attic was low and hot despite November. The stove downstairs had been stoked and smelled of dust, candle smoke, and wool. The windows were painted black; the single lamp wore a shade scavenged from a hat, pinpricked to give them constellations no German could read.

They had gathered at the behest of Father Antoni. Jadwiga, cheeks wind-chapped, jaw set. Helena, hair tight, eyes dimmer than usual. Wiktor the forger, ink ghosting his fingers like guilt. The seamstress with her thimble dent permanent in the pad of her finger. A half-dozen others who made up the spine and nerves of a movement that refused to die.

Samuel stood because sitting would make the urge to run more intense. The dog whistle lay at his wrist; he had forgotten it until it clicked against the table when he put both hands down to keep them from shaking.

"They sentenced her this morning," he said. He kept his voice in the register he used to teach frightened boys – flat, steady, unarguable. "Hanging. No date announced."

A ripple of breath went through the room, not shock because most of them had already known, but a collective tightening, the way bodies brace for a wave they cannot stop and intend to meet standing firm.

Father Antoni crossed himself; his fingertips lingered at his brow. "I went to the church behind Szucha at noon," he said. "I knelt and prayed for the men in that building to get stomach-aches. The Lord and I are still negotiating."

"Bribes," Wiktor said, as if naming a tool. "We cannot storm doors but we can purchase a look the other way."

"Madness," the seamstress whispered, hunger and hope knitting knots in her voice. "And yet, maybe."

Samuel leaned in. "We do it." He didn't give them time to gather objections into speeches. "We pay. We pay until the right pair of hands values coin over conscience."

Father Antoni's gaze was old. "Do you know what you are proposing?"

"Of course he does," Helena finished, not to argue but to measure. She had brought a small sack with her – a drawstring purse like any housewife's for market days. She untied it and tipped it once; the sound of coins on wood was an indecent clatter. "My husband's insurance money, the last of it. It won't be enough but it is yours."

Wiktor unrolled a wad of Reichsmarks so fresh they stank of

forgery. "The signatures are real," he said, deadpan. "The ink not so much."

Jadwiga pulled from her coat a narrow packet of German cigarettes. "Stolen," she announced, chin up. "From a man who will not notice."

Father Antoni set a bottle on the table, clear liquid, mean as winter. "From a parishioner who brews a few hours of oblivion. I will confess this myself in spring."

The attic went still. They were all looking at Samuel. He understood why. He was about to say the thing that would decide whether they did something that would be told as brave or stupid by people who had never lived in that moment.

"We can't abandon her," he said, and the words came like a bell rung from the centre of his chest, "there is no other option."

The sentence hit the beams and came back softened and stronger. It landed in Helena's eyes like a match to tinder; she did not look down at the coins again, she looked at him. Father Antoni's mouth lifted in a painful echo of a smile a priest once wore in good times. Wiktor exhaled, long. Jadwiga made a sound like a laugh.

"Vote," Father Antoni said, practical at last. "No speeches. Raise your hand if you agree with Samuel, or do not. God will count the absent ones."

Hands rose, reluctant and brave, in ones and twos. The seamstress's hand shook but she lifted it higher anyway. Wiktor's went up with theatrical disgust at himself. Helena's, of course, was first. Jadwiga's with a snap, as if slapping a face she'd never met. Father Antoni's slowest of all, because he would have to stand at the front of whatever came next and make it look like peacekeeping. Two hands stayed down; one hovered and then came up.

"Strong and sure," Wiktor said. "Like any good bridge that leads to freedom."

"So now we cross it," Jadwiga nodded as she spoke.

They bent over the table as if over a wounded body. The plan came in pieces, as plans always do: a name – *Bruno*, a policeman with a watchful wife and two young sons; a second name – *Klaus*, a guard who drank courage before noon and feared the night when it was all gone. Who would approach whom. With what words. With what price. Wiktor would forge a hospital order and a corpse report – two documents born on the same day. Father Antoni would visit a priest who heard confessions behind a door three corridors from the cells. Helena would provide a reason for a mother to be seen weeping conspicuously outside Pawiak's gate – visible, attention seeking grief, a cover for invisible commerce. Jadwiga would run the notes, foul her shoes in alley water, watch like a hawk.

"If it is to be done," Helena said, cool as a knife washed in cold water, "it must be done before the director chooses a date."

Samuel found himself relaying what he had not witnessed but relayed by the translator. The tilt of her chin in the courtroom, the faint smile that made a man like Ritter misplace his certainty for half a heartbeat. He saw it as he spoke, the way you see a remembered street not with your eyes but with your feet. The dog whistle clicked against his wrist again; he took it off and set it on the map, a circle of rubber anchoring a plan that wanted to skitter like paper in draft.

"Two envelopes," Wiktor said, counting money into piles. "One for the gate guard who checks the book. One for the man who holds the keys."

"Tomorrow," Wiktor said. "We start tomorrow."

"Tonight, we rest" Samuel said, and his voice frayed for the first time since he'd entered the attic, "and in the morning, I will go to Szucha and I will ask to deliver a letter to the director's clerk."

Father Antoni reached across the map and put his hand over

Samuel's fist, which was about to slam down again because it needed to be a thing other than a hand. "You will not go alone," he said. "We do not do alone here."

Helena gathered the money back into her purse, the cigarettes into a folded scarf, the bottle into a knitting bag no one would search because it looked like a woman looking after her life. Jadwiga tucked the forged orders against her ribs where her heart could keep them warm. Wiktor blew on the last of the ink as if it were a child's scrape.

They left in ones and twos, shoulders curved against weather and watchmen, each carrying a piece of a plan small enough to hide in a pocket and large enough to tempt despair. Samuel was last. He took the dog whistle from the map and looped it back over his wrist.

On the stair he paused, one hand on the rail, eyes closed. He pictured her in the cell, in the makeshift court, in the truck, and then he pictured a different thing, a thing so hideous the mind wants to spit it out.

"Tomorrow," he said into the wooden dark, and the house, old and practical, echoed it back without sentiment. Tomorrow.

18

November 1943

Mist lay over the yard while frost filmed the flagstones. The gallows stood at the far end, plain timber and a single rope already turning on its hook. Every swing made the beam creak. The condemned came out in a linked line, iron at the ankles, a chain running through them all. Irena limped in the middle; splints stiff inside boots that were not hers. Her wrists were free only because the chain did the holding. Breath smoked out of mouths and faded fast.

They shuffled forward. Boots hit stone in a slow, even beat. A guard on the steps blew into his hands, then checked the knot as if simply tying a shoe. Another guard watched the line without looking at faces. The captain barked a number; the column moved two paces.

The woman just ahead of Irena began to sob. The sound was quick and hopeless, the kind that slips out when the body is finished pretending to be brave. Irena edged closer until shoulders touched. Cold beaded on her hair. She kept her voice small and steady.

"They cannot kill our memory," she whispered. "Hold on to that."

The woman's breathing settled. The chain jerked, and they all took the next step. The rope swung once, slow, as if the gallows itself were impatient. Irena kept her eyes on it. She made herself see wood and hemp, not a symbol. The pain in her legs spiked with every shuffle and she let it mark time. In. Out. Names in sequence behind her teeth, Hanna, Dawid, Sura, Marek, something to put between her and the beam.

A crow dropped onto the crossbar and cocked its head. Dawn thinned the fog to a grey sheet. The line inched forward until the first step of the scaffold was only a few paces away. Death stood close enough to touch. She lifted her chin and took another step.

~

Inside the corridor cut the fog in two. Wet coats steamed on hooks. A ledger lay open on a table beside the door to the yard. The bulb overhead buzzed. Goods had changed hands twenty minutes earlier, when Żegota's packet slid under a latrine door with two cigarettes on top. Now the junior guard who had taken it stood by the ledger, face blank, heartbeat loud in his throat. The weight of the bribe felt like a hot stone in his pocket.

The guard captain stood near the yard door, listening to the chain scrape. They had expected Ritter to be there but some unexpected incident had him otherwise engaged. A clerk hurried up with a folder and the captain turned the pages once, nodded, then gave the smallest tilt of his chin. Begin.

The junior guard dragged the ledger closer and flipped two

pages very carefully. He frowned at a blank square in the stamp column, an invented error and lifted the book and angled it for the captain to see. The captain leaned in, swore, reached for the pen.

In that sliver of inattention, the junior stepped into the doorway and met the line as it entered the corridor. He touched the chain, pretended to untangle it, and used the movement to pull one prisoner one pace out of line, Irena, toward the wall. A slight pressure at her elbow, a bureaucrat's frown, the look of a man "correcting" a file. The rest of the prisoners kept moving. The woman who had cried once did not notice that the shoulder beside hers was gone.

A scuffle outside, someone stumbled on the first step. The captain snapped his head back toward the yard and his mouth thinned. He moved that way too, hunting the fault. The junior took his chance. He shoved Irena flat against the bricks, hard enough to knock breath from her, and brought the baton up in a short arc. One precise blow to the temple. The light overhead blinked; the corridor slid sideways. Her knees failed. He caught her under the arms before the chain could rattle.

The door to a service passage stood ajar, always sticking, never fixed. He dragged her through it into a narrow lane that ran behind the laundry. A handcart waited there, already piled with grey cloth and cabbage leaves for cover. The carter kept his eyes on the horse's shoulder. His coat pocket bulged with a bottle given to him an hour ago.

They heaved her onto the cart and pulled the cloth over her, layer on layer until she was only a lump among other lumps. The junior eased the service door shut with two fingers, wiped his palm on his trouser seam, and went back inside with the ledger under his arm and a frown that said the stamp had finally been found.

In the yard, the line moved. The first prisoner mounted the

steps. Rope brushed wood. The captain barked the order to continue. The machine of death liked to be told it was on time.

The cart rolled away from the wall. Iron rims clicked over the threshold lip and whispered along packed dirt. They took the first corner slow to look ordinary, then the long straight that led to the trees. Fog thickened into a kind of coat. The horse's breath blew white, then disappeared.

They left the road where the ditch dipped and the cover was close. The carter stopped by a wedge of birches. He listened. No boots. No voices. He lifted the cloth and saw skin and hair and nothing else he would have to remember. He tipped the load. The body slid into leaves and settled. He threw two cabbage leaves after it and a strip of grey cloth. The horse turned by itself, eager for the stable and the warmth that waited there. The cart rattled back toward the city, wheels singing softly on the hard ground.

Behind the door to the gallows, the rope stopped moving. A clerk drew a line in the ledger and dotted it. The captain smoothed a gloved hand over a folder with a red circle around a name and moved it onto the stack marked "completed," because paper always believes itself.

In the trees, the mist hung low. Leaves stuck cold to Irena's cheek. Pain pulsed in the exact shape of a baton, then withdrew enough to let sound in. A wagon's whisper faded. A bird tested a note and fell silent. She stayed still and counted to four. In. Out. The woods held their breath with her.

The gallows had stood waiting. Death had been inches away. Corruption made a gap wide enough for her body to fall through and live.

19

November 1943

Cold woke her first. Not pain, not fear, only bitter cold, precise as a blade laid along the spine. It had pooled in the hollow of her back, seeped through the damp wool under her, climbed the rungs of her ribs. When she tried to lift her head, the world slid and steadied, trees knitting back into their upright places. Leaves pressed to her cheek as frost bit her lips. Breath came in small, white threads.

She lay still and counted. In for four. Out for four. The numbers were the only thing that held when everything else was about to topple. A lace of branches made a roof, bare and black against a grey sky. Far off, a crow worked at something in the litter and scolded the morning for existing. Closer, a wagon creaked once and was gone. No boots. No voices.

She moved the right hand first. Fingers answered, slow, stiff, but present. The nail beds ached, raw as new mouths. The left hand trembled when she asked for it; she forgave it. Her legs lay heavy and helpless, splints biting where bindings had found bone again. When she tried to bend the knee, pain flared bright, then dialled back to a workable throb. She breathed through it. She had learned that trick in other rooms.

A strip of cloth slid off her temple. When she touched her hairline, her fingers found the raised welt of the baton's kiss. The skin was sticky with dried blood and forest dew. She wiped her hand on the cloak someone had thrown over her.

Alive. The word arrived without trumpets, a fact more than a miracle. Alive, and dumped where trees keep secrets. She rolled to her side, slow, careful, letting leaves work as a mattress, and pushed to her elbows. The world narrowed to the ground ahead: the ribs of roots, a snail-shell of ice, the ragged print of a deer's cloven foot. She rested, let the pounding in her skull settle, then inched again until her shoulder found the trunk of a birch and borrowed its strength. Bark scraped her cheek, hard and clean.

When the retching came, it was dry and quick and mean. She let it pass, then licked cracked lips and tasted iron and sour breath. Thirst announced itself next, not politely. Her tongue felt like old cloth.

A shape moved at the edge of the trees, a man's outline, halved by mist. He paused, listening, then stepped off the rutted track with the cautious tread of someone who has lived long enough to respect his freedom. A bundle of brush hung at his shoulder; a short-handled axe swung against his hip. His cap was pulled low, his collar high.

Her body had learned to make itself small. It did so now without asking. She pressed back into the birch and let the grey cloak take her colour. He would pass. He should pass. Better to be ignored than named.

The toe of his boot found a cabbage leaf. He looked down. His gaze followed the green to the hem of her cloak and stopped. In the same motion, he stepped back and crossed himself, fast and hard, fingers dragging a white streak through the breath that puffed from his mouth.

A ghost, she thought, and would have smiled if her lips hadn't cracked. She could feel what she looked like: ash pale, hollow-eyed, hair matted, the ruin of a city in one body. A woman-shaped warning.

He did not run. He shifted his grip on the brush and stood very still, as if sudden motion would tear some veil and let trouble see him. His eyes were washed-out blue, wary, the eyes of a man who had watched too much and kept too little.

"Woda," she said, when her voice would obey. Water. The word came thin but intact.

He stared a breath longer. Then his shoulders dropped a fraction and something in his face loosened. He set the brush down, unwound a leather strap from his shoulder, and opened a tin canteen by feel. He crouched, slowly, like one would settle gentling a skittish horse, and held the canteen close enough that she could smell salvation. The first swallow burned the cracks in her mouth; the second was a relief so clear it made her eyes water. She stopped before greed embarrassed her and nodded once. He tipped one more mouthful into her palm and she wet the hinges of her hands, the raw beds of her nails. He glanced away, giving her the courtesy of not staring.

His gaze returned to the bindings on her legs. Trained hands or farm hands, either way, he understood splints. His eyes climbed to the edge of the bandage at her temple and down again to the outline of the shackles' bracelets around her wrists. He put it together and did not say the word for it. Pawiak.

"Nie tutaj," he said softly. Not here. The warning sat tidy in two syllables.

"Nie," she answered. No.

He looked toward the road, listening, measuring. Morning hadn't fully made up its mind about the day; fog kept its grip. A small horse waited on the track, shaggy, patient, steam puffing from its nostrils; a low cart stood behind it, a basket for kindling already half full. He brought the cart as close as the ground allowed, the wheels bumping over roots. He did not ask her name. He did not offer his. He crouched beside her again and told his body what to do: one arm under shoulders, one under knees, lift with legs, let the birch take some of the strain. He counted for himself and for her, breath a metronome. Her head swam. The world narrowed to the hard bowl of his shoulder and the smell of linen worn and washed and worn again. Pain flashed white, then settled into a dull, reliable roar.

He kept the motion small, no swinging, no sudden drops, and lowered her onto the straw in the cart. His hands worked quickly, arranging the cloak, tucking straw around splints, making use of small comforts. He set his brush over her like a thatch and cane-strapped it down, enough to hide a shape without calling attention to the act of hiding. Experience spoke in each movement; fear lived in the care that didn't waste seconds.

They moved. The horse set a stubborn, ordinary pace. Hooves thudded soft; iron rims whispered. With each jolt, pain flared up from her shins and died back; she rode it like weather. The track bent toward open field. Beyond the fog lay a small, square house with a roof patched in two places and a smoking chimney. A plank fence sagged in the middle; a chicken pecked at nothing with missionary zeal. He led the horse past the house to a low barn whose boards didn't match, slid the door just enough, and brought the cart inside. The horse shook and the harness jingled once. He shut the door behind them.

Light fell in squares from two small windows. He set the brush aside, then the rope, then crouched to lift her again. A bed of hay waited in the corner; a blanket pitched over it like a tent. He made a soft tunnel with his hands and his body and the blanket, then slid her within, leaving a narrow slit for air. The hay stabbed and itched and smelled like stored summer. She breathed through it and listened.

He stood still a long moment, just inside, just listening, and then went. She heard the outer door, the metal click of the latch, his step on hard-packed earth as he crossed the yard, then the house door opening and closing, once, twice. Voices might have come next, his, a woman's, but none did. Only the small chores of a morning resumed: the scrape of a chair leg, a kettle set down, wood settled in a stove.

She slept, if the drift between pain and waking counted as sleep. The barn blinked, the light-shapes on the boards moved with the day. Once, a rat stitched itself along the wall; once, a hen wandered in and muttered an opinion to the straw and left.

When he returned, he carried a crock and a dipper, a folded cloth, and a bundle that smelled of chamomile and spirits. He didn't light a lamp. He moved by the light that was allowed, sat on a milking stool, and went to work with a farmhand's economy. Cloth dipped, wrung; the cool touch on her skull made the pain ring and then soften. He worked around the bandage the doctor had laid, adding fresh binding where blood had seeped. He examined the splints, nodded at them as if acknowledging good craft, and didn't touch them.

He offered a dipper of weak broth. She lifted her head with his hand at the back of it and swallowed slow, shivering at the heat. The second mouthful went down easier; the third met resistance from a stomach that had learned to expect nothing. He stopped at three.

From his coat, he brought a folded paper, torn from a wall, creased to quarters, edges black where fingers had handled it too long. He looked through the slit of the blanket to be sure she watched, then opened the sheet once and laid it on his knee so the light could find it.

Obwieszczenie. The word stamped the top like a fist. Beneath, in the clerk's careful hand and the printer's thin ink, the list ran down the page: names and ages, dates and places, a lie of order laid over murder. Her eye found its mark without her permission.

Sendlerowa Irena—wyrok wykonany. The room did not move. She did not feel the hay or the cold. She read it again. Sentence carried out. Official. Finished. The black print made her body a thing of the past.

He did not look at her face. He looked at the paper, then at his hands. One thumb had the permanent half-moon dirt of a man who worked and washed and still carried earth. He folded the sheet and put it away again inside his coat and shut his fist on the place where it lay, as if to keep it from speaking.

"Pod miastem," he said finally, voice low, for her and for the hay and for the horse that had begun to nose along the stall for old oats. In town. The lists were posted. People had read them. He gulped once. "Wszyscy widzieli." Everyone saw.

The name on the paper had weight. It pinned her like a hand on the chest. She tasted what it meant: no more permits; no address; no legal shape; not a person, not on paper. In the Reich's ledger, she was a line drawn through. To the world, she was already hanging and already buried. The first sensation wasn't grief. It was shock. The second was grief.

Ghost, she thought, and this time the word did not make her want to smile. Erased yet breathing. A shape that doors and lists could not admit, a body that could pass through some walls because those walls no longer recognised her. She let the blanket down a fraction so he could see her eyes. His flinched at the sight, startled again, still seeing a dead woman speaking and then steadied. He was terrified. He was also making a choice.

He went to the corner and brought back an old shawl and tucked it under her neck. He set his canteen where her hand could find it and pushed the crock closer to warm in the hay. He drew the blanket's edge down again to make darkness. His hands hovered, awkward, respectful, careful. He did not touch her face. He did not cross himself. He adjusted the slit a hair so she could breathe.

Through the narrow seam she watched him move: the square of his shoulders, the careful way he placed each thing back where it belonged so the barn would look unchanged if anyone came. He shook straw from the brush bundle and laid it where it must always have lain. He paused at the door, hand on the latch, and rested his forehead against the wood. The posture meant prayer or fatigue or simple bracing. Then he went.

Alone with hay and the horse and her own body, she pulled the folded corner of the blanket to her mouth and bit it until her jaw stopped shaking. The paper's words crawled under her skin: *wyrok wykonany.* The sentence had been carried out. Clean. Official. A stamp had taken a life and tucked it away.

Remember me, the world asks the living to say for the dead. *Don't remember,* her future now demanded if she meant to keep moving. The two imperatives braided, tight and strange. She felt them both and did not try to unpick them. Then she slept the way hurt people sleep – halfway between nightmare a delusion, in slices, waking to count, slipping back. Light shifted. Rain began, quit, began again. Once the barn door thudded and a boy's voice skittered through like a pebble, quick, curious, then vanished at a man's command she couldn't hear. Once the horse sighed and stamped, and she felt the tremor of it through the boards into her bones.

The farmer returned at dusk, bringing a heel of bread and a smear of something that wanted to be butter. He looked older than he had in the morning, as if the day had asked more than usual. He ate nothing himself. He watched her take small bites, saw her wince when her teeth met crust, waited each time before lifting the dipper again. After, he tucked the blanket tighter and sat in silence while the light drained out of the timbers.

When he stood to go, she put her fingers through the slit and caught a thread of his sleeve. He looked down, startled, then let his wrist rest in her hand for the time it took her to press and release. Thank you. He nodded once.

He left her a candle stub and a match. He did not light it. He set them by the slit, invisible to any eye that was not lying in the hay. Night settled. The barn breathed. Somewhere a fox called to its mate, was answered, then fell quiet as if shushed by a larger darkness. She lay awake inside her small tent of straw and wool and recited the names in order until they were a chain and then a ladder. Hanna, Sura, Dawid, Marek, Ania, Zofia, David. It steadied her hands. It made of her breath a page. On that page she wrote another word, one that had refused to die the first time they tried to kill it: *again.*

The morning would bring choices. She would be no one on paper. That meant she could be anyone in daylight, if she could stand, if she could walk, if the farmer kept choosing her life over his fear one hour at a time. She would be a rumour, a woman people swore they'd seen when no one could prove it. A ghost with work to do.

The hay pricked. The cold edged back in and nested along her spine. She pulled the shawl higher under her neck and let her mind reach toward a garden she could not visit and an apple tree where, under a wintering lawn, a tin waited. She pictured it, not the metal, but the paper inside, the curled truths, the thin defences. Those scraps belonged to the living. So did she.

~

They carried her like contraband up a staircase that didn't dare creak. The farmer lifted from below, Jadwiga from above, her small hands careful and sure. At the top, the trapdoor rose an inch; a line of lamplight cut the dark.

Samuel was there before the opening widened, already reaching. The first glimpse of the shape under the shawl, the pale strip of face, took his knees away. He caught the jamb with one hand and the floor with the other and held himself upright by will alone. Jadwiga's look warned him: keep it together.

They eased Irena in, back-first, onto the attic boards. Samuel slid in beside her on his side, afraid that if he used both arms he would shake her apart. The farmer set down the lower half of her splinted legs with the care of a man placing eggs; then he was gone, the trapdoor lowering, the bolt whispering home. The house settled around them.

Samuel's hands hovered, useless. Then he folded her in, careful of the splits in her hands and the stiffness of her legs and held on as if warmth itself could pull her back through whatever door she'd slipped under. She smelled of hay and damp wool and human functions. His cheek found her hair; her breath brushed the hollow of his throat. He didn't realise he was shaking until his teeth clicked once against the crown of her head.

Jadwiga laid a folded blanket over them and turned the lamp down to a steady amber. "Water," she said to herself, to the room, to the panic, and put a cup by Irena's hand. She pressed a rag to Irena's temple where the baton had bloomed purple, then set the rag next to the cup. Her mouth had gone thin like a person refusing to cry.

Samuel tried to speak. What came out was a sound from too far down. He swallowed it and made a sentence. "I thought –" His voice broke. "I thought I had been widowed without ever earning the word."

Irena's laugh was a breath with an edge. She reached out, slow, stubborn and found the V of his shirt and bunched it in her fist. The movement cost her; he felt the flinch run through her body. He made his hold gentler, a shelter, not a clamp.

Jadwiga knelt and slid a hand under Irena's head, lifting just enough for the cup. The first sip shook; the second steadied. Irena let the water sit on her tongue and savoured it.

"You can talk later," Jadwiga said, soft but brisk. "Not now. Now you breathe. You two just have to keep each other together."

She moved to the far corner to give them the illusion of privacy, busying her hands with neat, pointless tasks: folding a sheet that had already been folded, lining up three candles by height, checking the edges of the blackout paper on the tiny window. Her shoulders shook once; she flattened the tremor of a sob into stillness.

Samuel pressed his forehead to Irena's. He had her with both arms now, careful of every bruise. The locket stitched into her coat pressed faintly against his chest through both layers, a cool coin with a memory inside it.

"Alive," he said, as if the word could be a bandage.

"I am actually dead," she whispered, and the words came without drama, just fact. Her breath hitched once and went on. "But my soul is still alive. And the children's"

He closed his eyes hard. Salt burned. He let it. His tears threaded into her hair and disappeared. "Then we keep it alive," he said. "Yours, theirs. Every single one."

She nodded, small, against him. "They posted the list," she managed. "I saw it. My name, is finished." She pulled a breath through her teeth. "It might help us."

Jadwiga turned then, quick and fierce, as if the word had thrown a match. "Good. Let them tell each other you're gone. We will use their arrogance like a cloak." She came back, crouched, and brushed a stray hair from Irena's cheek with a knuckle. The motion was matter-of-fact, not tender, which made it tender.

Pain ran its circuits through Irena's face, flaring and fading. Up close, Samuel saw everything the truck and the cell and the yard had written on her: the split at her lip; the welt under her hairline; the raw crescents where nails should have been; the way her shoulders held themselves as if expecting rope. He touched the unhurt places with two fingers, the hinge of her jaw, the ridge of her brow, the warm damp corner of her eye, and felt her relax a fraction.

"Her legs?" he asked, voice low.

"They must have set what they could," Jadwiga answered. "Then the farmer. He found her after the wagon. Brought her to a barn, brought me the news, brought her here at dusk. His life sits under this room with us tonight."

Irena's mouth shaped thank you and didn't try to send sound with it. Jadwiga saw anyway. "He'll sleep lighter for knowing he was useful but still worry until we leave" she said. "Tomorrow I'll replace their broth and tell his wife a lie, that we will soon be gone, and hope she hears truth."

Wind shouldered the roof, found a seam, and spoke down the rafters. A floorboard somewhere deeper in the house answered with a tired tick. The three of them listened to the ordinary noises, letting them build a fence around the moment.

Samuel eased onto his back and drew Irena with him so her weight could settle without fighting bones. She lay partly on his chest, partly on the blanket, breathing where his heartbeat lived. He turned his face into her hair and let the smell of hay and weather fix the moment.

"You kept the locket," he murmured.

"Sewn into my coat," she said. "A foolish miracle."

"Keep it there." His hand flattened over the spot, then

wandered until it found her bandaged fingers. He kissed the gauze. “Tomorrow we’ll move it someplace safer.”

“Tomorrow,” she echoed, and it sounded like a password.

Jadwiga tucked the blanket snug around their shoulders, then sat back on her heels, her eyes shiny in the dim light. “I’ll sit the first watch,” she said. “You sleep like people who meant to die and didn’t. We’ll plan when the day returns.”

No one argued. The attic grew small and warm around them. Samuel felt the tremor leave his muscles in slow waves, each second confessing how close he had come to dropping into a place he could not have climbed out of. Irena’s breathing evened, then hitched, then evened again; each time, he matched it, a metronome lent to her.

She startled once, hard, and his arms tightened before he could think. Her face cleared; she found him and the attic and the lamp and came back. “Rope,” she said, almost not saying it.

“You’re safe,” he answered. “Under a roof and a bad blanket. With us.”

Her mouth tilted. It wasn’t a smile. It was a promise to try.

When sleep finally took her, it came like a truce, not a mercy. Samuel lay awake awhile, counting the seconds between the roof’s complaints, learning the attic’s language so he could hear danger when it muttered. Jadwiga’s silhouette kept watch by the trapdoor, knife tucked into her boot, chin on her knees, stubborn as a mule and twice as useful.

He looked down at the woman in his arms and felt the rough joy of a thing stolen back from oblivion. He pressed his lips to her hair and tasted salt and dust and the edge of tomorrow.

“The names are alive,” he whispered into the dark, not to wake her but to teach the room. “So are we.”

20

November 1943

Helena opened the garden gate with the slow care of a woman easing a door into a sleeping room. November thinned the air to glass and the moon was a pale coin. The apple tree stood in the middle of the small plot, its limbs stark and patient, roots heaving the soil as if straining to lift the world back into place.

"A week," Helena murmured, locking the gate behind them. "You should still be in bed."

"I'm done lying down," Irena said. She worked her crutches over the threshold. Each step sent a clean nail of pain up her shins; she welcomed it. Pain meant the body was still in attendance.

Samuel hovered close enough to catch her if she faltered, far enough to pretend he wasn't counting her breaths. He kept his head low, hat brim shadowing his face. The city, beyond the fence, rasped under curfew, the sound of distant boots, a muffled engine, a train going who knew where, into the night.

Helena's windows were dark, blackout paper neatly pinned. In the flower bed, frost made lace from dead stalks.

Irena crossed the narrow path and stopped at the tree. Moonlight silvered the bark; the scar where they had dug last spring showed as a darker seam in the earth. She tipped forward, set the crutches against the trunk, and lowered herself to her knees. Samuel reached, but she shook her head. "No," she said. "I dig."

Helena passed her a hand spade, then a second, then wordlessly, her own gardening knife. Irena's hands, still tender where nails had been, curled around the wooden haft. Dirt crumbled cold and damp under her fingers. It packed under the raw crescents; she felt the sting and kept going. The scent rose, metal and apple rot and clean loam. She cut through roots as thin as thread, pressed her palm flat to thicker ones and whispered, "Excuse me." The tree said nothing, but the ground yielded, grudging and then willing.

"Let me," Samuel tried again, voice low.

She didn't look up. "You can keep watch," she said.

The spade scraped against tin with a small, singing sound. All three went still. Irena dug with her fingers now, scooping the soil away until they settled on a rusted lid. Another scrape, there, the second, set at an angle, exactly where she and Helena had pushed it months ago when the ground was warm and the world was only half broken.

"Hold the light," Elena whispered.

The moon was a thin thing, but Helena angled a pocket torch behind her palm, a cup of glow that didn't travel farther than their knees. In that small circle, the metal showed freckled with rust, wax-sealed at the rim. Irena pried a lid loose. It gave with a sticky sigh, like a jar that had decided to forgive you.

Inside: oilcloth, beeswax, string. And under that, the thing that mattered, the folded scraps of paper pressed tight as a heart pack. Names. Jewish names written in pencil and ink, steady and careful even where the hand had shaken. Infants disguised as saints, toddlers renamed for angels, siblings given twin initials so they could find each other again someday.

Irena let out a sound that wasn't a sob, more a guttural cry. It came from the bottom of a well and climbed up her. She pressed the tin to her chest, shaking with the effort not to let the papers rustle in the cold air.

"They tried to make me give you up," she said, tears running straight and hot into the dirt on her face, "but I never will."

Helena bowed her head as if at a grave and an altar. "God willing," she echoed.

Samuel went to his knees and put his hand on the tin and then on Irena's shoulder, anchoring both. He couldn't speak. He didn't need to. The three of them stayed that way a moment, tree, earth, hands, breath, while the city beyond the fence continued its lie of order.

Irena set another tin in her lap and unwrapped the inner pack. She checked each fold like a mother checking fingers and toes: no damp, no mold, edges crisp. She pulled one slip free at random. A girl's true name. Her parents' names. The parish name she had invented for her. The address where she'd been placed. The tiny notation in Irena's hand – *mole on left cheek; loves cats*. The details that made a child a person and not a memory.

"They've kept," Helena said, relief and pride braided tight.

"We rewrap," Irena answered. "More oilcloth. The second tin too. Deeper this time."

Helena was already moving, quick and silent, to fetch a square of old table oilcloth and a candle stub. Samuel cupped his hands around the match as she lit it; wind licked the flame and then surrendered. The softened wax glazed the new wrapping. Irena sealed edges with the side of her thumb, leaving half-moons. When she reached for the second tin, Samuel slid his hands into the hole and placed the tin reverently. He didn't insist, and she didn't thank him; both were understood.

They had come armed with a sack of sand to bed the tins away from damp, and with coarse salt to ring the cavity—a superstition or a science; either way, something to make them feel less at the mercy of worms and weather. The roots pressed close, like ribs around a lung. The hole looked like a mouth closing on a secret. Then she and Helena folded earth back over, smoothing it flat. Samuel tamped the soil with the heel of his hand, then scattered last summer's leaves so the ground looked unchanged, uninteresting.

Irena sat back on her heels, palms filthy, breath visible. The throbbing in her legs had settled into a rhythm she could stand inside. She leaned her forehead to the trunk. The bark was cold and alive. "You're saving them with me," she whispered to the tree. "Watch over them always."

Helena put a folded cloth in her hand and then, as if remembering herself, allowed one heartbeat to stroke Irena's hair. "Tea," she said, voice rough. "Inside. I'll leave the back door unlatched." She glanced at Samuel, and a hundred practicalities were in the glance –watch, stay, listen. She slipped towards the house, feet silent on the path, leaving them to the quiet.

The garden settled, as gardens do after a necessary violence. Somewhere a neighbour's window whispered shut. Samuel sat beside Irena, his shoulder to the tree, his hand closing over hers where her dirty fingers still gripped the cloth.

"You should be in bed," he said, finally.

"So should the world," she said. They smiled, a brief, honest thing that made room for the next breath.

He took the crutches and set them against the trunk, then turned to face her. The lamplight from Helena's kitchen made a pale square on the ground through the blackout seam. Under the blanket of the moonglow, the garden felt temporarily serene.

"Come away with me," he said, the words catching like a match and then burning clean. No preface, no detour. "Tonight. We can vanish. To the country. To the convent, they'll hide us. We'll wait out the winter, the spring, make ourselves useful elsewhere, and when it's finally over –" His hand moved, helpless. "We'll walk back into a world that isn't trying to hang you."

She looked at him and saw the whole map of his hope and his terror. It would be so easy to say yes and mean it for an hour. She reached and touched his cheekbone with the pads of her ruined fingers, feeling the grit he hadn't washed away, the life under the skin.

"If I stop now," she said, voice small and steady, "all those names are wasted."

He shut his eyes. It wasn't anger that crossed his face; it was grief for a future he wanted to steal and couldn't. He opened them and leaned in until their foreheads met. "I know," he said. "I knew before I asked. I ask anyway because I love you, and because the thought of losing you twice is a thing I do not know how to survive."

"You will," she said. "And if I go first for real, you will water the tree, and you will keep the names moving like a river."

He made a small, broken sound. She pulled him in with her hand curled in his collar, and he kissed her, not the gentle kiss of convalescence, not the rushed kiss of corridors, but a fierce, anchoring thing like a vow that only the body knows how to make. It hurt her mouth and healed something older.

When he drew back, his breath shook. He took her face between his hands and spoke into her hair, her temple, her mouth, vows scattered like seeds that would find their holes. "Then I'll follow you," he said, voice gone rough, "until the end. Into the alleys and the gates and the dark. If the world says you're a ghost, I'll haunt the world with you."

She smiled, small and unstoppable. "That would suit me."

They sat with their backs to the apple tree, her head on his shoulder, his arm around her waist, both of them looking at the ground they had made holy with their labour. The tins lay in the earth like lanterns snuffed for safety, still warm at the core. The roots held them in their skeleton. The air yearned the memory of apples.

Helena's kitchen door creaked, then closed again. Tea would be steeping, the good leaves she saved for births and deaths. The gate's latch lay quiet under the moon. The apple tree lifted its branch against the sky. Around them the city kept its terrible time. Under them, the names waited.

When they rose at last, Samuel slid the crutches under Irena's arms and steadied her while she set her feet. She touched the dirt once more with her fingertips, then wiped them on her skirt and left the smudge there on purpose. They moved toward the house in step. At the door, Irena looked back and breathed a word for the tree to keep. "Watch."

The apple tree didn't answer. It didn't need to. It had its orders. And so did they.

21

November 1943

Frost filmed the inside of the courtyard windows, turning Warsaw into a blurred postcard beyond the glass. Ritter's office door stood open to the corridor's chill. He preferred the cold rage that had an edge to it.

"Show me," he said, and held out his hand.

The captain of guards placed the ledger in his palm. Ritter read the top line: *Transfer – interrogation, Szucha.* A neat signature. Beneath it, in another hand, another ledger's certainty transcribed: *Execution carried out.* Two truths in one day. One had lied.

"Where is the body," Ritter asked, the way an accountant asks where a decimal went, "if the sentence was carried out?"

Silence. The captain's eyes slid to a spot two inches left of the window latch.

Ritter closed the book, not with a slam – slamming belonged to men who were losing control – but with a precise finality. It was the sound of his voice that carried. Typists two rooms away stopped their keys for a heartbeat and then resumed, softer.

"She fell," the captain tried, voice low. "Possibly before the door. There was confusion – another prisoner – then she was executed..."

"The lack of a body in the pit tells me otherwise, unless somebody has lost the ability to count,'" Ritter said.

He lifted the corner of a folder and revealed the red circle he had drawn a month ago around a name that should already have been buried deep or burned and not his preoccupation. *Irena Sendler.* Her name was missing from the list of bodies to be disposed of. Either a small oversight or plot to outsmart him. The circle did not fade with handling. Obsession, well-tended, never does.

"Posters," he said. "Before dawn. Everywhere. Find her."

The captain blinked. "But she is –"

"Dead, yes." Ritter let a smile touch his mouth without reaching his eyes. "And yet her body is nowhere to be found. I am no longer interested in what paper believes. I want that body found, alive, and brought to me."

He snapped his glove's button and began to dictate; two officers crowded the doorway with pads and pencils, summoned by the friction in his voice.

"Headline: *Terrorist in Disguise.* Use her municipal cover of being a *welfare officer*. A photograph of her arrogant face underneath. A thousand zloty or five hundred Reichsmark for information leading to her capture. Twice that for a name that stands up under questioning. Polish and German, side by side, clean fonts. Include penalties: harbouring earns death. Include kindness: informers earn clemency for past irregularities." He paused, savoring the mechanism the way a clockmaker admires gear teeth. "Place them at tram stops, bread queues, parish gates, the university noticeboards, the clinic on Elektoralna, the courthouses, the dairies. I want Warsaw to carry her face in its pocket whether it loves her or hates her."

A young junior lieutenant cleared his throat. "Herr Oberst, the photograph –"

"Use the permit clip," Ritter said. "Grainy is fine. Grainy makes every blonde in a scarf my quarry."

He turned to the captain. "And your men?"

"Questioned," the captain lied too quickly.

"Questioned," Ritter repeated, considering the weight of the word. He had built his career on calibrating it. Too little and rot spread; too much and the floor gave way and swallowed the righteous along with the guilty. He set the ledger on the desk edge, parallel to the blotter, and looked up. "The junior who stands at the corridor door, the one with the ledger in his hand. Bring him now."

Boots retreated, then sprinted. Ritter remained standing. Sitting made men think meetings were over. The junior guard arrived, ashen skinned and white about the lips. Cigarette smoke and fear clung to him. He stopped exactly where training told him to and not one step farther.

"Your ledger," Ritter said mildly. "Has an error."

A flicker moved under the guard's eyelid. Ritter watched it with the cool interest of a man examining a specimen.

"Ritter went on. "Here is what happens next. You will accompany an officer tonight through every corridor you touched. You will remember precisely what you did. You will point to the door that sticks, the latch that sings, the corner where men don't look. If your memory pleases me, you will continue to breathe. If it does not, you will learn the difference between mercy and accounting."

The guard bobbed a nod that was almost a collapse. Ritter dismissed him with a flick of gloved fingers.

When the door closed, the captain ventured, "Posters alone will not –"

"No," Ritter agreed. "Posters only wake the city. Bounties loosen tongues. But we will also squeeze where she once stood. Welfare. Parishes. Clinics. The courthouses that kiss both sides of the wall. The convent that pretends to be holy. I want a list of every woman with blonde hair. I want their bread rations counted and their husbands' overtime checked against our files. I want confessions bullied from priests who think Latin can save them from German."

He stepped to the wall map that he regarded as his own private city and fixed a pin at the ghetto gate, another at the courthouse door, a third at Elektoralna, a fourth at a random location that he did not know but suspected was as guilty as a thousand pins on one map. A red thread linked points into a web.

"They don't want me to know their names," he murmured, to the map, to the room, to himself. "Of the children they have taken."

The captain shifted. "Sir?"

"And children are the key to catching her." Ritter's eyes were bright in the lamplight; pupils narrowed to dark commas. "She is proud of what she has done and will therefore do it again. She can't stop. It is the flaw in believers: they are reliable. You will see."

With the merest nod, the captain was dismissed and Ritter took a seat at his desk, steepled his fingers, knowing it was only a matter of time. He didn't have to wait long.

He had been in his office only minutes, his breakfast settling nicely when a runner arrived breathless with a telegram from the district office: rumours in Wola of a "ghost woman" seen under a shawl; a farmer asking for liniment without saying for whom; a boy at a tannery swearing he tipped his cap to a dead lady. Ritter read, folded the sheet once, and tapped it against his knuckles until the paper softened.

"Print an additional notice," he said. "Describe her as *dangerous, wounded, may seek aid from women and priests.* Offer the same money for rumour that proves true. And send plainclothes to the markets with onion money and the patience of a hungry cat."

He turned back to the red-circled name. In his head, he heard his father's voice levelled at a younger Ritter who had misread a line of Virgil – *precision, Karl, makes victory inevitable.* He had made a life of that sentence. Precision would bring him this woman.

"I will find her," he said, not loudly and not for effect. It was the tone in which he told a clerk to fetch a file. "Not because of posters. Not because of coin. Because she has made me a promise by surviving. She intends to continue. I intend to end the intention."

He slid the file into his valise, as if proximity to the name mattered. It did. Obsession prefers talismans: a circled word, a clipped photograph, a map threaded tight. Outside, a truck downshifted at the corner; the building's old bones took hold of the vibration as if they recognised it.

The captain saluted. "At once."

"And captain," Ritter added, as the man turned, "if anyone in your chain has learned to love money more than he fears me, I want him before dawn. Understood."

The corridor received the officer and his orders and swallowed them. In the composing room below, the pressman rolled his sleeves and fed paper, the first poster taking ink: *TERRORYSTKA – NAGRODA.* Sheets lifted and dried on lines like laundry. The city would wake to her face. So would the men who would swear they did not know it and then whisper a name to a friend, and then to a stranger, and then to a man who would write it down.

Ritter stood alone in the cold office and let the rage settle into something more useful. He drew the drape half an inch, looked out at the rooflines and chimneys, and imagined the alleys as veins. Somewhere in those veins, the mouse moved quickly and carefully, convinced that righteousness made her invisible.

He smiled without warmth. "Not invisible," he said to the glass. "Just late."

He shut the drape, turned off the lamp, and left the door open to the corridor's chill. Let the building keep its breath sharp. The hunt worked better that way.

The cellar of another safehouse was a square of warm breath in a frozen city. Frost pinched the tiny windowpanes white; blackout paper fluttered at the seams. The lamp wore a shade pricked with holes, throwing a poor constellation over a table scarred by a hundred arguments.

They were already talking when Irena and Samuel descended the narrow stairs –voices low, urgent, braided with the scrape of chair legs. Wiktor had ink under his nails and a fresh stack of permit blanks at his elbow. Father Antoni's collar was open one button, the priesthood loosening only enough to make room for fury. Jadwiga paced, the stone trapped in her sole thumping a steady accusation against the loose board. Two couriers from the south district hunched over a city map that had been folded so many times the creases were white scars.

On the table lay the morning's truth: a fresh poster taken off a wall still wet at the corners. *TERRORYSTKA –NAGRODA*. The grainy clipped photograph – her face, nearly but not quite hers – stared up from the paper. A second line screamed reward in both languages; the small type promised clemency to snitches and death to saints.

Samuel tugged the poster aside with two fingers, as if it were filthy. "Ritter's rage has teeth," he said.

"Sharp teeth," Antoni agreed, "and a printing press as an ally."

Irena took the last three steps without help and stood at the edge of the circle, the cane set lightly. The room turned toward her, relief blooming and then hardening into calculation. She saw it, accepted it. Love and logistics had learned to share the table.

"No," Wiktor said, as if answering a question she hadn't asked. "Whatever you're here to demand – the answer is no."

Jadwiga stopped pacing. "You're officially dead," she said, not unkind. "Let's keep it that way."

Irena looked at the map. The ghetto wall sliced it like a dull knife; their routes threaded the paper in faint pencil, courthouse, clinic, tram, courtyard, church, yard. She could trace them blind. Her fingers ached to.

"Children are still waiting," she said.

"Not you," Antoni said. "Anyone else. Pick a dozen 'anyone's' and I'll bless all their names. But you must vanish. That is your job now. You will not withstand another capture."

Wiktor's hand found the bounty poster and flicked it with his thumbnail. "He'll buy the city's eyes if he has to. The bounties will double in a week. Men will see you at their breakfast tables just to taste the reward."

"Then I won't show them me," she said quietly. "I'll show them a laundress. A nun. A bored clerk pushing a box. I can be all of these. I have been all of these."

Samuel's voice was careful, the way you speak while you carry a hot pot that must not spill. "Do you ever learn?"

"Yes. I learned I can live through whatever they do to me and if there's a next time I suspect they will forgoe the pain and end me swiftly, just to be sure I am really gone and I am not afraid of it," she said.

Silence pulled the room tight for a beat. Then the couriers started at once.

"The courtyard route is watched now –"

"– the tannery street has been closed off

"– Klaus at the bread shop is jumpy; he's either bought or scared–"

"–the convent door is safe only if you arrive as laundry and still it is under suspicion."

Jadwiga cut through. "Doesn't matter what is safe or compromised. You're not going back onto the streets."

Irena reached for the map, found the tiny X's she herself had pencilled months ago –the "quiet corners," the friendly doors, the tolerant gatekeepers. Her fingers left a smudge where sweat met graphite. "If I disappear, holes open in the pattern," she said. "The papers at City Hall? The sanitation permits with the violet halo? The men who only trust 'the blonde' because she has always been the one to look them in the eye and say the lie like truth?" She tapped three points, gentle and exact. "If I go to ground, we lose time teaching my ghosts to walk those rooms. Time is children."

Antoni pushed his palms against the table, as if to keep the wood from moving. "You are not a symbol in a story. You are a person I have to bury if this goes wrong again."

"No I'm not a symbol," she said. "I'm a tool. Put me where I fit."

Wiktor swore under his breath.

"Listen to me, please," she said. She set the cane back,

stepped close, and laid a list beside the poster – fresh pencil, cramped neat: three infants needing placements, two sisters with measles, a boy with a limp who could be a cobbler's apprentice by next Tuesday if the right paper appeared. "This is today. Tomorrow will be more."

"You can dictate from an attic," Jadwiga said. "We fetch. We carry."

"And when a guard says *where is the sanitation lady, the one I trust?*" Irena asked, voice cool. "When the door opens because my face has always opened it? It won't open for your anger, Jadwiga. Or your charisma, Father. It will open for habit. Habit makes fools of tyrants."

Antoni's jaw worked. "Ritter's habit now is you."

"Then let him chase the habit while we work," she said.

Samuel moved to her side, not to argue and not to endorse – simply to stand where she was standing. His presence steadied the floorboards.

The south-district courier, a boy too young for the depth of his eyes, cleared his throat. "She's right about habit," he said. "The baker at Żelazna gives scraps to 'the blonde's' basket that he wouldn't to mine. He's superstitious. He thinks her touch blesses the food against searches."

Wiktor's head snapped toward him. "Do not encourage–"

"Enough," Antoni said, and the word held. He turned back to Irena. "You want to go back through the courthouse. Through City Hall. Through a gate that is now a mouth that knows your taste."

"Yes."

"You will be caught."

"Maybe," she said. "If I am, you already proved you know how to cheat a rope."

No one laughed. Even the lamp seemed to pull its light in, waiting.

Irena took a breath, lifted her cane, and laid it on the table between the poster and the map. The thunk was small and final. "I may limp," she said, voice steady as a ledger line, "but I am not done walking."

The room went still. Jadwiga's eyes flooded and didn't spill. Wiktor looked away first. Antoni's shoulders lowered a fraction, a priests surrender, not to hubris, but to vocation.

Samuel closed his hand over the cane where it lay and squeezed once, as if sharing oath through wood. "Then we plan for a cripple who is more stubborn than any mule that ever lived," he said.

Wiktor groaned. "God help us, we're doing this."

Antoni drew the poster toward him and tore it cleanly in half, then into quarters, then into pieces the size of confessions. "God can keep watch at the door," he said. "We will do the rest."

Maps slid closer. Routes redrew themselves in pencil and breath. They cut her face from the poster and burned it over the lamp, ash blooming like a mean flower. Outside, the city shifted in its sleep. Inside, a broken woman and the people who loved her fitted her back into the machine she had built – not because they believed she could not break again, but because the lives of the names beneath the tree outweighed the body that guarded them.

22

October 1944

Snow came down once more, soft and guilty, and turned the gutted streets into a filthy ribbon. The winter of 1944 had a hard, endless surface that scraped at the bones of anyone who dared press a foot into it. The wall that had once divided the ghetto from the rest of Warsaw was mostly rubble now, a jagged lip speckled with ice; patrols traced its ghost line anyway, boots ticking a dead perimeter. Within it, the city had been emptied, burned, bulldozed, then repopulated by what refused to die: families welded to cellars, children with the cunning of cats, old men who could make soup from water and memory. Hunger bleached the faces to one shade. Irena moved through it like smoke.

Her hair, once braided and tucked, was chopped close to her scalp with kitchen scissors, the ends bristled under a worker's cap. A coarse jacket hung from her shoulders, too big, sleeves rolled, collar turned up against the wind. Trousers belted with rope. The limp was there but subtle, folded into a workman's shuffle. Her breath fogged and vanished. She kept her chin tucked and her mouth full of lies.

The paper said she was dead. It was the only document she carried now.

She passed a doorway where frost had stitched lace over the hinge and found, under it, a child seated on a brick, gnawing bark. The girl's eyes were too large, irises floating in winter; her shoes were two different sizes and neither hers. A woman crouched beside her, forehead to the lintel, as if the door might open to someplace with heat if she willed hard enough.

Irena did not stop. Stopping was a point on a map; points drew eyes. She drifted, a bored apprentice with nothing urgent in his hands, until the corner turned and the shadow of an arch ate her. There, under her coat, she worked. The loaf had been baked too quickly, the crust a little scorched – perfect. Inside, the crumb concealed medicine nested in waxed paper, well, what counted for medicine now: sulfa powder in a paper twist, a thumbnail of aspirin, two tablets of yeast, a folded scrap with instructions she had written last night by the attic lamp. She pressed the loaf back together with the wet of her breath, rolled it in a rag that had once been blue, and slid it into the crook of her elbow.

German voices came and went in the air like a disease that had learned to sing. She let the refrain set her tempo and stepped back out into the street. They were everywhere. The guard on the corner stamped his feet; his breath made a pattern in the air; the black line of his rifle cut the falling snow. Two more walked abreast along the tram track, heads cocked, boredom scabbed over cruelty. Behind them, a wagon made tracks the colour of coffee grounds and iron.

Irena's face remembered the expression she had spent a year teaching it: empty, a little tired, a little cold, deeply uninteresting. She was a man named Norbert today, a municipal runner with nothing of value to carry and nowhere better to be.

At the doorway, she stumbled, a clipped toe on the brick the girl sat upon, and used the motion to kneel. The loaf slid from the crook of her elbow as if she were clumsy. The girl's hand flicked and missed; Irena's palm nudged the bread against her thigh, pinning it to bone, inviting the claim. The woman made a sound, a mother sound that had learned not to cry, and covered the transfer with her body.

"Mind your feet," Irena muttered, voice lowered a note into a man's register. She didn't look at the child. She looked at the brick and at the rusted hinge and at the way her own glove had lost its fingertips. The rag wrapped around the loaf was already another colour under the girl's hands – grey, like snow.

A patrol's shadow lengthened over them. Irena rose into it.

"You." The soldier's gloved hand hit her shoulder, a shove with the casual violence of a man who has never been refused the space in front of him. She staggered a step, let her weight go where he sent it, allowed her mouth to pull into a small, irritated line, the kind men make when affronted by idiocy rather than power. Too bold and she would be brave. Too meek and she would be prey.

"I'm on the book," she said in rough German, and patted the pocket where a permit lived when she used one. There was no permit now. There was only the lazy confidence of habit. "Waste unit."

The soldier's eyes flicked to her cap, to the rope belt, to the way her hip rode the trouser seam. His gaze slid off. He had seen a thousand of her. She was all of them.

"Move," he said, and pushed again, automatically harder, because the body in front of him had resisted the first instruction by existing.

She moved. The shove telegraphed through her legs and

woke the pain in her bones. She let the grimace be private, turned the corner on it, and put a wall between herself and the doorway she had left behind. Behind her, bread met hands; hands met mouth; sulfa would meet blood. She pictured none of it. She kept walking.

The city ground its teeth. Wind worried loose paper along the street, folding and unfolding it like a creature trying to breathe. In an alley, a pair of boots stuck out from under a half-collapsed stair – greyed laces, a trouser cuff frayed to threads, toes rimmed in ice where breath had frozen and fallen. Once there would have been a cart for bodies. Once there had been men whose entire job was to stack the dead respectfully. Now there was only weather and a small calculus: *someone will move him when they can; I cannot; walk on.*

Irena walked.

On Nalewki, a boy's fingers worked at the bark of a plane tree like a beaver; the child leaned into the trunk with his cheek, tasting whatever the tree had once known. Across the street, an old woman knelt beside a puddle that had frozen and thawed and frozen again; she scraped at the edge with a spoon to free the water that wasn't yet ice and let it melt on her tongue. A man limped past with a guitar that had no strings, carrying it like hope.

The snow thickened, then thinned to a fine, dirty sift. Upstairs, in a window with neither glass nor blanket, lungs coughed a long time and then didn't. Irena kept to the line of shadow cast by a wall and adjusted the lay of her belt with a workman's gesture and cut left to the rubble of a courtyard where a warren of families had sunk themselves into the ground like moles.

Hands reached out of dark holes. She let three tablets drop from a matchbox into a palm; took, in return, a name she would carry back to the ledger and bury under the apple tree when the ground thawed. She could not promise spring. She could only promise to keep the name until there was a place for it to live.

Feet approached – fast, too fast for the cold. She stepped out of the mouth of the courtyard and into the open just as a pair of soldiers turned into it, rifles at their shoulders, eyes bored and alert in the same glance. One scratched his nose with the back of his glove. The other yawned like a boy in a dull class. Snow clung to her lashes. She did not blink.

"Papieren," the first one barked, reflex.

She patted her pocket again; a piece of theatre played so many times it had the truth of habit. She let the glove ride low on her wrist so the blood-raw crescents of her nails sat under the soldier's line of sight like ordinary raggedness. He frowned, found nothing to be interested in, and dismissed her with his eyes.

She went. Behind her, a child's voice brightened once, brief as a matchhead, and then fell into the thick winter air. By the time she reached the break in the rubble that served as an exit, her feet were blocks and her breath a pinched thread. She had not been recognised.

Outside the ghost wall, Warsaw stretched itself in a different posture: Germans on corners that used to have bakeries; Poles with heads down; cold banks of snow piled against sandbags. She kept the limp that wasn't a limp and took small streets that looked like decisions and were routes.

In her pocket, folded to a sliver, lay a note inked in the hand they used for Żegota business. She'd picked it up from a crack under the butcher's door by the church but did not read it yet. Reading was for rooms that had doors you could lock and hands that would hold you if the news stripped your breath.

She passed a poster. Her own dead face, grainy. She didn't look. The snow stuck to the paper and made a cowl. She kept walking. Walking. Always walking.

The apartment didn't look like hers anymore. It looked like a set a stagehand had struck and half rebuilt: the table pushed off its mark; the stove used as cover for documents; the bed a place no one slept as lice lived there. The windows had their blackout paper; the radio sat under a shawl; a single lamp threw a puddle of light onto the table and left the corners to their own devices. The room smelled of poverty, and of fear less faintly, and of fabric that refused to dry at the edges.

Samuel was already at the table when she came in, chair dragged so he could see the door and the window at the same turn of his head. He had a scarf still looped at his throat, hair damp from melted snow, hands wrapped around a cup he had forgotten to drink from. When he saw her, his face did a whole year's worth of expressions in a heartbeat – relief first, then anger for loving her, then joy at the ridiculous luck of the return, then worry like a lid put carefully on a boiling pot.

"You look like a bad boy," he said, voice gone low with the work of calling his heart back to his chest. "A small, mean one."

She took off the cap and shook the snow on the mat, then put the cap back on because the room was colder than a word could fix. "I like that look," she said.

He tried to smile and failed. "You met trouble on the way."

"Only the usual," she said, crossing to the stove and setting her hands toward its sullen heat. Feeling came back into her fingers with knives. "I wasn't recognised, anyway."

He tapped the folded sliver on the table. "You should read this while you're making plans to die of stubbornness." He placed the note where the lamp could warm it, as if the words needed help. "From the south cell. Coded by someone who loves bad poetry."

She unfolded it. The thin lines resolved: banal talk about

bread and flour and a cousin's wedding, then – there – letters that didn't quite belong in the words they were asked to occupy. They made a second poem under the first, and this one had fewer jokes. *River rises east. Iron singing nights. Red coats ask the road to Warsaw. Not yet. But soon.*

Her heart did that small, traitorous lift. Hope wasn't a flame; it was a brightening of the air. Dangerous if you let it change your step. Necessary if you wanted the next step to exist.

"Russians?" she said.

"Maybe." He leaned in, forearms on the table, as if proximity could make news work faster. "Guns heard in the east. Locomotives stalled by orders from men who have started to imagine failure and hoard what they can."

She sat. The cap made her shadow a different shape on the wall. "Soon is a fool's word," she said.

"It is," he agreed. "But it's the first soon I've heard since summer."

He reached across the table and laid his finger on the line that mattered most. *Not yet. But soon.* He had ink on his knuckle, a smear where a nib had bled into skin. "We could go," he said, voice steady.

She looked at him. He held the look. "Tonight, if you say so. I know the route. Wiktor has papers. Jadwiga can get us past the second checkpoint with a crate that smells like fish and a story she's been saving for a night like this. The farmer who brought you will take cash and keep a secret. We leave at dark, we sleep in a hayloft, we wake in a village that has forgotten how to pronounce your name. We wait a week. Or a month. Or until this ends."

"When the children are safe," she said, "then I will rest."

He shut his eyes. It wasn't weariness that passed over his face – he didn't have the luxury. It was the wrench of loving a woman whose spine had more vows than sense and knowing that sense wasn't what had carried any of them this far.

"The children," he said. "Yes. And the ones whose names you haven't written yet. You are a river now, Irena. You will always say 'there is another.'"

"The river keeps cities alive," she said. "Or it drowns them. We have no choice in the matter."

"I want to be your bank," he said, and his voice was wrong, broke upward; he swallowed it back. "I want to put my hands on both sides of you and hold until the flood lessens enough that you can lie down without listening for boots or the fear of drowning."

She reached across and took his wrists. The bones felt sharper under her fingers; he'd lost weight, carved himself down to a set of angles. "You are," she said. "If you weren't, I would have already gone under."

He shook his head, a quick, frustrated motion. "Then let me be selfish. Let me say I cannot love you and send you back into the mouth of that place that has already learned the taste of you once. Let me say I want your breath next to mine in the morning more than I want to be remembered well by whatever children live to ask about us."

"You may say it," she said softly. "Then we will fail to obey it."

"Don't," he said, the word tearing out of him. "Don't make me the one who watches you go and pretends to be brave about it."

"You are brave," she said. "That is why you can say this to me and still wait for me in this room."

He laughed, a thin, angry sound that didn't want to be laughter. "We could be two cowards together. It sounds like heaven."

She couldn't help it; the smile got past her guard and did its small work. "It does," she said. "And it would kill me in a week."

He tipped his head back and looked at the ceiling. The lamplight poured up his throat to where his pulse lived. He lowered his head and leaned forward until their foreheads touched, until the breath she had saved for the ghetto shared its last warmth with him.

"I am offering you a life," he said.

"I am offering you a purpose," she said.

"I want a life with you," he said.

"You have one," she said. "It simply isn't the one people usually mean."

He made a sound, almost a curse, almost a prayer. Then the argument which had been a line on the table between them tilted and slid and became something else entirely. He stood so fast the chair legs squealed; she was already up without knowing how she'd moved. He reached for her and she reached for him and they collided in the middle: cap knocked sideways; scarf pulled loose; hands at shoulders and hair and jaw, mouths meeting hard. The kiss wasn't gentle; it apologised later, with the second and the third. He tasted of cold and of the tea he had not drunk; she tasted of bread she had not eaten and of winter.

She laughed into his mouth and cried in the same breath when his hands found the bandaged places and went careful without needing to be told. They kissed like animals and like saints who had learned restraint and abandoned it for a minute.

When they stopped, the room returned slowly, as if embarrassed to be itself after watching that.

"I will not run," she said, voice roughened into honesty, "until I can run without stepping over a child I left behind."

He nodded. It was the kind of nod that is exactly half consent and half despair. He reached up and set the worker's cap back on her head, a ridiculous, tender gesture that broke and mended something inside both of them in the same heartbeat.

"Then I will walk where you walk," he said.

"Occasionally," she agreed, and took his hand and kissed the ink on his knuckle. "Tomorrow we go back. I need a new box with a false bottom."

"Wiktor has improved the hinges," he said, because promises take many shapes, and one of them is a hinge that doesn't squeak at the wrong moment.

He gathered her into his arms and sat with her on the floor in the single patch of warm the lamp allowed. Outside, the city scrabbled in its sleep. Between the world and the window, the blackout paper trembled once in the wind and held.

"Soon," he said into her hair, not an order, not a prophecy, just a loaned word they could spend to buy themselves an hour of steadiness.

"Not yet," she said, and it didn't hurt this time to say it. It felt like the truth paying its own way.

They stayed where they were until the lamp coughed and reminded them oil had become another ration. He stood and banked the room in dark; she stood and found his hand exactly where it had been the last time she reached. The apartment settled, rearranged itself around their breathing. On the table, the coded letter lay open to air, and the line that mattered most kept its own small light. Not yet. But soon.

23

November 1944

They came by the alley that smelled of coal and human waste. Snow sifted down like a thing they used to sprinkle of pastries. Samuel flattened his palm to the cellar door, felt the chill through the wood, then eased it a thumb's width. Cold and dark breathed back.

"Wait," he murmured.

Jadwiga was already halfway down the steps, knife in her boot hilt-warm against her ankle. Irena caught her sleeve. Pain ran its bright wire from her shins up through her ribs, but she took the next tread anyway, one hand on the rail, the other carrying breath steady – four in, four out – until the floor took her weight. The lamp by the jamb answered the match with a weak circle. The room stepped forward out of the dark.

The safehouse had been opened like a mouth. Chairs on their backs. Crates kicked in. The stove door yawning. A scatter of paper across the flagstones. Wiktor's stamp kit upended and pulverised, violet ink bled to a bruise on the table, the municipal seal face-down in the puddle, crushed by a boot or the hilt of a rifle, like a drowned eye. A coil of wire unrolled. A cupboard with its false back pried and left ajar. In the corner, the hand press – a brave little thing lay on its side, smashed like a felled animal.

No grey clad bodies. No angry voices. Just the aftermath of destruction.

Jadwiga's face went narrow. "They took them away. I saw."

Samuel was already moving, slowly, precise. He touched a chair leg and turned it; he crouched at the stove and found ash still faintly warm; he held his hand above the ink spill and felt it tack his skin. "What a waste," he said.

Irena stepped carefully, reading. Boot marks in the ink, narrow heels, two pairs, one a thicker tread. The chalk in the joist where they marked rendezvous times had been wiped, not the way a hurried hand wipes, but with a damp rag until the wood grain let go. A small smear of blood dried to a penny-brown crescent on the edge of the table. Rope fibres clung to the chair back, too few to tell a story and enough to write one anyway.

She put her fingertips to the rim of the stamp pad. Violet darkened the beds of her ruined nails. She let the sting come and go. "They knew what to leave to frighten us."

Jadwiga kicked at the crushed crate, then knelt and sifted the pieces as if a miracle might be hiding under splinters. "Someone told them which cupboard. Which boards. Which hour we change the hand that holds the key."

"The neighbour could –" Samuel started.

"No," Jadwiga snapped, not at him. "They don't know this door exists. We built it out of nothing."

Irena crouched by the press. The plate still held a half-inked permit for a sanitation inspection; the letters were crisp where the roller had kissed and ghosted where a hand had hesitated. She peeled the paper free and read the name she had invented, Norbert Krawczyk, the man she had been all morning. He stared up at her from the black type as if asking which of them was real.

"They didn't torch it," Samuel said. "They didn't want smoke."

"They didn't need to," Jadwiga answered. She had found a scrap that had fallen between floorboards: the corner of a map with a pencil X and the tail of a street name. She crushed it too quickly, then opened her fist and smoothed it, angry at herself for wanting to keep evidence. "They'll wait at the doors and the corners that X means until someone's hunger learns to talk."

She used the word *someone* the way you use a match, dangerously and on purpose.

Samuel looked at her. "We don't know this," he said quietly.

"We do." Her jaw jumped. "Look at the seam on the cupboard back. Who pries here on the first try? Who goes straight for the ledger shelf? Who leaves the loaded stamp but takes the blank paper? Not a patrol. Not a neighbour who saw too much by accident. This was a hand that knew where we keep our secrets."

Irena picked up the stamp by its wood handle. The seal face shone violet-black. She set it gently into the clean corner of the blotter so it wouldn't stain more than it already had. "Ritter has someone inside the inside," she said, and the words were a measured truth, not a panic. "He learned how we breathe. We have to stop breathing the same way."

They went about the room because staying still would let fear root itself. Jadwiga checked the cache behind the stove, the one she and Irena had made after the arrest, shallow and mean, enough for a knife and two folded notes and a coin stamped in 1927 for luck; the knife was gone; the notes were gone; the coin lay where they had dropped it because superstition doesn't bribe. "They touched everything," she said.

Samuel pulled the cupboard fully open. The hollow they'd built behind it was empty. He reached up to the lintel on habit and came away with nothing but dust. "Passwords?" he asked.

"Taken," Jadwiga said. "If they were worth a damn."

Irena squinted into the crawlspace under the steps. Children had hidden there once, breathing like birds. Now it held a crate of blank ration cards half-stamped into belonging—spoiled by muddy boots tromped across them in the struggle or the search. She lifted a corner. The print held a partial seal and a smear of heel. She let the fabric go.

"Wiktor?" Samuel asked, not because he wanted to put doubt on a friend, but because inventory steadies people.

"Alive or taken," Jadwiga said. "Either way, not here."

"They could have gone to ground," Samuel offered. "A signal –" He stopped, because the chalk had been scrubbed, and because the signal they might have used lay in someone else's pocket now.

Irena knelt at the table and gathered what paper had not been turned to confetti. A timetable she herself had written in a too-tidy hand, now smeared. A list of parishes that had said yes and no, now shredded at the margins. A child's name – Anita, half-torn across the middle, as if violence had reached for her and missed.

She laid the torn halves together and let her palm warm them. "No more names in any room," she said. "Ever."

Jadwiga's mouth went white. "This was ours," she said. the room, the shelves, the stupid press we loved like a dog. "We kept people alive from here."

"We keep them alive from somewhere else," Irena said. "If we argue about this room, he has won."

Samuel crouched, caught Irena's eye, then Jadwiga's. "Listen. We accept the loss. We assume the worst. We do not speak what we think out loud where walls can hear it." He touched two fingers to his lips and then to the table where the ink had pooled. "We start again."

Jadwiga lifted her chin, anger draining into something colder. "You think it's the south boys."

"I think nothing," Samuel said. "We don't point. We reduce contact. We change the routes."

"And we meet under the tree," Jadwiga added, fierce through the crack in her voice. "No paper. No ceiling. No cupboards with backs."

Irena put her hand flat in the ink and pressed it once, hard, onto the underside of the table where only a crawling thing or a desperate one would find it. A dark palm print bloomed. "For the next poor fool who thinks a room can save him," she said. "Let him touch it and get up and go."

Samuel wiped her hand with his scarf. "We have to move," he said, listening. "The street has eyes."

They left as carefully as they came, lamp cold, door pulled, alley swallowing their prints. Snow had gathered in the stair treads; their steps unstitched it back into blankness. The safehouse didn't wave goodbye and they didn't look back to see.

On the street, posters hunched under snow. *TERRORYSTKA –NAGRODA.* Her grainy image stared through the flakes. Jadwiga spat once at the curb, a mean, small offering to a city that had bitten them again and set her shoulder into the wind.

"Ritter has another set of eyes," Irena said, low, as they walked toward the seam in the night that meant home or something like it. "Closer this time."

"Then we blindfold those eyes," Samuel said.

They didn't talk again until the stair conceded to their weight, and even then the conversation was hands: a door locked, a kettle set, a match shielded; the new liturgy of a people in retreat who intend to be advancing by morning.

~

Ritter's office was warm like a winter carriage, its heat paid for, contained, and not to be questioned. The frost on the courtyard windows had been scraped into clean half-moons; outside, the sky was the colour of foundry smoke. He sat with his back to the radiator and his face to a man in a chair.

The courier had been handsome before someone decided to teach him obedience. Even now, his cheekbones painted a picture of defiance under the bruises. The rope on his wrists cut a slice into the meat of his hands; his mouth had learned to hold spit and blood until neither mattered. His name could have been anything. To Ritter he was the useful intersection of fear and information.

"Lift your head," Ritter said, conversational. The gloves made small noises when he flexed his fingers. "You will want to see me when you answer. It helps a man tell the truth if he's forced to look at what he's lying to."

The courier lifted. The motion cost him. He showed his teeth without meaning to.

"You run messages for the council," Ritter continued, as if reading a grocery list. "You have hands that know paper and feet that know streets. You have a priest who tells you your sins don't matter if you confess in the same week. And you have a woman."

A flicker. Human faces always confess before their owners do.

Ritter smiled with his mouth. "Yes. The woman. The one who should have learned her lesson in October." He slid a page across the desk, the poster, her grainy face like a thumb smudge. "They call her the blonde when they are afraid to say her name. Irena Sendler when they want to pretend courage. And yet even though she is dead she still walks. Imagine my surprise."

The courier stared at a point over Ritter's shoulder.

"Do you know," Ritter mused, "why hanging is preferable to shooting?"

The guard by the door shifted; he had the look of a man who would prefer not to know the answer to this again. Ritter continued anyway. "Shooting is noisy. Democratic. Men miss. Men feel brave with guns in their hands. Hanging is precise. The rope fits the neck; the neck breaks or it does not. It's honest as gravity." He leaned forward, not menacing, interested. "If you tell me enough to make my precision neat, I can promise you this: not today. Maybe not this week. The rope can wait for a better audience."

The courier swallowed, Adam's apple sliding bruised under the skin. His voice came gravel-dry. "There is no woman."

Ritter ignored the lie like a stain and brushed a speck of dust from the poster. "A man with a limp was seen in the quarter today," he said. "Short hair. Cap. Rope belt. Moved like he was in pain." He lifted his eyes. "We both know what body that costume wore."

Silence. The kind that announces itself. Then, too quick to stop, a glance, a flinch, when Ritter said *limp*. He had his thread.

"Where does she hide when she is not playing at being dead?" Ritter asked softly. "In whose rooms does she fold herself into corners? Who keeps water near her hand, and a shawl at her neck, and foolish vows in his head?"

The courier's mouth hardened. "I don't know," he said, and the sentence had the mournful truthfulness of the partially honest. He didn't know *which* room. He knew the man who kept it warm.

"Then tell me the near-things." Ritter's voice went patient, coaxing, as if with a child whose stubbornness had started to bore him. "A church whose bell you hear too often in your messages. A street name half written and crossed out. Familiar hands. A girl who is never hungry when she should be. A dog who barks at the wrong times."

The courier's eyes slid sideways, the smallest betrayal. Ritter caught the movement and filed it next to a courtyard he had not yet found on his map. He made a small sound of pleasure in his throat; the guard flinched.

"You see?" Ritter said. "We are both tired men. Why make the winter longer than it needs to be?" He leaned back and let weariness colour his words, as if he hated this work and needed only cooperation to be allowed to hate it somewhere else. "What do you carry in the bread?"

The courier's lips cracked into a smile that was not a smile. "Bread."

"Medicine," Ritter answered himself, the lesson a foregone conclusion. "Powder and hope and lies baked into crumbs." He sat up, the mildness gone. "Where?"

The courier lifted his chin. If death had posture, it was this: dignified defiance in a dirty chair. "In God's pocket," he said.

Ritter's face didn't change. Men who lose their temper lose their questions. He tapped the poster with one gloved finger, then folded it once and slid it into his breast pocket, close to his heart like a photograph of a sweetheart. "This is the arithmetic," he said. "You do not leave this room until I can draw a line on my map from her breath to my hand. When I have that, you will have hours. Not freedom. But hours. You can use them any way you like."

The courier's mouth moved around the word *hours* and then let it go. "Saints are made in minutes," he said. "Not hours."

"Saints were corpses once," Ritter said, tired again. "I prefer living witnesses."

He stood, smoothed his jacket, and moved to the wall map and beheld the private city he had driven pins into for months. Red thread linked the ghetto gate to the courthouse to Elektoralna to a point he had not yet earned the right to mark. He added a new pin, a tannery street, not because he believed in the street, but because belief made men stupid and he preferred to make it work for him rather than against him.

Behind him, the guard bent, murmured in his ear: a rumour from Wola of a farmer seen late with an empty cart; a priest at a convent with bloodied hands. Ritter listened and let the information sort itself into piles. Useful. Later. Irrelevant. He picked up a pencil and wrote three names in a narrow column: *Bruno. Klaus. Leon.* He underlined none. He circled nothing. He kept his handwriting tidy.

The courier coughed, blood flecking his lip. Ritter offered a handkerchief. The man didn't take it. Ritter laid it on the desk where it could be accepted later, privately, and look like a victory.

"You will bring me the blonde," he said finally, using the name as a leash. He didn't raise his voice; he didn't have to. "If your mouth won't, your eyes will. If your eyes won't, your friends will. If your friends won't, your hunger will. If hunger fails, my precision will not."

He reached into his pocket, touched the folded poster, and let his obsession find its shape out loud at last. "I will see her hang with my own eyes."

The courier closed his. A muscle in his cheek jumped once and was still. Ritter signalled. The guard lifted the chair and the man together and took him to the room where precision kept its tools. The door shut soft.

Ritter stayed with his map and his red thread and the cold

pinprick of winter at the base of his skull. He drew a line in air he could not yet mark on paper: from a woman with a limp who refused to do the merciful thing and die when asked, to a place he did not know, to a street he would soon learn by heart, to a rope that waited for a name to hang from it.

Outside, the city made the sound of people trying to sleep while waiting to die or be saved. Inside, the predator paced.

24

November 1944

Snow fell on Warsaw, soft, incessant, and already filthy before it touched the ground. Steam bled from couplers and hissed under carriage wheels; a switchman's whistle cut the air, iron clanged in short, impatient fits. The winter of 1944 had pared down to sound and breath and the sting of metal against skin. Lantern light carved circles in the gloom and turned every exhale into a small white sign that you were still alive.

They slipped in along the coal stacks where the wind bit less cruelly. Irena moved in a man's coat, cap pulled low, trousers tied with rope. Helena had wrapped ten children into hay, two per cart, the smallest diapered in rags and tucked deep with air holes cut along the slats and warmed bricks hidden at their feet. Samuel wore a foreman's armband and in his pocket, forged orders bore stamps drunk on violet ink.

"Here," Helena breathed, kneeling by the first cart to check the little mouths. The lantern threw her fingers into long bones over straw. "Two taps if you need air. Not three. Two." She looked at Irena and smiled a tight, bright thing that had room for nothing but belief. "We meet at the barn. If it goes wrong –" She didn't finish. There wasn't a verb for that they were willing to use.

Irena squeezed her wrist. "It won't." Her breath made a small cloud that vanished, which felt like an omen and she refused to let it be one.

They pushed. Wheels squealed softly, straw whispered, wood protested. They timed their movement to the steam bursts and the shunt clangs, letting the yard's own noise wrap theirs like a blanket. Between tracks the snow was thin and mean; underfoot, cinders ground to black grit.

The guard at the east spur was the tired kind, the worst: bored enough to prod, cold enough to be cruel just to feel some kind of heat. He stamped his boots, breath pluming, rifle slung easy. His lantern landed Samuel's chest and climbed to their faces.

"What's this?" he said in German, as if nothing in the world had ever surprised him and this wasn't the night it would start.

"Umlagerung von Stroh," Samuel snapped back, businesslike contempt in the vowels. "Transfer of straw. Cold damages the bearings. Order came at dusk. Your office was told and, as usual, failed to read the print." He fanned the top sheet, letting the stamp show and the rest blur. "Sign here then we can out of your way. The depot manager complains when his horses freeze."

The guard took the paper, his eyes slid over the letters without drinking them. Violet halo. Double signature. A seal that looked like it believed itself. He grunted, unimpressed by stamps on principle.

Irena kept her head angled as if nursing a yardman's stiff neck. Beside her, the second cart trembled like the small life inside it. She felt the tremor through the wood the way a musician feels a wrong note. A patrol turned the corner of the shed. Two more guards: one yawning behind his scarf, one with the taut meanness of a man looking for someone to hurt. Their lantern washed over the carts. Straw gleamed. A tiny sneeze, barely a feather—escaped the second cart.

Irena didn't think. She stumbled hard, flinging herself forward into the lantern light, shoulder taking the full smack of the guard's hip, a grunt ripped from her throat. The lantern skated; its flame guttered and flared, everyone's attention pulled where it shouldn't be.

"Idioten!" she barked, in a yardman's rasp. "You spill that and the whole siding goes up." She bent into the shove, caught the lantern wrist, righted it with rough competence, glared like a man used to being obeyed. The mean guard stepped into her space, eyes narrowing.

"Papiere," he said.

Samuel was already between them, his own lantern up, orders out, voice turned to the precise boredom of hierarchy. "Herr Unteroffizier. The rail load to Praga is halted for a straw transfer. I have a stamp from Versorgungsamt and the yardmaster's initials." He let the paper flap, thwack, thwack, like authority beating its wings.

The yawning guard huffed a laugh he didn't mean to let loose. The mean one bristled, hate and calculation in his eyes. He snatched the top sheet, turned it toward the lantern – the violet bled prettily – and ran a gloved thumb along the bottom where Wiktor had drawn a second line just messy enough to look written in haste.

"Which track?" he challenged.

"Three, to the east spur," Samuel shot back and leaned in, man to man, petty tyrant to petty tyrant, sharing the warmth of his contempt. "It is too cold for the hierarchy to come out and oversee the real work so they send us to freeze instead."

The guard's chin tilted. He liked being told a truth by someone who might have been of his tribe, albeit on the other side for now: the brotherhood of men disdainful of work they didn't invent. He gestured with his rifle like a wand. "Move."

They moved. The patrol's lanterns swept on. The sneeze became history. Helena, behind the third cart, met Irena's eyes for a fraction, astonishment, gratitude, and then returned to guarding her straw.

They reached the shadow of the water tower where the yard's din. Beyond, the service gate showed as a darker rectangle in the fence. A lock hung on it like a dare; the chain was slack and thanks to a trick Jadwiga knew and had passed to Samuel that afternoon, with a look that said *only God will judge you*, he worked it with mittened fingers. The latch muttered and gave.

"Two by two," Helena whispered, pushing the carts' noses into the gap. The children lay inside, under the straw and the smallest flicked a finger against the slat twice—air—then settled. Irena crouched and put her mouth to the wood. "Cicho," she breathed. "Quiet. We are almost at the barn."

Boots scrunched on snow behind them.

"Hey!"

They all felt the word hit like a thrown stone. Samuel pivoted, papers up again, face already set to the next lie. Irena's hand found Helena's sleeve and urged the cart through the aperture; wood rasped on chain. The "hey" grew into a shape. A boy, no, a young soldier, cheeks raw, rifle held like a broom, trotted toward them from the coal pile. His lantern swung, and yellow chased blue. He looked barely sixteen but wanted to do his job right.

"There's a curfew," he said, breath fogging. "After twenty-two hundred, only –"

"Depot orders," Samuel snapped, holding the same paper as if it had multiplied authority since the last inspection. He stepped into the boy's space the way teachers do to startle obedience out of it. "Do you think we'd have got this far without your men waving us through?" He jabbed at a line that Wiktor had underlined in a flourish: *Späte Umlagerung genehmigt.* Late transfer permitted. Samuel lowered his voice as if imparting a secret men share to feel important. "We're late because a Hauptfeldwebel with a pretty stamp forgot to tell his wife he was meeting his mistress and now he's also late for his dinner."

The boy's mouth opened and closed. Everyone in the yard hated someone with a pretty stamp. He scratched his ear through the wool and glanced at the gate as if to be sure the guards were still there.

Helena's cart had cleared the gap. Irena moved the second into the slot behind it, body a wedge of breath and grit. The next pair rolled. The boy's eyes ticked to the straw just as the tiniest foot pressed the slat from inside and then vanished.

Irena sneezed. Loud, ridiculous, spectacular. She doubled with it, hand to chest, made her face run. The boy recoiled, survival instinct went before training, and waved a useless hand in front of his nose.

"Verdammt," he muttered. "Go. Freeze somewhere else."

They went. The gate returned to itself without a sound. Samuel's knees softened after three steps; he didn't let it show. Irena's shoulder throbbed where she'd taken the lantern collision. Helena's hands were raw meat inside her gloves. The carts rolled on wood ruts that couldn't wait to get away.

Behind them, the yard resumed its song: steam, iron, whistles. If God was awake, He decided to ignore them on purpose. They pushed into an alley that led to the barn that stored the straw. The door gave at the shoulder, old wood, compliant to need. Inside, straw smelled like summer and hard work men prefer to talk about after it's done. They closed the world out and cracked their lanterns to fist-sized suns.

Helena went to her knees and dug with both arms into the first cart. A little face, pale and slick with sweat in spite of the cold, came up through the straw, eyes wide, mouth opening on air like a fish at the surface. She pulled the girl against her chest and sobbed a single, angry sob. "There," she said into the child's hair. "There."

One by one they lifted the small bodies out – two girls with scarves tied tight; a boy who counted while he breathed; a pair of brothers sound asleep from the shock of being parted from their parents; a toddler with cold-numbed hands; a quiet one who stared a hole through the wall. Irena checked fingers, toes, the long bones of shins; Samuel poured a thimble of hot tea into each mouth, then another; Helena made a nest in the straw and built children into it like a mother hen.

They worked until everyone had been wiped and wrapped and warmed. The oldest girl, the one who had sneezed, found Irena's sleeve and tugged. "I tried to catch it," she whispered, ashamed.

"You did," Irena said, touching the child's forehead with the back of her fingers. "And you were brave, that's what mattered." She kissed the small, cold forehead that tasted of winter and courage.

Helena's lantern faltered but she coaxed it back. "I'll sit the first hour," she said, eyes already scanning each damp scarf, each shiver.

Samuel put his hand over hers and pressed once. "We'll wake you at the turn." He looked at Irena. "Come."

They crossed to the far stall where straw had been banked to make a hollow. They folded themselves down and gave up their weight. Laughing came up through them like a cough, ugly and beautiful, half hysteria, half giddy gratitude. It spilled out and didn't wake the children; it left them lighter.

“If we die, at least we die together,” Samuel whispered, forehead to hers, breath warm in the inch between them.

“Yes.” She caught his face in her palms, straw crackling under her wrists. “But tonight we live, because they must live.”

He nodded, because she had made the truth sound easy. “Then we live,” he said, and sealed the promise on her mouth for a second, then a third, as if layers made anything more likely to hold. The kiss was an inventory: yes, mouth; yes, heartbeat; yes, you.

The barn closed in around then as Helena’s soft singing joined the winter and invented words to an old tune, vowels laid like blankets over shivers. One of the boys muttered the end of a prayer and fell into sleep. A mouse scuttled then hid. Somewhere far, a train coughed and started and dragged its long weight toward a place that was elsewhere.

“We could still run, after this is done,” Samuel said finally, because hope had put its finger on the door again and he could not pretend not to feel it.

“We already are,” Irena said.

He laughed once, quiet, into her neck. “Stubborn woman.”

“Stubborn man.” She tucked her head under his chin and let his arm become both bank and blanket. “Tomorrow we do it again.”

“Ten more?” he asked.

“As many as the night will carry,” she said, and felt him shiver at the ambition and settle against the necessity.

Outside, snow kept falling. They did not sleep so much as drift at the edge of it, listening for boots that did not come. When Helena’s hour slid into theirs, Irena lifted her head, checked the small bodies’ rise and fall, then settled back. Samuel’s hand found her bandaged fingers and threaded carefully between them, as if to teach them flexibility. She squeezed, gentle.

"Thank you for bearing my weight," she said into the straw.

"It is light and my honour," he answered.

They let the dark envelop them while ten children's breaths stitched a seam across it. By the time the lantern finally died, the wagon tracks outside were already filling with snow, erasing the line they'd left across the yard. The world likes to wipe itself clean. They would write another story again tomorrow.

25

Winter 1944

Dawn came and the snow that had fallen all night turned pewter in the early light, already bruised by soot. Irena and Samuel moved shoulder to shoulder down Krochmalna, heads bent, a drab couple the city had learned to ignore. Just two tired people with nothing worth stealing. They counted their steps because counting steadied breath and hearts.

The safe contact's door sat midway down the block, an old dressmaker who stamped city vouchers in her kitchen and hid medicine in button tins. Three windows. One lamp. The blackout curtain on the far pane never quite reached the sill. On quiet mornings, steam curled from the tea she would set for those without names. Irena pictured the steam. She let the picture be a prayer and not a distraction.

Samuel tightened his grip around the folder in his arm, work orders so perfect they bored the eye. He leaned close, brushed his mouth against Irena's temple through her cap, and murmured the plan: in, swap the papers, out by the courtyard, never two routes in a row. She gave the smallest nod. Pain gnawed at her shins; she let it be a metronome. Four in, four out.

Half a block away, a truck idled where trucks did not idle at this hour. Samuel felt the wrongness first. He slowed, shifted the folder so it could be dropped or offered. Irena used the pause to read the street the way she read rooms: shutters too carefully closed; a neighbour with her scarf tied too neatly for a morning this cold; a cat that should have been prowling frozen gutters tucked instead into the jamb of a door and staring with round, waiting eyes.

"Back," Samuel breathed.

Too late. The street became iron. Soldiers spilled from thresholds and alley mouths, rifles up, breath turning the air white as they shouted men into doorways and pushed women against walls. A whistle shrieked. Boots pounded. A truck rolled forward a pace and stopped as if it had found its mark. A boy ran and was caught by the collar, feet scrabbling uselessly on ice. The smell of coal smoke thickened. A paper lifted from a post and slapped back, the grainy face on it a joke that wasn't.

Ritter stepped from the shadow of a doorway as if the house itself had decided to birth him. Cap perfect. Gloves immaculate. A certain kind of smile. He didn't raise his voice; he never had to.

"Ah," he said, looking straight at Irena as if the disguise were a child's trick. "The dead woman walks."

Samuel didn't think; he moved. His palm hit Irena's shoulder and threw her into the seam between buildings, the narrow throat of an alley that smelled of excrement and old piss. "Run," he said, and the word was the first honest thing either of them had been allowed all day.

Shots cracked – one, two – ricocheting into brick with the mean sound bullets make when they find something harder than flesh. Samuel's gun was in his hand before the echo faded. He fired twice toward the nearest patrol, saw a soldier stagger, shouted, “There!” as if directing help past himself and toward some other target. He stepped to the alley mouth, made his body big, drew the gunfire that was meant for her.

Irena scrambled, palms skating on ice, shoulder smashing into damp brick and pushing off again. The alley bent, bent again, hemmed by the backs of tenements and their skinny drainpipes. Behind her, the street flowered with commands: *Halt! Links! Zu!* – boots and steel and a hunter’s breath about to become laughter.

She glanced back. Samuel stood square in the mouth of the alley, left side turned toward the street to narrow his frame, forearms locked the way a good shot holds protects life. Ritter’s men fanned to either side, trained in a day to avoid crossfire and still clumsy at it. Samuel fired again, not wild, not brave, efficient. A rifle jerked. A man went down on one knee in slush. The rest swarmed.

A shot found Samuel, low and mean. He jolted, a grunt torn from him as if someone had dropped a stone into his gut. His gun hand stayed steady, another shot, another, and then he dropped only when it had to. He slid one step into the alley and flattened himself against the wall, leaving a bright smear that steamed in the cold. He sucked a breath through his teeth and took another shot into the white blur of breath and uniforms.

“Go!” he barked at Irena; more anger than voice.

She moved because he had ordered her to. Her whole body shook with the effort of leaving, but training was a cruel teacher: you obeyed or you died. She ran, limping hard now, hate at her own weight hot behind her ribs. The world narrowed to brick and snow and the scrape of her boots. She hit the elbow of the alley and went to pound out into the next street, then stopped – because it was wrong too. Wrong in the exact same way: quiet that wasn’t peace, a cart abandoned, a man standing too still.

Back, then, it was the only option. Through her fear.

Through the guns. She turned and slid, biting ice with her soles, hands out like a blind woman. She came around the bend just as Samuel's knees buckled and he slid down the wall, leaving a dark ladder behind him. He had a little time left. He was spending it well. She dropped to him. Blood ran like ink from his side, warm enough to steam, thick enough to scare. Her hands went to the wound and pressed, a useless, necessary ritual. He made a sound that was not a complaint. His mouth shaped her name and then chose a different word.

"Names," he said. "Remember... the names."

"I will," she said. She didn't cry. There was no time for grief's theatre; there was only time to tell the truth and make it stick. "I will. I swear it. Every single one. And yours. Always yours." She sealed the oath with her mouth on his brow, on the locket through his shirt, on his mouth because love is a sacrament that requires touch.

His hand found hers and gripped, harder than a dying man should have had left. He pulled her palm flat to his chest, made her feel the beating that had carried them through cruel winters and would not carry him through this one. "Please," he managed. "Go."

"Together always," she said, because she was still a fool in the important ways.

He smiled the small, lopsided smile she had kissed a dozen times in rooms that were not theirs. Then his eyes went heavy, slid shut, fought once, opened again because he would not leave her without permission. "Live," he said. The word weighed nothing and everything, air and iron.

Boots hammered the mouth of the alley. A shadow jumped across brick. A bullet cut the corner and spat stone dust into their faces. Irena flinched and put her body over his, spine curved, skull tucked, instinct older than prayer. The next shot scored the wall above her ear. Someone shouted for a grenade.

Another voice, cool, irritated, refused. Ritter. He'd want her face intact for the rope.

"Now," Samuel breathed, and the word was a last order, not a plea.

She kissed him once, hard, and tore herself away. His hand slipped from hers like a rope end sliding off a cleat. She didn't look back. She crawled, low and fast, letting the uneven bricks tear cloth and skin. A drainpipe bit her palm and then held when she needed it. She used it to haul herself up onto a broken stoop and over a collapsed frame into the next yard. Behind her, a gun coughed three sharp syllables and then stopped. The world held its breath. Then one boot scuffed in slush and a man swore under it in disappointment. They had him. They did not have her. Yet.

26

Winter 1944

Dusk gathered early. Frost gritted the path. The apple tree stood black against a leaden sky, limbs bare, roots lifting the soil in slow heaves, as if the earth itself were trying to breathe.

Irena came through the gate without seeing it, only the hollow of her body telling her to move forward, one step and then the next. The cap was pulled low; the coat hung on her like a sentence. In her fist, Samuel's locket had pressed its oval into her palm so long it had made a red brand there. She couldn't open her fingers without feeling it tear.

Helena was waiting, scarf tied tight under her chin, a lamp cupped in both hands so the light wouldn't travel. She said nothing as Irena crossed the bed of dead marigolds and went to her knees at the trunk, the way she had a hundred times with names and lists and hope. Knees into cold, hands into colder. Breath she didn't trust at first, then the second, then the third.

"Do you want –" Helena began, the question too large for words.

Irena shook her head.

She stumbled towards the scar in the earth. The world had narrowed to the small circle she made with her body and the tree, to the rhythm of nature. Helena set the lamp closer and knelt beside her, the old bones of her hands sure. She touched Irena's back, one palm, steady; lifted it when Irena's shoulders hitched as if struck; set it back when the shaking let her.

"Here, you buried their names," she said at last, voice about to fall apart and refusing to. "Now you bury his."

Helena helped her dig and find a tin and once it was brushed free form soil and the seal broken and the lid removed, Irena's fist opened, disobediently slow. The locket lay in the cup of her hand, dull in the lamplight. She didn't look at the picture inside because she knew it like she knew the map of her palm. A coin-weight of him. The metal cold enough to hurt. She lifted it to her lips once, then placed it inside the oilcloth amongst the folded names.

"You will be safe now," she whispered. "With the children. Here, close by." She drew the oilcloth up and over, tucked it like a blanket around a child. Her hands couldn't stop moving, tucking and smoothing, smoothing and tucking, making it right in the only way left. Helena passed her the candle stub; wax warmed in her fingers; the seal gleamed and dulled. Irena pressed the lid back on and felt it seat itself with a small, decisive click.

She used both hands to lower the tin into the earth. Roots laced the hole like ribs. She laid the tin among them. "Guard him," she told the tree. "Guard them." The lamp made a small sun on the soil and then stepped back into shadow as she pulled the ground over, pressing, patting, making plain. They sat a long time after the hole was gone, backs to the tree, shoulders touching. The locket's absence burned hotter than its metal ever had.

"Say what you feel. Don't hold it inside," Helena murmured, after the silence had done what it could.

"I don't know how," Irena said. The words tasted like acid.

"Then say anything," Helena coaxed. "He's listening."

The first words were useless things, sorry and why and please, shards she turned over in her mouth and put down again because they cut. Then something simpler:

"Your hands," she said, eyes shut. "They were always warm." A small, terrible gift of a sentence. Then another: "You laughed with the back of your throat." She let herself remember the weight of his arm when sleep finally came and the way he always knew where to stand when the street turned dangerous and that he would have hated how clean the snow looked tonight.

Grief came like a storm, sudden, impossible, absolute. Her body bowed under it. Helena's hand moved to the back of her skull and stayed, holding the pieces inside.

"Breathe," Helena said. "And then we go in and you eat what I put in front of you and tomorrow you get up and you go about your insane business." She meant it tenderly. "He would break your legs himself if you stopped now."

Irena made a sound that might have been a laugh if laughter had lived in her anymore.

Helena went on. "Come, let us keep walking at least as far as the house for tonight," she said.

A wind came up and stirred the dead leaves, a dry applause. The lamp hiccupped and steadied. Irena put her palm flat to the ground where the tin lay. She tried to measure the distance between surface and memory. Impossible. She stood, slow, the way you stand after kneeling too long, and leaned her forehead to the bark. "Keep vigil," she told it. "Do it for me."

The tree did not answer. Trees do not. Even so, she felt the sense that something vast and patient had accepted the order.

They went inside with the lamp caged between them, light a small prisoner. In the kitchen, Helena set a bowl in front of her and another beside it and sat until both were empty. The room was quiet except for the scrape of spoons and, beneath it, the drum of Irena's heart slowly remembering it was supposed to beat. When the bowl was clean, Helena took Irena's hands and washed the dirt from under her nails. The water turned brown. When it ran clear, Irena pulled away.

"I have to work," she said.

"Yes," Helena said. "But not now."

"I need to do *something*," Irena said. Her voice was a wire pulled too tight. "Because the world just took something I cannot afford to give it."

Helena looked at her a long time, then nodded once. "Then we will make a deal. Tonight we rest then tomorrow we find something for you to do."

Irena, riddled by grief and exhaustion could only nod and allow herself to be led to the cot where she lay down and closed her eyes. There they slept, wrapped together for warmth like sisters, comrades, friends.

A boom rolled the air flat, then another closer, then many, until the city seemed to be pulsing with detonation, like a beast discovering its heart. The ground shook. Plaster sifted from ceilings. Windows that had survived the winter shivered themselves to death. Someone shouted a name in the street; someone answered with "Here!" then wasn't.

The first day of the uprising came heat-hot, smoke-thick, wild with men who had run out of words and reached for guns, and men with better guns answering, and women with nothing but empty hands between them and the end.

Irena tied a scarf over her mouth and staggered into it. The sky had turned the colour of a hell. Flames walked the rooflines. The air tasted like nails and ruin. She could not hear her own breathing; the fire filled her ears. She moved toward the corner where the school had once been, where the children had once darted under the fence and back again, toes quick with mischief and shoes too big. Now only bricks and stairs to nowhere. She found a boy under a beam, small and furious, and wedged her shoulder under the wood. The old hurt sang. She shoved until something shifted. He came out like a birth, dirty, blood soaked but alive. She handed him to a man who had become a father on sight and kept walking before relief or fear could slow her.

At the tram stop, two men in armbands fired from behind a sandbag wall, faces black with soot, mouths grim as saints. German armour clanked into the square with calm timing, the way clocks climb toward noon. A shell hit the bakery she had hidden in yesterday and tore it open like an orange. Flour leaped to the air and turned the fire white. She could smell bread, somehow, in the ruin – a hallucination or a cruelty God allowed. For a moment her knees went out from under her and she thought she had dropped to pray. She hadn't.

An old woman stood on a stoop with her hands open and empty. "My son," she said to no one, to everyone. "My son. He was just here." Irena gave her a command to sit, because orders sometimes work even on mothers, then turned to the next cry. The city widened and narrowed, widened and narrowed: a child's face, a doorway falling in, a man hurling a bottle that blossomed into heat.

Smoke slapped her. She coughed until her ribs hurt and then coughed again until the cough became nauseous. She learned to breathe on the beat of blasts. She saved a girl with glass in her cheek by pressing her kerchief there, then saved the girl's mother by shoving her toward a cellar door and snarling until the woman was scared enough to live.

When the first building across from Helena's caught, the garden fence burning, Irena ran, scarf down so the tree could see her face, and stood under its black limbs while sparks fell on her coat and died. She wanted to rip the ground open and hold the tin in her hands and run with it to anywhere that wasn't this. Instead she stood and spoke to it with the calm of a woman reneging on every instinct she had.

"I will not move you," she told the earth. "You are safest where you are." She spread her arms as if to shield more than root and soil. Helena came behind her and flung a wet sheet over the lowest branches, as if the tree were a man wounded in the street. Together they beat at sparks with their coats, two ridiculous women daring fire to argue.

For a moment there was a mercy pocket: a lull between shells like the breath the world takes before it shouts again. Irena leaned her shoulder to the trunk. The bark was warm but not alight. She turned from the tree and went back into the smoke. Men fell and stood and fell again. A boy ran messages in shoes that slapped the pavement like applause. German soldiers moved in grey, as if they were the only ones immune to flames in a world that had delighted in catching fire.

When night finally came, it did not mean dark, only a new colour of flame. She and Helena sat on the garden steps with a bucket between them and their skirts wet to the knee, watching the horizon against the sky.

"I thought it would hurt less," Helena said without preface. "All of it. The boy, my brother, the city. But it keeps finding new places to hurt."

"It will run out of places eventually," Irena answered, too tired to soften the lie.

"Yes," Helena said, as if agreeing to take turns with suffering. "Eventually."

They slept in chairs with their heads tipped toward each other so a stranger would think them sisters. In the earth at their feet, the tin kept quiet, the locket within it cool as a moon. In the city beyond the fence, people lay down in cellars and on stairwells and under tables and on holy floors and earned their courage. In the morning the smoke would find new paths, and so would she.

Before Irena closed her eyes, she said his name once into her coat, once into her palm, once into the dirt at the tree's roots. Then she said the children's names until they braided, until they made something that could hold a woman together long enough for dawn.

She slept, and the apple tree kept vigil. The roots did not read lists. The soil did not pronounce sentences. And under all the heat and noise, the ground took care of those who belonged to it.

27

January 1945

Snow went sideways all morning, a grey swarm driven hard by a wind that smelled of metal and ashes. The road into Warsaw had become a trough of churned ice and frozen mud carved by caterpillar tracks. From the outskirts came a new sound – engines like furnaces; the hoarse bark of commands in a language that was not German. Civilians stepped from cellars as if unthawing from hibernation, scarves pulled high, eyes narrowed against the sting.

Irena climbed the last mounded drift with Helena's arm braced under her elbow and saw them: squat, soot-streaked tanks nosing past collapsed buildings, red stars iced white, soldiers riding the hulls with scarves flapping, rifles upright like fence posts. A truck wobbled behind, canvas roof patched, men hanging off the tailboard and grinning like boys who had survived a dare. Someone on a tank threw his cap in the air and laughed; someone else lit a cigarette from a burning rag. Relief reached the ruined street and turned into noise.

A young soldier jumped down, boots hitting hard. He was nineteen at most, cheeks raw from wind, cap yanked crooked. From a sack he handed out bread heels and fistfuls of makhorka cigarettes. He pressed a crust into Irena's palm, another into Helena's, grinning with a sort of stunned kindness as though generosity itself were a weapon he had only just been issued. Around them, people reached and cried and touched metal the way pilgrims touch relics. "Spasibo," someone said by guess, or memory. "Dziękuję," someone else whispered against the bread, as if it had an ear.

A woman to Irena's left crossed herself, then crossed herself again. A boy, no more than ten, hugged a tank's track and was hauled away before the engine crawled forward. A sergeant barked at him in Russian with a father's impatience, then passed a cigarette to an old man who had lit his last one a year ago and kept the memory of smoke as a companion.

Suspicion travelled with gratitude, a thin, practical rivulet under the flood: the way a soldier's eyes moved over doorways and into pockets; the way another's fingers lingered on a girl's sleeve before his friend slapped his hand away; the unsmiling men in long coats sitting in the back of a staff car, faces shuttered. Liberation and a new, wary fear, arrived on the same trucks.

"You see?" Helena breathed, voice incredulous. "They came."

Irena held the bread but didn't lift it. The cold had made her hands wooden; her scarred fingers couldn't feel the crust's promise. She tried to taste joy and found only a kind of stunned emptiness as though the body understood survival but grief had not yet been told to rejoice. Through the engines' roar, through cheers and shouted questions, through the slap of canvas and the dry cough of a misfiring truck, one thought rose like a flare through fog.

"The apple tree," she said. "The names are waiting."

Helena looked at her, then at the road, then back. She nodded once, the way women agree to carry madness because they know it is not madness at all. “Go,” she said.

They turned away from bread and cigarettes and the red stars and limped toward the quarter where gardens kept secrets better than houses. A lieutenant called after them in Russian, something about shelter, about soup later. Irena lifted a hand without looking back. She could feed later. The tins fed her now.

They moved through ruins that used to be streets, past doorways that opened onto rooms where sky lived instead of ceilings. A page from a prayer book, scorched into lace, skittered past her boot and vanished under a rib of ice. Shell casings shone dull in the slush like coins without kings. A poster showing a grainy image of her face peeled from a wall and fell to the snow facedown.

At the corner where the school had been, a tank slowed to avoid a crater and an old man laid his palm against its side as if feeling the beat of a new heart. Irena pressed her teeth into the bread at last and swallowed without tasting; she needed the strength, not the pleasure.

They reached Helena’s gate and found it leaning but still on its hinges. Frost furred the curly stubble of last summer’s growth. The apple tree stood in the centre – bark scorched on the westward side, a limb cracked and healed into a strange elbow, roots lifting the ground in slow, patient pulses. Snow had drifted against the trunk. Something small had nested once in the crook of a lower branch; a tuft of straw clung there like a remembrance.

Irena went straight to her knees.

Her bones protested, an old chorus. She didn’t heed them. She pulled off her gloves and pushed her fingers into the drift, into the frozen crust under it, scraping down to the older earth that remembered spring. The cold bit to bone; it stung like truth. Helena crouched opposite, hands ready, breath pluming.

"Here," Irena said, passing her a trowel and pointing, locating the scar of their last burial, the way you find a child's face in the dark by touch alone.

They dug with the trowel and then with a spoon when the trowel struck a stubborn ice vein. Dirt lodged under her nails; blood came where skin split; she welcomed both.

"Slowly," Helena warned gently, though her own hands were already in the hole. "We don't need to rush. They will be there."

"It's like I can hear them calling," Irena said through her teeth. "They have been waiting too long."

Metal sang under spoon. They stopped breathing for one small, perfect second.

Rust showed under the earth, freckled and honest. Irena scraped it free while Helena cleared away roots fine as hair. The first tin lifted in both their hands and Irena set it on the snow, fingers shaking. Helena steadied the lid. It resisted, then gave with the familiar wax-pop, a little sigh like a secret leaving a mouth.

Inside: oilcloth, darkened by time and cautious water; a fold of beeswax paper; string swelled with damp. Irena unwrapped carefully, breath shallow, the world narrowed to the circle in her lap. The first scrap showed ink blurred at a corner where a tiny leak had tried and failed to become a flood. The name held. The letters swam and settled back into clarity, stubborn as weeds.

She sobbed once, an animal sound ripped up from a place language never reached, and then another, smaller, as if something inside had learned to breathe again. She pressed the sheet to her chest, against the cold coin of the locket sewn under her seam. "You are alive," she said, the words breaking and mending as they left her. "You are still alive."

Helena laughed and cried in the same breath. "Open the rest."

They did. One by one the scraps came out, damp from the cold at the edges, legible in the centre, a miracle of human engineering: wax and faith. Children rewritten as saints and cousins and farmhands and nieces. Birth names paired to new ones, an umbilical of pencil strokes tying past to future. Parents' names. Marks on cheeks. Favourite lullabies. The tiny notations that declared a person a person: *hates cabbage*; *sings to chickens*; *could count by two*. Irena's handwriting looked back at her from another year as if she were receiving letters from the past.

She found the second tin and worked it free, and then the third they had added in the worst month, when night had been crowded with boots and the city's breath learned to move around fires. They opened both, laid the papers in careful stacks on Helena's apron, turned pages in the lamp's trembling light and read aloud into the blue air of evening – the names like beads passing through their hands.

Hanna. Dawid. Sura. Marek.

Ania. Zofia. Jakub. Róża.

David again, another David, from another mother, already spoken for by a shoemaker in Praga who had sworn to keep his Sabbath as a secret inside his Sunday.

"Count them," Helena said, practical even now.

"I don't have to," Irena answered, wiping her cheek with the back of her wrist. "I know how many. Almost four hundred."

"Count them anyway," Helena insisted. "For the joy of a number."

They counted. Each digit rung like a bell, striking bone. When the last page was set down and the last name said into the small faithful circle of lamp and tree and kneeling women, Helena let out a long breath. "Then we begin the next work," she said. "We draw them back."

Irena nodded. Her knees hurt. Her hands shook with hurt and relief. Her heart had learned a new rhythm: grief in one chamber, victory in the other, the muscle between them doing what muscle must, squeeze, release, go on.

Beneath the folded papers, her fingers brushed the locket. Cold, familiar. She drew it out by the chain and held it up. Helena didn't speak. Irena opened it with her thumbnail. Inside, Samuel looked up from the square of time where he was still alive, eyes laughing, collar crooked, a softness around the mouth she had kissed the night the city taught them both a new language.

"Stay," she whispered to him, to the tin, to the dirt, to the air. "Stay with them for a while."

She laid the locket on the topmost fold of names – his memory among their futures. From the street beyond the fence came shouts, the exuberant sloppiness of soldiers who believed they had earned an hour of foolishness, the sharp commands of men in long coats who distrusted joy, the sobbing laughter of civilians drunk on the idea of living another day. A tank backfired. Somewhere, a woman sang two bars of a hymn before her voice broke.

Irena pressed her dirty fingers to her mouth and tasted earth and wax and salt and the ghost of bread. When she spoke, her voice was low and full and steady. "Tomorrow," she said, as to a partner already nodding. "We go to the parishes. To the convents. To the farms. We knock on doors and we say they can go home and their names belong to them."

Helena stood, knees creaking, and offered Irena her hand. "Eat first," she said. "Then sleep in the bed, not the chair. We need our strength for what comes next and Samuel would say the same. Rest now, heal."

"He would scold me if I didn't," Irena said, and felt how the sentence warmed her from inside, like tea moving through a body cold too long.

They stood and turned toward the house. Snow skittered over the garden, thin and new. The apple tree stood and took its vigil up again, no more dramatic than a soldier at a post. Its black branches wrote their old script against the sky; below, the ground remembered exactly what had been asked of it and what it had promised to keep.

On the road, tanks idled and moved; the red stars blurred under fresh flakes; a new army rehearsed how to become an occupation while it called itself liberation. In the garden, two women closed the door and banked the stove. Between those truths lay the work. Irena washed the dirt away and dried her hands, and, for the first time in months, allowed herself a full breath without counting. She let it out slowly and felt the space it made.

"Alive," she said, not to be contradicted. "All of us who can be."

Outside, the wind shifted. Snow thickened. The apple tree stood proud and in the house, paper slept. Ink held. Names waited, stubborn and exact, ready to be spoken back into bodies.

28

April 1945

The sign on the door was a scrap of cardboard inked in a shaking hand: Komitet – Names & Records. The building had once been a school, then a barracks, then a shelter; now it was a place of order. In the corridor, boots tracked thawing snow over cracked tiles. A child coughed; someone hugged him kindly. The air trembled with paper.

Irena climbed the last flight with Helena's steadying palm at her elbow and the canvas satchel tight against her ribs. The stairs were steep and uneven; her cane ticked time. Above them, voices braided, Polish, Yiddish and Russian.

In the room the committee had claimed, desks faced one another. A stove sweated in the corner, irrelevantly heroic. On the far table, a tin of pencils stood like a meagre bouquet. The men and women behind the desks had librarian faces both tender and ferocious, eyes that measured not lies but losses. They looked up when Irena entered and their gazes softened, then squared; they knew her story, or the outline of it. They knew what she carried.

She slid the satchel free and placed it on the table. The straps had been replaced three times; the canvas still held the faint sweetness of apples from a life when fruit had been an ordinary miracle. Her fingers fumbled the buckle; Helena's steadied them. Together they lifted the rust-stained bundles as if they were a sleeping child who must not be woken.

The room stilled. Irena unwrapped the oilcloth. Wax released its quiet, faithful scent. Pages lay beneath, scraps and slips and margins and makeshift registers, ink blurred at the edges, names written in her careful hand and in Jadwiga's bold one and in Father Antoni's sideways script, birth names yoked to baptism names, parents to children, streets to parishes, tiny notes about moles and lullabies and nightmares. She had read them a thousand times in the dark; daylight made them new again.

She did not hand them to the committee like a file. She passed them as a sacrament with both palms, steady and slow, each stack to a pair of waiting hands. "This is Zofia K –" she said quietly. "Placed under *Zofia Kowal*. Sister *Ania* under *Anna*. They will answer to both until we teach them otherwise." She turned the next: "Dawid now *Jan*. Left cheek scar from measles. Loved by a cobbler." Another: "Hanna, now *Helena* – four in 1941, pink ribbon in her hair when it was safe to wear one. Her mother wrote a poem about her life and hid it. I could not save the poem but I saved the girl."

The committee chair – an elderly man with a scholar's spine and a labourers' hands cradled each page as if heat might rise from it. He nodded his gratitude; his lips trembled once and found control. Around him, others sorted, cross-checked, murmured, added notes to the margins as if speaking to the future. The stove ticked. A fly tested the window and failed and kept trying.

Survivors gathered, gaunt, bundled, eyes too large, bodies already leaning toward the table. They reached for the lists and then hesitated, as though touching might alter the words. One by one they pressed their forefingers to the columns and moved down them slowly, naming in whispers the dead who might yet be the living. Some found nothing and went quiet in a way that made the room colder. Others found a single line, just one and broke open with a sound that made the hardest soul allow their eyes to shed a tear.

A woman with a kerchief tied hard under her chin read *Jakub, b. 1938 – now Kuba, parish Św. Krzyż* and sank to her knees beside the table. No one lifted her; a kindly woman slid down and sat on the floor next to her, the list spread between them like a small fire.

A man with ash on his cuffs read a name and looked up, suddenly younger, suddenly taller. "Here," he said to no one and everyone. "Here he is." He put the page to his chest, left a dark print there, and did not apologize. "My boy."

The room made room for both kinds of news, joy that shook, silence that burned. People stood for one another without a word. Someone refilled the tea kettle. Someone opened the window when the heat and grief thickened.

Near noon, a boy approached Irena. Eight, perhaps nine. His coat had no buttons; his wrist bones were articulate under the skin. He held his breath in that careful way children do when they expect to be told the truth and fear it will hurt. In the thin voice of a child who had learned not to expect much, he said, "But Mama isn't coming back, is she?"

Irena knelt. The strain climbed her splints; she welcomed the honesty of pain. She took his cold hand between both of hers and lifted it to her cheek. She didn't answer right away, because answers deserve their silence. When she spoke, it was to the whole room as well as to him. "I don't know what door the world will open for us," she said softly. "But her memory is in you, and your name is hers and no one can take that. You are who she said you were."

He frowned, concentrating, as if the sentence were a complicated set of directions. "So if I say her name..."

"She hears it," Irena said. "And so do we."

"Mama," he whispered into the dark fabric of her coat. She gathered him in. He cried with a dry sound, as if tears had to be invented again; she let his head knock against her shoulder until the rhythm soothed him. When he stopped, she gave him bread and a name card, the small, stiff sort they were making for the children who had few things of their own, and watched him walk it to the door as if he were carrying a passport to himself.

Afternoon leaned into evening. Records multiplied. The stove's heroic heat faltered and was fed and faltered again. Snow drifted sideways past the window and stuck to the glass in a lace of tiny hands. Helena dozed upright in a corner, mouth open, while Jadwiga came and went like a storm, rage and love electric in her wake, snapping orders. Names left the room in pockets and hands and against hearts.

When the last petitioner was ushered out and the chairs had been set on their aching legs again, the room emptied itself into dark and quiet. The committee took the lists to the vault – a closet with a door that didn't lock but understood the burden of trust. Helena kissed Irena's temple and went to make soup for men who wouldn't taste it, just gulp it down and hope for more. Jadwiga pressed her forehead to Irena's for one breath and said, "Tomorrow, we do it all again," because there was no other benediction left.

Irena remained.

She drew the last lamp low and pulled a chair to the table. The satchel lay open, limp with relief. She took from her coat's hidden seam the locket and placed it on her knee. The scratched oval glinted, then dulled. She rested her fingertip on the metal. It was cold. She opened the locket.

Samuel smiled from the tiny square—soft mouth, eyes laughing at the joke they had made of living. The room shifted; sound drew back; winter pressed its face to the window and listened. She pressed the locket flat to her heart. His voice came up through the quiet, not magic, not madness, only memory. *Remember the names.*

"I have," she said. "I do."

She folded her hand over the locket and closed her eyes. What rose behind her lids was not the alley or the blood or the last word *Live* (though that lived here, too); it was Samuel's face turned toward a child he would never meet, the way his shoulders softened when he listened, the way he turned his body to take the blow meant for someone else. The children's names braided themselves through him until she could not tell where one ended and the other began. Love had been their private rebellion and she would cherish it, always.

By winter's end of 1945, Warsaw had taught itself to walk again. It limped and staggered and tilted, but it moved. The river shrugged off ice; the bridges that survived stood proud; trams squealed in cautious circuits through streets lined with the facades of houses that hid nothing behind them. The city looked like the skull of itself. People merely threaded through the eye sockets.

In late 1945 the snow came early and mean. Irena took to the streets with her cane and her satchel and a pocket crammed with rolls of bread. She had learned a new country of corners, doorways that gathered orphans, stoops that collected old men, church steps that warmed under the bodies of the stubborn. She knew whom to nod to and whom to let pass without acknowledgment; she knew which checkpoints wanted a paper and which wanted a story.

Children wandered in packs or singly, empty as cracked teacups. She found them under scaffolds and in the lee of brick piles, two to a scarf, three to a crust, their eyes already too old. She gave them food first and asked their names second – quietly, reverently, like a physician applying salve.

"Be proud of your name," she told a stiff, thin girl with a stubborn chin. "You are *Róża*." The syllables floated in the cold and settled. The girl blinked. The name fit around her like a coat.

She taught them where to go to be counted and where to go to be loved; sometimes the same place managed both. She wrote down parish addresses and the names of aunties who were not related except by vow. At night she returned to Helena's and let her body tally the day: knees and shins, hands and scalp, the ache behind the eyes that numbers cannot measure. She slept when exhaustion argued louder than grief. She woke to the city asking again.

Spring came without apology. It burst, as if to prove it had not been killed, and dragged the city with it. The first stall selling tulips made people stop and stare as if they'd seen a miracle performed with knives. Rain arrived that was only water and not ash. On a Tuesday, three trees on Nowy Świat shook open weak blossoms; Irena stood under them and then went to the cemetery.

The gate sagged; the path had learned a new route around a

crater where a bomb had decided to lie down and breed daisies. Trees in the farther rows wore pale blooms like bandages that healed from the outside in. She passed names carved in stone and names written on boards and stumps of wood or stone that nobody had gotten around to carving or writing yet. She carried her cane, her satchel, her notebook, her locket. She wore her best coat because he would have teased her if she hadn't.

Samuel's grave was new and stubbornly modest, just his name, the letters cut with care by a man who charged less out of love. Irena brushed snowmelt from the stone with her sleeve and sat. The ground was cold and the blossoms overhead made a thin, foolish halo against the grey.

She set the cane aside. "You were with me," she told him, simply. "All the way. You helped save them. You saved me." Her throat closed around the last word and she pried it open gently, the way you open a child's fist. "I love you. I will miss you every day there is."

Wind moved the blossoms; a few let go and flattened white against the dark earth, briefly perfect, briefly foolish. She laughed once, softly, because beauty can be brave and ridiculous at the same time. She spoke to Samuel, about what life was like now and what she hoped it would become until the bird in the next tree answered with a line of its own, and she accepted the duet.

When she finally finished, she did not feel emptied. She felt full of voices, of days, of a city that had chosen to keep breathing. She pressed the locket to the stone, cool against the carved letters, then tucked it back into her coat.

"Tomorrow," she said to the grave, to the trees, to the names that made a life. "We go again."

She stood, gathered her cane, and looked once more at the blossom-salted earth. The evening air carried a faint, clean sweetness, from trees that had no business blooming and did anyway, from bread that might be baked later and shared, from children who would answer to both the names that saved them and the names that were theirs. She stepped into the future, and the city that was saved.

EPILOGUE

August 1965

Summer had taken its time and then arrived all at once, warm enough to loosen the knots in hearts and memory. In Helena's garden was hers now, though the city had changed hands and uniforms a dozen times, the apple tree wore its crown of fruit, deciding at last to be extravagant. Branches bent under the weight; the grass below was sweet with windfall.

Irena sat underneath on the old bench with its flaking paint, a cushion under her hips because her creaking bones had become opinionated. The cane lay beside her, not quite needed, not to be argued with. Her hair, once a stubborn brown, had gone to the dignities of silver; her hands had thinned, blue rivers close under the skin. The locket small, scratched, faithful, rested against the hollow of her throat where her pulse still kept arguments with time.

Children ran the length of the path, their shouts skipping over the fence. One skidded to a stop at the gate to peer in, judged the old lady and the tree harmless, and scooted on, a red ribbon flashing at the nape of her neck. Another bounced a ball; it hit a car root and leapt sideways.

Twenty years, Irena thought. Enough distance for names to grow into lives. Still not enough for forgetting. Above her, fruit thumped softly as it let go. A wasp found a split apple and worried it with the mindless devotion of appetite. The tree's leaves shifted in a wind that cooled her skin. Even now, when night pressed hard, she could feel the iron circle in the earth where the tins had slept, the old bed of paper and wax, emptied at last to offices, to synagogues, to registers and reunions and funerals. The ground had held; the tree had remembered.

She tipped her head back against the trunk and let Samuel's name arrive the way it always did, not with trumpets, but with the accuracy of memories held dear. He would have laughed at this fat summer, she thought, would have filled his pockets with apples and then stolen the a spoonful of pulp from the edge of the pan when Helena wasn't looking. He would have taught some child to throw a ball as if aim mattered more than speed. He would have grown soft at the temples and unembarrassed about tenderness.

Her fingers found the locket without looking. The chain had been replaced twice, then repaired with a bead of solder that looked like a lump of moon. She opened it. His face, no bigger than a fingernail, smiled from an age that now felt mythical. She pressed the cool oval to her lips, then to the inside of her wrist where the skin was thin and the beat was honest.

Her father's sentence came whole, as if he had just spoken from the next room: *If you see a man drowning, you must jump in.* He had added, always, the necessary cruelty: *Even if you cannot swim.* She had not known it would mean alleys and ropes and names in tins and a city under fire. She had not known it would mean a bench twenty years on, with children running free and a locket warm from skin and an ache that had learned to be quiet but never obedient. She only knew that the command had never released her, and she had never asked it to.

A girl's laugh cracked the heat; a boy chased his shadow, bravely losing. From the tenement nearby came a radio turned too high, a waltz flattened by static. The world, as usual, offered its small, imperfect mercies.

She thought of the ones who had not come back, of voices that hung in rooms that were no longer rooms, chairs that had learned to be empty. She thought of the ones who had, those boys who now carried briefcases; girls with babies and the tired pride of miracles performed and old women who had slipped real names into ledger columns with hands that shook until the pen touched paper and steadied them. She had watched faces bloom when a word fit; she had watched faces collapse when none did. The human register was never balanced. You could not balance it. You only showed up and carried the deficit forward with care.

A fruit let go above her, struck the grass, split on impact. The smell rose sweet, bruised, immediate. She cut it with Helena's old pocketknife, still sharp, and ate it bite by bite, juice on her wrist, a luxury earned by no one and granted by summer anyway. The taste brought faces with it. Hanna's fierce eyes, Dawid's stubborn jaw, Sura's cautious smile – and the little notes she had written once as if faith could be archived: *mole on left cheek; sings to chickens; hates cabbage; counted to ten by the age of two.* She had been right about this, at least: details were life vests. Children wore them back to shore.

She closed the locket and kept her hand there, palm to metal, as if blessing or borrowing heat. "We did it," she said into the leaves, into the afternoon.

Again she leaned her head against the trunk. The bark felt like an old friend's shoulder. The tree stood tall – fruit heavy, leaves whispering, roots sunk deep into soil that had learned the solemnity of paper and promise. If there were monuments worth having, this was one: a living thing that asked nothing and held everything.

She closed her eyes. The names moved through her like a tide. When she opened them, the garden was the garden again, and the children were only children, and the apple tree remained, branch-laden, unastonished, exact. She sat with it until the shadow reached her knees, and then a little longer, lips still working, counting the saved and the missing with equal care. They would be her legacy, always and forever.

AFTERWORD

Irena Sendler (1910–2008) was a real Polish social worker who led one of the most daring rescue operations of the Second World War. Working in Warsaw under the German occupation, she used her position in the city's Social Welfare Department and later, her membership in the underground Council to Aid Jews (Żegota) to smuggle Jewish children out of the Warsaw Ghetto and hide them on the "Aryan" side in convents, orphanages, and with vetted foster families.

Sendler received special permits as a sanitary inspector to enter the ghetto under the pretext of combating typhus. With a small, trusted network, she moved children out in every way they could: carried under coats, in tool crates or boxes, through service entrances and courtyard gates, in ambulances and work carts, and behind false walls. On the outside, she arranged forged identity papers and Catholic cover stories, then trained families and nuns on how to keep the children safe if questioned.

To give the rescued a path back to their identities after the war, Sendler wrote down each child's real name, the names of their parents, and their new identities. The lists were sealed in jars and buried beneath a tree in a friend's garden. After the war, she used those lists to try to reunite children with surviving relatives. In most cases, their parents had been murdered, primarily at Treblinka, and the children remained with their rescuers or in children's homes.

In October 1943, the Gestapo arrested Sendler. She was brutally tortured, her legs and feet were broken and she was sentenced to death. Żegota managed to bribe officials so the guards listed her as executed and her comrades slipped her out of Pawiak Prison. She lived in hiding for the rest of the occupation and continued her work under a false name. By war's end, Sendler and her network had rescued approximately 2,500 Jewish children from the Warsaw Ghetto, and she had personally saved 400, an extraordinary collective effort that relied on dozens of couriers, priests and nuns, doctors, and ordinary families who chose to risk everything.

Sendler's moral compass was shaped early. Her father, Dr. Stanisław Krzyżanowski, a physician who treated the poor, including many Jewish patients. He died of typhus and is often credited with telling his daughter: "If you see a man drowning, you must jump in and save him, even if you cannot swim." She carried that instruction through the war and the difficult postwar years. Under the communist regime, she was questioned and restricted because of her ties to the wartime underground, and her story was rarely told publicly.

Recognition came slowly. Yad Vashem honoured her as Righteous Among the Nations in 1965. Poland awarded her the Order of the White Eagle in 2003. In 2007 she was nominated for the Nobel Peace Prize. She died in Warsaw in 2008 at the age of ninety-eight.

This book blends history with fiction. Irena's courage, her Żegota network, the forged papers and convent placements, the buried lists in jars, her arrest and escape from execution, and the postwar search for families are all drawn from historical record. Certain characters (such as "Ritter") and specific scenes have been invented or compressed to carry the emotional truth of what happened. The core remains: a small group of people chose action over fear, and thousands of children lived because of it.

Made in United States
Orlando, FL
09 March 2026

79210662R00146